NATIVE WARRIOR

A Novel by

Mark Reps

This book is a work of fiction. Names and characters are products of the author's imagination. Any similarities between the good people of southeastern Arizona and tribal members of the San Carlos Indian Reservation are purely coincidental.

BOOKS BY MARK REPS

ZEB HANKS SERIES

Native Blood

Holes in the Sky

Adiós Ángel

Native Justice

Native Bones

OTHER BOOKS

Heartland Heroes

Butterfly

ACKNOWLEDGEMENTS

A writer does not stand alone in his or her writing. We paint ourselves into corners, we forget minor details that make the story whole and complete but, most of all, we need a backup team that edits our work and reminds us when we go off the rails. I would like to give special thanks to John Omps for his critical eye for detail and general input. I also want to thank my wife, Kathy Reps, for her ability to encourage, edit and help me in the evolution of the Zeb Hank series.

1

INVASION

Helen didn't even bother to look up as the wind jostled the front door of the sheriff's office. The slightest wind blowing down the hallway of the old building created a recognizable creaking sound a dozen times a day. As she turned to grab a freshly sharpened pencil, her elbow caught the heavy duty Swingline stapler sitting on the edge of her desk. In a fraction of a second the stapler hit the floor, burst open and sent staples flying in all directions.

"Dang it all." Helen spoke aloud even though no one was in the vicinity.

Those words were as close as she would ever come to swearing. She bent to her side, swept the staples onto a piece of paper and grabbed the Swingline with her other hand. As she lifted the mess back onto her desk, from behind and out of nowhere a latex gloved hand compressed itself over her mouth. Across from her desk in the mirror she could see a person in a mask standing behind her. The left hand of the intruder covered her mouth. The right hand held a gun directly against her temple. An ominous warning followed.

"Be completely quiet or something very bad is going to happen. If you make any noise, you're going to have a dead sheriff on your hands, and you won't be doing so well yourself. For good measure I'll kill anyone else who walks through the door. Everybody's' lives depend on you, Helen. Think hard about that."

The person, whom she automatically assumed to be a man, called Helen by name. He had a high pitched voice and, more importantly, knew who she was. Her heart began to quake and tremble. She tried to take a couple of deep breaths to calm herself. No luck. She fought with every prayer she could muster to quell a rising panic attack, a panic attack that could kill her and others.

"Where's Sheriff Hanks?"

Helen chose to try and stonewall her captor by offering no reply. If she was going to meet her maker, she wasn't going to allow some fool with a gun pointed at her head to take anyone else along, at least not on her account.

"Where is he? I won't ask again. I want you to think of what might happen to your grandchildren if you don't tell me the whole truth and tell me right now."

Panic raced between her heart and her brain. How could anyone even think such thoughts? She was dealing with the devil himself.

"I'm going to count to three..."

The devil reached into his pocket and twisted what Helen suspected to be a silencer onto the end of the handgun. He spoke methodically like he had done this before.

"...then I am going to pull the trigger. This bullet will make a small hole in one side of your head and a rather large one on the other side. It will look really ugly at your funeral, especially for your family. Oh how they will feel your suffering. So, for one last time, exactly where is Sheriff Hanks?"

Facing certain death if she said nothing, Helen spoke. Her voice was but a fear-filled cracked whisper.

"He's in the bathroom."

"I know," replied the high-pitched voice. "I was just checking to see what sort of value you put on your own life. You passed the first test with flying colors."

In a flash the masked intruder taped her mouth shut. She counted. He wound the tape around her head three times. Then, calmly, the devil walked in front of Helen and made another command.

"Clasp your fingers together and push your wrists tightly against each other."

Almost instantly handcuffs bound her at the wrists and hands. She recognized them as Monadnock double cuffs. They were identical to the ones she had ordered for the office many times.

"On the ground."

Helen was confused. What did that mean?

Before she could decide what it meant, a hand underneath each armpit lifted her to the hardwood floor. Surprisingly, she was lowered gently. Nevertheless, her panic converted itself to anger. This time her ankles were bound in cuffs. She was trussed and hogtied like a farm animal ready for the slaughter. No decent human being deserved this sort of treatment. Helen felt her cheeks glowing with the fire of infuriation. For the first time in her life she felt as though, given the opportunity, she could hurt someone and hurt them badly. The evil one offered her some advice.

"Stay calm, Helen. Take it easy if you want to live and keep others among the living."

Helen looked at the eyes behind the mask. They were dark. That was all she could tell. She searched them for reason or meaning but found none. She studied her vile interloper. The long sleeve shirt was partially untucked and not buttoned at the wrists. The pants were work style khakis, pressed with a perfectly straight line. The boots were sand colored, military style. The tops went three or four inches above the ankles. They were like those sometimes worn by the young men and women coming back from Iraq and Afghanistan. The laces were double knotted. Her neck began to ache. Helen turned her head and spotted a second pair of shoes. These she could see only from the ankles down. They were red with a circular logo at the anklebone. They were classic Keds. Her own children had worn them faithfully for years. They were well worn but in great condition. A vaguely familiar voice came from above the red Keds, a second voice, different from the person who held the gun to her head.

"Is all the office information from the criminal files on your computer?"

With her mouth taped shut, Helen couldn't reply. The man with the high pitched voice leaned closer to her ear. Helen smelled something on his breath. Was it sulfur? She knew that to be the smell of the devil? Maybe it was bad breath from a rotten tooth? Was it the foul odor of an ulcer? She remembered the stench of Zeb's ulcer breath. Something else too stirred her nostrils. Sage? A dark whisper interrupted her thoughts.

"You are exactly two seconds away from having that hole I was talking about blown through your brains." She felt the barrel of the gun in her ear. "If I kill you, I am going to have to kill your sheriff."

The voice was muffled by the stocking mask, but she clearly understood every word. Helen made direct eye contact. She nodded her head, indicating the information was on the computer. She didn't want to die and she didn't want Zeb to die.

Helen rolled her head in despair. With her ear pressed against the floor, suddenly her faith was renewed. She could hear the pipes from the bathroom rattle. Zeb had just flushed the toilet. Now he would be washing his hands. In vain, Helen scraped her shoes across the old oaken planks of the flooring. Hoping against hope, she was praying Zeb would hear the scrapes. She hadn't moved them six inches when a hand grabbed them, holding them in place.

"Bad idea to warn Sheriff Hanks. It might buy him a bullet."

Helen looked up at the eyes behind the mask. She saw only evil. Glancing toward her desk, she saw the red Keds reaching to her computer. She noticed he also wore latex gloves. His hand pulled a green flash drive from her computer. Helen quickly considered how long the flash drive might have been downloading information. It had probably been five or six minutes. Ample time to get what they needed if they knew what they were doing, and it appeared they did.

The intruders pulled Helen out of sight, on the side of her desk. Red Keds hid behind a half wall. The larger invader stood behind a half opened door with his gun held professionally in his hand, waiting for Sheriff Hanks.

2

DANGER

Zeb couldn't remember feeling this good for at least a year. The feelings of clarity and calmness seemed to come out of nowhere of their own volition. After using the men's room down the hall from his office, he washed his hands and scrubbed his face with hot water and Helen's homemade lavender soap. He felt clean, refreshed and somehow rejuvenated. As he dried his hands, he gave himself a good, long look in the mirror. His reflection was the ear-to-ear grin of a man whose life was about to change for the better. This feeling, wherever it came from, was a gift. Was the spirit of his eternal love, Doreen, sending him good vibes from heaven? This was the first moment since her murder that he felt temporarily, maybe even totally free of the pain and suffering of her death and the consequences it had brought him. Life was good, maybe even great. His recent election campaign for Sheriff of Graham County had been a breeze. He smiled as he realized how effortless it was to run unopposed and have the backing of the local media.

All around him life seemed to be clicking with a rare synchronized rhythm. Kate and Josh had gotten engaged. They seemed to truly be in love. He felt happy for them in a way that only one who has felt true love can feel for others. Former Sheriff Jake Dablo, now Zeb's deputy, was at the peak of his game. Despite his age, Jake was proving to be more of a mentor than ever. Helen ran the office like clockwork. She never missed a beat and he, Sheriff Zeb Hanks, with the breezes of a newly won election firmly flying at his back, felt hardly any weight on his shoulders. This strange freedom had its roots in so many things that at this moment he could hardly contain himself. He began to whistle a Guy Clark tune, *Some Days You Write the Song, Some Days the Song Writes You*, arguably the best song ever written if you asked Zeb. As he opened the bathroom door, he truly believed that today he was writing his own song and the tune was a good one, a damned good one if he said so himself. He stretched his arms toward the ceiling and arched a kink out of his back. With a little time on his hands he felt like taking a short walk down to the Town Talk Diner. He'd pick up a sweet treat for Helen, press a little flesh, thank a few of the locals for their votes and have a late lunch. He glanced at his watch. It was exactly two-thirty.

"Helen," he said. "I'm headed over to the Town Talk. Blueberry muffins? One for now and one for later? I'm buying. How's your sweet tooth today?"

When she didn't answer, he figured she was either on the phone or perhaps at a loss for words, wrapped up in the delight of getting her favorite sweet treat. As he stepped around the corner into the front office, his world shifted with lightning speed. Helen hadn't answered because she couldn't. The room suddenly became shadowy dark as a fast moving cloud slid off the eastern tip of Mount Graham and blocked out the sun.

At that precise moment Zeb's eyes landed on Helen's cuffed feet jutting out from beneath the edge of her desk. Instinctively, Zeb reached for his weapon. The instant realization that his gun was hanging in his office, next to his hat, stirred his heart and tightened his chest. A wave of anxious hypervigilance swept through the sheriff. He moved quickly and decisively toward Helen while simultaneously surveilling the room. She was bound at the hands and feet with standard cuffs, probably from his own supply. A piece of silver-gray Duct Tape, tightly wrapped around her head, covered her mouth. Her terror filled eyes shot daggers of anger and fear.

Attempting to reassure her, Zeb whispered, "Everything's going to be okay. Stay calm."

Even as he spoke those words to Helen, Zeb felt a tinge of doubt. Reaching to the sheath on his belt, Zeb deftly withdrew his Randall knife. He bent forward to cut the beveled edge of the cuffs from her feet, using the hardened blade as a tool rather than the weapon it was designed to be. He smiled and spoke gently.

"I'll have you undone in no time."

She returned his smile and kind words with a darkened glare of shock. For a fraction of a second, before he realized she was signaling him with her eyes, Zeb's hint of doubt turned to faith all would quickly be well. Then suddenly and without warning he departed the world of amplified awareness and dropped off the cliff into a world of total darkness. The knife dropped in slow motion from his hand and landed next to Helen's bound feet. Its sharpened tip stuck in the wood floor. Blood squirted from the back of Zeb's skull as he fell on top of Helen, who not only had fainted out of pure fright, but also had the wind knocked out of her by Zeb's massive body.

In the millisecond between intense alertness and complete loss of consciousness, Zeb realized one of three things had likely happened. He'd been shot, blackjacked on the head or burst an artery in his brain. The speed at which things were happening didn't allow him time to choose among the options.

3

HELP ARRIVES

Zeb and Helen lay in an unconscious heap for five minutes before Deputy Kate Steele walked through the door of the sheriff's office. The instant she saw Sheriff Zeb Hanks lying in a pool of blood on top of the injured Helen Nazelrod, she drew her weapon and thoroughly scanned the room. Kate assessed that they were both unconscious but, after checking their pulses, quickly determined they were alive.

An ugly, angulated cut on the back of Zeb's head had already begun to show the first signs of clotting. Kate concluded the jagged cut had pulled back the scalp, producing a profuse amount of blood inconsistent with its appearance as a serious, life threatening wound. The skin and hair flapped down, mostly covering and closing the injury. The protruding lump next to the cut had already grown to the size of a golf ball. Kate's EMT training had taught her it likely looked worse than it was, but she made a mental note to do a quick concussion check on Zeb when he was conscious again. Kate surmised that when the sheriff came to he was going to have one nasty headache. Behind closed lids Helen's eyes moved back and forth erratically. From what the deputy could see the only damage to Helen was likely from Zeb's body falling on top of her. Kate removed the tape from Helen's mouth just as the secretary opened her eyes. Kate placed a pointer finger over her lips, signaling quiet. Then the deputy searched the office room by room. When she was certain the office was empty of any intruders, Kate gently rolled Zeb off Helen. She freed Helen's hands from the cuffs with Zeb's knife after freeing it from the floorboard.

"What happened?" asked Kate.

"My shoulder," replied Helen. "I think it's broken. My arm hurts like the devil took a bite out of it."

Kate gently ran a finger along the area of Helen's shoulder where she described her pain. Kate could easily feel the fracture in the collarbone. The clavicle had a full half-inch separation, with the part of the bone closest to shoulder joint dropping toward Helen's back. Thankfully, no bone was poking through her skin. The arm didn't appear broken, but blood was pooling below the elbow, blackening it beneath the skin. It was ugly but probably looked worse than it was.

Zeb stirred. His groans sounded like those of an old man. When consciousness returned, his hand immediately moved towards his aching head. Zeb's finger inadvertently slipped beneath his torn scalp, landing on his exposed skull bone, provoking new bleeding. "Ouch." A wave of nausea trickled through his aching body. He pushed the feeling away.

Noticing the blood on his hand, Zeb muttered angrily, "What the hell is going on? What happened?" He spit out a drop of blood as he spoke. He had bitten through his lip in the fall. His mouth tasted like iron. A line of blood continued to dribble down his lip as Helen began explaining to Kate what had happened. He wiped the red fluid away with the back of his sleeve.

Helen began to jabber at a thousand nearly incomprehensible words a minute. As she listened to her own description of what had happened, the shock of the near death experience began to sink in. Helen started to shake uncontrollably. Both Zeb and Kate reassuringly put their arms on her back. Their combined calm soothed her only temporarily as she began to gulp in deep gasps of air. Her brow was quickly covered with cold sweat. A fresh look of terror rose in her eyes. Clearly she was diving headlong into a panic attack.

Zeb got her a glass of water. "Drink this."

She tried. It helped a little. Kate and Zeb waited as she attempted to calm herself down. At this moment their words were not reassuring.

"Take your time," said Zeb.

After several minutes of deep breathing, the acuteness of Helen's fit of terror slowly began to subside.

"I think I'm better now," replied Helen. "But my heart won't slow down. You don't think I'm having a heart attack, do you?"

Kate spoke softly, assuring Helen that she was just shook up and probably not having a heart attack. Kate offered to call Doc Yackley. Helen pointed an unsteady finger to the blood on the back of Zeb's head.

"Yes, call Doc," ordered Helen. "Do it now."

Kate grabbed the phone and dialed Doc Yackley's private number at the Safford Medical Clinic.

"This is Deputy Kate Steele. We have an emergency involving the sheriff and Helen Nazelrod here at the office."

"I'll send Doc Yackley right over," replied his nurse.

"Doc is on his way, Helen," said Kate.

"Okay. What happened next?" asked Zeb.

"The intruder asked me where you were." Helen looked at Zeb as though what she was about to say next would grievously disappoint him. She burst into tears as she answered. "I stalled as long as I could, but with a gun pressed against my temple I said you were in the bathroom. I'm s-so so-sorry. I could have gotten you k-killed."

"You absolutely did the right thing," said Zeb. "We're both alive. That's what matters. That's what really matters right now."

"I guess so." Helen paused and looked at Zeb and Kate. "Yes, of course you're right. We are blessed to still be alive. We should be grateful for that."

"Please tell me whatever you can remember," asked Zeb.

Helen gathered her thoughts before continuing. The room swirled. Her pain deepened with each spoken word. She said a quick prayer that God give her the grace to remain resolute and thanked Him for letting her survive so that she might see her grandchildren grow. As she detailed what had happened, Helen's panic turned to anger. The rising rage made her cheeks glow like fire.

"Rotten scumbuckets," said Helen. "Treated me like an animal."

Kate silently mouthed 'Scumbuckets' to Zeb. Helen noticed Kate mimicking her words. Kate saw that Helen noticed the interaction. Helen may have been down, but she was definitely not out.

"Yes, I said scumbucket. The person who whispered in my ear smelled funny and had tattoos. The intruders threatened a woman and struck an officer of the law," replied Helen, turning to Kate. "If that doesn't define scumbucket, what does?"

Zeb and Kate exchanged a glance. Both were clearly curious about Helen's choice of words.

"Scumbucket or scumbuckets? Intruder or intruders? As in one person or more than one person?" asked Kate.

"Two. I think. Yes, there were at least two of them. There might have been more. I never saw the second person until I was on the floor. I only saw the shoes on the second person. They were Keds tennis shoes, well-worn but cared for. They were red."

"Large or small feet?" asked Zeb.

"Medium," replied Helen. "The Keds were medium sized, bigger than a boy's shoe, but smaller than a man's. They were red."

Kate wrote it down.

"Red Keds wanted to know if all the criminal cases handled by the office were on my computer. I couldn't answer because of the tape. The other one pointed the gun at my head and threatened to kill me and then you, Zeb. I was scared right down to my bone marrow. I didn't want to die. I didn't want you to die either, Zeb."

Helen began to cry at the horrifying memory. Kate put a soft hand on Helen's neck. Her softest, most loving touch did little to calm the sheriff's secretary.

"Take a deep breath. Tell me what happened next," asked Zeb.

I heard the pipes rattling and knew you had flushed the toilet. I tried to signal you but I knew you couldn't hear me." Tears began to rush down Helen's cheeks.

"I know you did your best, Helen," Zeb said reassuringly.

"Red Keds pulled a small flash drive out of my computer. I think he got what he was after. It seemed like all eternity passed by, but it must have been only five or so minutes."

Zeb glanced at his watch. That amount of time seemed accurate.

"Did the one in Keds sit on your chair?" asked Zeb, hoping for some forensic evidence.

"No, I'm fairly certain he remained standing. That's when I heard you shut the bathroom door. They heard you too. I could see by the way they acted they heard you coming. The one with the gun whispered in my ear again, threatening me with a bullet to the brain if I made a single sound. The whispering scumbucket said it didn't matter if I died or if you died or if both of us died. Oddly, together they laid me very gently on the floor, like they didn't want to hurt me. Then Red Keds moved behind the half wall and the other one hid behind the door over there."

For a moment Helen stared intently as if the intruders might still be there, somehow hiding. Zeb recognized the look of shock on her face.

"Helen. Helen are you with us? Are you okay?"

"Yes. Yes. I'm fine. When you came around the corner and bent over me, the one in the military boots clubbed you in the head with the pistol grip. I think it was a .45."

"Did you recognize the gun specifically?" asked Zeb.

"My husband has one just like it. It was a big gun with a big handle. It had a cylinder, not a clip. Then you fell on me. I passed out from the pain in my shoulder and arm."

Zeb eyed Helen's broken, bent shoulder and blood darkened arm.

"I am so sorry," said Zeb. "I didn't mean to hurt you."

"Of course you didn't," scoffed Helen. "It's probably just a broken bone. By the grace of God, we both are alive. Good Lord, Zeb, come to your senses and be grateful."

The sheriff responded to the righteous scolding with a humble nod. His aunt/secretary always did have a way of putting him in his place. How often he wished he carried in his heart the same faith she did.

"That's when I came in," said Kate. "You were both unconscious. I checked to see if you both had pulses, then I cleared the office. No one was present."

"You didn't see anyone leaving the building as you arrived, did you?" asked Zeb.

"No. No one. Are the interior and exterior security cameras up and running on a regular basis?" asked Kate.

"I assume so," said Zeb.

"Probably not," said Helen.

Her glib response surprised Zeb and Kate. Their reaction was spontaneous and unified.

"Why not?" they asked.

"The installation technician has been here on and off over the last few days. He said we had some minor, but very real, problems with the cameras. He told me he knew about it because part of his contract is to remotely check their working status once a week. He said the cameras were producing nothing but static."

"I didn't see him coming or going," said Zeb.

"Neither did I," said Kate. "Which is odd considering my office looks right toward your desk and the front door.

"He has been in and out two times. Now that I think about it, he was here when I was the only person in the office. The last time I saw him he said that he would have it fixed in one more trip, but he had to order a couple of parts first. I doubt he got it fixed before we got hurt. I really don't think anything was recorded," said Helen. "In fact, I know it wasn't because he said nothing would be recorded until he got them fixed."

"Kate, check on those security cameras and see what you come up with," said Zeb.

"Could the security camera technician be involved? Do you know him?" asked Kate.

"He's a young kid. According to his mother, he's obsessed with computers, computer gaming and computer security. She's an old friend of mine. He lives in his mother's basement. She told me that since he graduated from Safford High School a couple of years ago all he's basically done is take one class at Eastern Arizona University and play video games. She told me he's had a couple of jobs involving computers and security cameras. I thought I could help both of them out--him by offering some real work and her by seeing that her boy could be a productive member of society," said Zeb.

"I'll look into him, but being twenty-one years old and living in your mother's basement should set off an alarm bell or two," said Kate.

"There are extenuating circumstances," said Zeb.

"What's his name?" asked Kate.

"Curtis Lowe," replied Zeb. "His mother's name is Angela Lowe. His father, Levi, is serving five years in the Safford federal prison camp for defrauding the United States government. He was a federal contractor for a BIA committee headed by Senator Russell. The contract had to do with the purchase and distribution of supplies and food to the San Carlos Reservation schools. Seems he got caught with his fingers in the till, over-billing, money in an off-shore account, not delivering products the government paid for and re-selling products after he stole them. He was in prison the same time Tribal Chief Nations Wentsler was. I'm sure they know each other. Talk to Nations for the inside dope on Levi, if it comes to that."

"Zeb, any chance you remember how he got the federal government contracts?" asked Kate.

"He bid on them in the usual manner," said Zeb.

"Is federal contracting to the Rez his business?" asked Kate.

"No, he's a computer guy. Don't know exactly what his specialty is, but I suspect he got the contract because he was the local chairman of the committee to re-elect Senator Russell," said Zeb. "Why do you ask?"

"It's probably nothing, but I've got a bad feeling about a kid who might have a chip on his shoulder because of his dad being in prison. It just seems too coincidental that the security was down when this happened," said Kate.

"And, as I recall, you played a role in helping put Levi away," added Helen.

"I did," said Zeb. "However, I don't know how we're going to tie all of that together. But, it's a starting point. It seems loosely related at best to me. I agree as unrelated as it seems we still should have a look into it."

Jake sauntered into the office, unaware of what had just happened.

"What the hell is going on here?" he asked. "Looks like I missed out on all the fun. I gotta drink my coffee a little faster."

"We had an intruder. I got bonked on the head and fell on Helen who was hog tied and Duct taped."

"I think I broke her shoulder, probably damaged her arm to boot. Doc is on his way over now," said Zeb.

"Good thing we spent all that money on that fancy security camera get-up," said Jake. "I bet all that expensive modern technology did most of our investigation for us."

"Don't bet your retirement on that," said Helen.

"It's out of order," added Kate. "A technician is working on it."

"Check out the techie," said Jake. "You can almost bet that he's involved somehow."

"I'm already on it," said Kate.

"Did Zeb or Helen see anything?" asked Jake.

"We're right in the middle of that," said Kate.

"Well, don't let me stop you," said Jake. "How you doing, Helen?"

"I'll be all right," replied Helen. "Thanks for asking."

"Zeb, it looks like someone transplanted a golf ball into the back of your skull."

"It feels more like a softball, but I'll be fine."

Zeb returned to quizzing his secretary.

"Did you recognize anything else about the two intruders?"

"Only the one did most of the talking. The voice was kind of in the high range for a man. If he sang in the church choir, which I highly doubt he does, he'd be a high alto. There was no accent to speak of. I would say from the voice that the person seemed to be roughly forty some years old. Not old, but not young. Hard to tell because all I heard were whispers. The one who did the talking had a military tattoo on the right forearm. Helen tapped her own right arm just above the wrist.

"Military tattoo?" asked Zeb.

"Yes, most certainly military. The tattoo was a rifle stuck in the ground with a helmet resting on top of it. I've seen the image many times," said Helen. She paused. "This one had initials or a name tattooed near it."

Zeb could see Helen was thinking back to the incident itself. He was concerned she might self-trigger another panic attack, but he knew she was tough as nails when she had to be.

"What are you remembering, Helen?" asked Zeb.

"When the whispering in my ear was going on, I could smell something. It was like an herb or something like that. I didn't recognize it. It smelled like dirt and herbs combined. It was strange. It didn't smell bad, but it didn't smell good. But, then again, I am not much for herbs. I don't like to use them in my cooking. Neither the kids nor my husband cared for spices other than salt and pepper."

"You sure it was herbs you smelled?" asked Zeb. "Maybe thyme, sage, cinnamon, nutmeg, chamomile, like the tea I drink? Any idea of which herb?"

Helen sighed loudly. She was in pain and gave Zeb a stern look. He backed off.

"Sorry, I don't mean to push you."

"Oh, you're not," replied Helen. "It's just so frustrating. It seems like I should remember everything, but I was so scared."

"Take a breather," said Jake, placing his hand on her uninjured shoulder. "It'll all come back to you. No sense pressuring yourself."

"Thanks, Jake, but I know it's best not to let too much time pass as it might make my memory faulty. I learned that a long time ago at a sheriff's secretaries' convention up in Las Vegas."

"I believe I was sheriff back then," said Jake. "You thought you might want to be the first woman deputy in Graham County, maybe even sheriff."

"You're right, you were sheriff, but I never wanted to be sheriff. You did get me to play the penny slot machines between meetings."

"If I remember right, you quit after losing fifty cents."

They both laughed at the memory. Helen relaxed and once again felt at ease enough to tell her tale.

"When the intruder whispered in my ear, there was something about the breath. I can't really place it. It wasn't like it was bad breath or good breath. Maybe like someone with a bad tooth, not a rotten tooth, but a tooth problem."

"Herbs, tattoos, high voice, something strange about the breath and the security system down," said Jake. "It's a good starting point. Any other tidbit you might remember, Helen?"

"I didn't recognize much else," said Helen. "The cadence of the voice seemed vaguely familiar, but I couldn't really place it. The person was definitely primarily an English speaker but may have had a bit of Hispanic or Native American accent, but only a little tiny bit. Wait a second. The military boots were soft sided. They rode three or four inches above the ankle bone. They seemed to be genuine military issue, like I've seen soldiers wear. They were identical to the kind National Guard soldiers wear when they're on duty. You see guys and gals with them all the time when they are at the Safford Armory on weekend warrior duty."

"What color were they?" asked Zeb.

"The color was light sand-brown, but like I said, they were camouflaged. I'd say they were about size nine or ten. They looked about the same size as my husband's boots and shoes. He wears a size nine and a half. I can't say how tall the person was because I was on the floor most of the time, and I was scared half out of my mind. The intruder had a pretty good build, square shoulders and seemed in good shape. One odd thing is that the fingernails were clean. I could have sworn they had a clear coat of polish on them, but men don't do that, do they? Or do they these days? I remember thinking it was strange, the combination of strange breath and cleanly polished fingernails. In fact, now that I think about it, the hands were almost effeminate, like a woman's hands."

"Every detail matters, Helen," said Kate. "What about the tattoo? Can you describe it in more detail?"

Helen finished her water and asked for more. Zeb was amazed at how quickly she was apparently shaking off the ill effects of her harrowing near death encounter and how well she was holding up under the pain of a broken collarbone.

"I remember the tattoo had a United States flag in the background, and the rifle was stuck into the ground between a pair of boots," said Helen. "That's about all I can remember. Wait, there was something, some letters or a name near the tattoo. It was half covered and I didn't see it very well, certainly not well enough to read it. But there was something else there."

Her description of the tattooed intruder was interrupted by a phone call. Helen quickly regained her work demeanor and answered with her undamaged arm.

"Graham County Sheriff's office. How may I help you?"

"This is Senator Clinton Russell's office. The senator would like to speak with Sheriff Hanks. Is he available?"

"One moment," replied Helen, holding the receiver against her body to block out her voice.

"Zeb, it's Senator Russell's office," she whispered. "He wants to speak to you."

Zeb nodded as he pressed a wet towel Kate had brought to him against the back of his head. He headed to his office, shut the door halfway, glancing at his hat and holstered gun before sitting at this desk. He cursed himself beneath his breath for not having been carrying his gun. He picked up line one just as Doc Yackley came bursting like a cannon shot through the front door of the sheriff's office.

"What in the name of the jumpin' Jehovah is going on here? Helen, I heard you broke your collar, your arm and are damn lucky you didn't break your neck. Why aren't you lying down and taking the pressure off your injuries. This damn office will run well enough without you trying to kill yourself by doing everybody else's jobs when you're injured. Now tell me what in the hell happened?"

Zeb kept one hand over the receiver as Helen calmly explained what had happened. Doc's examination took about one minute to come to a conclusion.

"You're coming to the clinic, pronto. I've got to take an X-ray, set your broken collarbone and bandage you up," said Doc. "You're going to be out of commission for a while if I have anything to say about it. Knowing you, I probably don't have much of a say in it, but that doesn't mean you shouldn't follow my orders. Come to think of it, if you did, it would be the first time."

Helen offered no protest and, uncharacteristically, barely took the time to glance back toward Zeb's office where he held the phone in his hand, Senator Russell on the other end. She only briefly attempted to stall Doc Yackley from taking her to his office so that she might hear a word or two of what Zeb and Senator Russell were discussing. Doc would have no part of her shenanigans and hustled her out of the office into his oversized classic Cadillac.

4

SENATOR RUSSELL

"This is Sheriff Hanks."

"One moment please. Senator Russell is waiting for you." The senator's aide was cordial yet professional. "I will connect you with the senator now, Sheriff Hanks."

"Zeb? How goes the state of my State?" asked the senator.

"The state of Arizona is likely running just fine, but at this exact moment I've got a pounder of a headache," replied Zeb. "My secretary..."

"Helen?" asked Senator Russell.

"Yes, Helen. She has a broken collarbone and maybe a fractured forearm."

"Didn't she just answer the phone?"

"Yes."

"When did she get injured?" asked the senator.

"Within the last hour," replied Zeb.

"Good lord, Zeb, don't you think you should let her go to the doctor?"

"Doc Yackley is looking at her right now."

"Sounds like you've got more than a little trouble down your way," said Senator Russell."

"We do," replied Zeb.

"Sometimes it just goes with the territory, doesn't it?"

"It does. Some days you write the song and some days the song writes you?"

"Not quite sure I follow you, Zeb. How hard did you get hit on the head?"

"Not that hard. What can I do for you, Senator?"

"Two things. First of all, my son, Sun Rey, has wandered away from the treatment center. I think he might be headed back to your part of Arizona. Can you keep an eye out for him and let me know if shows up?"

"Why'd he leave the treatment facility?' asked Zeb.

"Too confining, at least that's my take on it. He was always bitching that it felt like being in prison. Being confined with other troubled people and the anti-psychotic drugs they were having him take seemed to suck the life out of him. He hated those drugs with a passion."

"Why would you assume he's coming here?" asked Zeb.

"Just a hunch. I suspect it was the only place he ever felt at home. I don't know. Frankly I'm worried that he might do something crazy again. I talked with his counselor, and she's convinced he is a paranoid schizophrenic. We got a second opinion that said he was a social deviant with tendencies toward sociopathic behavior."

"That's a pair of unhealthy diagnoses," said Zeb.

"He absolutely refuses to take his medications as prescribed. He claims they make him feel not like himself, which in his case is a good thing. But, on the other hand, who wants their brain to feel differently than it normally does?"

"Does he have a tattoo on his forearm by any chance?" asked Zeb.

"Not that I know of. Why?" asked Senator Russell.

"Nothing. Just a thought running through my aching head. I'll inform everyone on my staff to keep an eye out for him."

"Thanks."

"You said there were two things."

"Yes, do you remember FBI Agent Rodriguez?" asked Senator Russell.

Zeb's skin crawled at the mere mention of Rodriguez's name. He was one of only a very small number of people who could connect Zeb to the retribution he had personally delivered to Doreen's killer. For many reasons, some legitimate and some unknown, Zeb and Rodriguez stuck in each other's craws like sideways chicken bones.

"Hell yes, I remember him. Why?"

"He had a complete nervous breakdown after I had him transferred to Alaska. You do remember that I had him transferred as a favor to you?"

Zeb didn't like the little game Senator Russell seemed to be playing. Of course he remembered. It was a personal favor delivered by the senator for Zeb.

"I do," said Zeb.

"Rodriguez is back in Arizona, working as an agent again."

"How is that possible if he is unstable?"

"You ever try to fire a federal employee? Especially an FBI agent? They practically have to murder someone to lose their job."

"Right, I forget how strong the federal unions are," replied Zeb.

"I think he's still gunning for you," said Senator Russell.

"What makes you say that?"

"He called my office and asked if I could put in a good word with the regional FBI director and help him get his old job back. I owe him a few favors, so I did. In passing he asked my chief-of-staff if you were still the sheriff of Graham County. It might mean nothing at all, but I thought you should know."

"Thanks. Does he have a military tattoo on his arm?" asked Zeb.

"What?" asked the senator, though Zeb knew he had clearly heard him.

"A military tattoo."

Zeb heard the senator bark out an order to a staff member to pull up the file on Agent Rodriguez and check it for arm tattoos. In thirty seconds he got his answer.

"Yes. He got it after the first Gulf war. It's on his right forearm. Why do you ask?"

"What's the tattoo?"

Once again the senator shouted out a question to his aide. The assistant must have brought Senator Russell a picture of Agent Rodriguez and his tattooed arm.

"It's a Fallen Soldier Battle Cross tattoo. Helmet atop a rifle butt that is stuck in the ground between a pair of combat boots. Flag in the background. Like I said, it says in his file he's a veteran of the first Gulf War, an Army Ranger. He served as a sniper with twelve confirmed kills. He often operated behind enemy lines. He earned a Purple heart and numerous other combat commendations."

"Fuck," grumbled Zeb.

"What's that, Zeb?"

"Nothing. Thanks. We'll keep a good eye out for your son. I'll have one of my deputies check into his known associates and places he was known to frequent."

"Good. Thanks. I think that will be helpful."

"I'd like something in return," said Zeb.

Senator Russell's response was stern.

"This is my son we're talking about."

"I am well aware of that," replied Zeb.

"What do you want in return?" asked Senator Russell.

"A copy of Agent Rodriguez's work discharge, his military records and all his medical and dental records including his mental health disability discharge," replied Zeb.

"You're assuming I can get them in the first place."

"You know you can."

"Giving you a copy of his medical records would violate HIPPA," said Senator Russell.

"Yeah, so what? You, yourself, said he was gunning for me. It would help if I had some background information on his physical and mental states."

Senator Russell hesitated fifteen seconds before answering. Zeb found the lack of a quick response irritating. It was the least Senator Russell could do for him, considering the circumstances.

"Okay, I'll have everything faxed over today," said Senator Russell. "And Zeb..."

"Yes?"

"Please find my son before he harms himself or someone else."

The pleading in Senator Russell's voice sounded like that of a loving father genuinely concerned about his son who was definitely disturbed and very likely in some kind of trouble. Zeb hoped he or Jake would be the ones who located him. If Kate found him and he confronted her, it wouldn't take much, based on how she felt about Sun Rey, for her to put a bullet in him if the situation called for it.

"I'll do my best," said Zeb. "Please mark the fax as confidential so my secretary doesn't get too snoopy. She's had a bad day, and God only knows what she'd think if she read the file."

"Why is that?" asked the senator.

"The person who tied her up and bonked me over the head had the same tattoo on his forearm as Rodriguez does," said Zeb. "I don't want her jumping to any conclusions."

"On second thought, I'll have it sent it overnight by Fed-Ex. I'll make certain it's marked private. That way no one should see it but you."

"Thanks, Senator Russell."

"Thank you, Sheriff Hanks. Good luck. Please keep me in the loop the minute you learn anything," said the standing senator from the state of Arizona.

"I will."

"And since your secretary broke her collarbone on the job, you might want to give her a couple of days off to heal up."

Zeb shook his head at Senator Russell's suggestion.

"It'll take more than that to keep her from working. She's a tough cookie. I wouldn't be surprised if she came back to the office later today after they set her broken collarbone."

"Then you're lucky to have her. I could use some of that kind of loyalty around here. Speaking of loyalty, did you remember to vote for Devon Dawbyns for state senator?" asked Senator Russell.

A curious chain of events, including the sudden death from a heart attack of the standing local state senator only ninety days before the election combined with the deep financial pockets of friends of Senator Russell, led the relatively unknown Devon Dawbyns to a seat in the Arizona state legislature.

"I stopped by his victory celebration to congratulate him," said Zeb. "As we both know, there is nothing quite like winning your first election."

"Nothing quite like it," said Senator Russell, "After a taste of victory most men and women will go to any length to make certain they maintain their power."

"Devon seemed more comfortable heading to the legislature than he ever did as a deputy sheriff," said Zeb.

Having expertly placed a bullet between the eyes of a vicious criminal was all the gun advocating, heavily leaning Republican region needed to make him their man. He had even garnered well over sixty-eight percent of the Democrat vote.

"I think he'll do all right in the legislature," said Zeb. "It seems like a good fit for him."

"Oh, I'm certain that young Mr. Dawbyns has the killer instinct of a politician," said Senator Russell. "By the way, I'm going to be at my lodge, between Safford and Tucson, in a couple of weeks. I'm giving a little shindig for Devon, Tribal Chief Nations Wentsler and a few other local folks. It would be nice if you could come and even nicer if Sun Rey were there to celebrate with us. I've had my son on the payroll doing odds and ends for a while now. I kept him on the payroll while he was in rehab. The kid can't sit still. He's always got to be multi-tasking."

"Sounds like he's a lot like you in that way," said Zeb.

"He's my son. What else could I do? Speaking of support, have you found a suitable replacement for your former deputy, State Senator Devon Dawbyns?"

"No, not yet. We have someone in mind. The guy's name is Sawyer Black Bear."

"Apache?"

"No."

"Native American?"

"Mixed. Lakota and White."

"If he's a good fit, you should hire him. I hate to think of you being understaffed," said Senator Russell. "Especially now."

"Sawyer Black Bear is the son of an old buddy of Jake's, from way back. Jake is doing most of the work on it. If he's as good face-to-face as he is on paper, I probably will make him an offer. I'm not much for doing a lot of interviews. I like to think I can spot a good man or woman when I see one."

"Good. Don't get caught shorthanded. I've got to run. Keep me in the loop on Sun Rey, please, and good luck to both you and Helen with your injuries."

Zeb had no more than hung up the phone when there was a knock on the door. It was Kate.

"Zeb, we found this jammed into the outside doorjamb. It had your name on it."

She handed Zeb a single piece of paper.

"You read it?" asked Zeb.

"I found it, so naturally I looked at it. You might say I could hardly avoid reading it. I had to find out what it was." said Kate.

"Do you think one of the intruders left it behind?"

"Maybe as they were leaving. Anything's possible. My gut tells me it's from someone else."

"What does it say?"

Kate didn't pull any punches on the injured sheriff.

"It's short. It's a threat aimed directly at you."

Zeb looked at the single page. His name was scrawled across the top. **SHERIFF ZEB HANKS**. A terse message was written in bold letters just below. Its few words could only be construed as a direct, dark and twisted threat.

THE BEST REVENGE IS REVENGE. THIS ISN'T OVER. WE WILL MEET AGAIN!

5

DEAD BODY

Zeb's cellphone rang. The ringer reverberated with a pounding drum beat. The musical intonation had been a tongue-in-cheek, re-election gift in the form of a downloaded phone app. Anyone who had ever seen an old western cowboy movie knew this as the music that played in the background when Indians were attacking. Musicians knew it as the *Apache War Dance Song*. Zeb knew it meant Tribal Police Chief Rambler Braing was on the other end of the line.

"Rambler."

"Zeb."

"You busy?" asked Rambler.

"Always."

"Got a minute?"

"For you, hell yes."

Zeb flipped off the television. He had been enjoying re-watching the first season of *Justified* on Netflix. He recently had become invested in daydreaming about becoming a United States Marshal should he ever be voted out of office.

"What's up, Chief?"

"How's the bump on the back of your noggin'?"

"How do you know about that?" asked Zeb.

"A friend sent me some smoke signals," replied Rambler. "They said 'Heap big White law man getting old and too slow to get out of way of gun handle'."

"You are a funny dude, Rambler, a regular comedian. What's the real reason you interrupted my favorite television program?"

"You watching Raylan Givens get his man?"

"You bet," answered Zeb. "I love that show. I take it you watch *Justified*?"

"I've seen every episode three times. Man, if real life only operated that way, our jobs would be a lot easier," said Rambler. "That boy can shoot a gun."

"Got that right. To what do I owe the pleasure of this call?"

"Big trouble. Trouble that I'm certain involves you."

Zeb eased back into his chair and lifted his feet onto the coffee table. His motion caused the threatening note he had received earlier that day to fall from his lap and zig-zag its way to the floor. He let it lay. From the sound of Rambler's voice some sort of trouble was headed down the path toward Zeb's door.

"Aha, the bearer of bad news. Are you going to make my day even more complex?"

"Yup, I guess I am."

"What is it?" asked Zeb.

"Jimmy Song Bird..."

"Is he all right?" asked Zeb. "I've been having the strangest thoughts about him lately."

"Whenever I get that feeling, he's got something up his sleeve that involves me, but he's fine. No need to worry about him."

"Good. What is it then?"

"Song Bird was doing a ceremony with one of our returning military veterans at the edge of San Carlos Lake just a few hours ago. They found a body floating in the lake," said Rambler. "To be precise, Sergeant Skysong of the United States Army found the body."

"Okay," replied Zeb. "The body must be covered in white skin if you're calling me."

"It is, but that's not why I'm calling you. I think this is going to be an issue for you, not because of skin color but because of who is dressed in the white skin."

"Why all the suspense?" asked Zeb. "Who is it?"

"Well, therein lies the rub. It's a male in his twenties. He was on the receiving end of two shotgun blasts, one to the neck and the other to the groin."

"Ouch," said Zeb.

"He ain't feeling a thing now," said Rambler.

"Pellets or slugs?" asked Zeb.

"Both," replied Rambler.

"That's odd," said Zeb.

"What's really more unique about the situation is that one of the shots was from a significant distance, an almost impossible distance to make a decent shot from. A shot that would require an expert shooter. The second shot was about as up close and personal as it gets."

"What are you talking about, Rambler? What you're describing doesn't make much sense to me, but then again my head still hurts and I'm a touch foggy," said Zeb.

"The kill shot, the one to the neck, was from a distance of roughly two hundred twenty-five yards," said Rambler. "And, as you have already surmised, that shot was the slug. I don't think the dead man felt much. It blew away half his neck, part of his jaw and some of his face."

"Two hundred twenty-five yards is one hell of a long shot for a shotgun slug. I don't know that I could make a shot like that with any degree of accuracy," said Zeb.

"You couldn't. I couldn't. Most people couldn't. Only a real pro could make that kind of shot, unless they were just damn lucky," said Rambler.

"How did you figure the distance?" asked Zeb. "I don't know that I could figure something like that out so quickly."

"Sergeant Skysong had some fancy military method that determined the distance. It was damn clever. Can't say as I understand how the calculation was done. When we had the distance figured, we backtracked and found a set of footprints two hundred twenty-five yards from where the body fell," said Rambler.

"Did Sergeant Skysong help you with that one too?" asked Zeb.

"I never turn down the help of an expert," replied Rambler. "I'm just a humble tribal chief of police, serving at the request of the voting public of the San Carlos Apache Nation."

"I don't think I'd say humility is your strong suit," said Zeb.

"You're entitled to your opinion, even if it's wrong."

"And the second shot? Where did it come from?"

"A couple of inches away from the body. It really was up close and personal. He's got two hundred or so pellets where his private parts used to be."

"Used to be?" asked Zeb. "Jesus, that ain't good."

"It looks to me as though someone killed him with the long shot, then they walked up to the dead body and, somewhere on that short march, chambered an upland small game shell in the same gun. They stuffed the barrel of the gun right down his pants and let him have it. It blew away everything that used to be there."

"Double ouch on the dead man. I'd say that tells us we've got one angry shooter on our hands," said Zeb.

"Good call. You figure that out from your training or watching *CSI*?"

"Just thinking out loud, funny man."

"Any ID on the body?"

"That's why I called you," said Rambler.

"Let me guess, this is where the bad news part comes along?" said Zeb.

"It is," said Rambler. "The dead man's billfold has two driver's licenses."

Zeb knew most professional criminals frequently carried multiple IDs.

"Yes," said Zeb. "Same name or different identities."

"Pretty much the same."

"What've you got on the IDs?"

"One is from the District of Columbia and one from Arizona. The Arizona license has the name of Sun Rey. The D.C. license has the name of Sun Rey Russell."

"Shit," said Zeb.

"Kind of thought that might be your reaction."

"Goddamn it. I just heard from Senator Russell today. He was looking for his wayward son."

"As in Sun Rey Russell?"

"One and the same," replied Zeb.

"That's the way I had it figured. I don't think the senator is going to take this too well," said Rambler. "This is the kind of news no one wants to get."

"When I told him I would keep an eye out for his son, I never expected this."

"Zeb, you couldn't possibly have known something like this would happen."

"He was a wildly troubled young man. It didn't take a lot of figuring to realize bad news was going to bite him in the ass sooner rather than later."

"The grapevine on the Rez says that Sun Rey was a terribly wounded spirit. In fact, the rumor is that more than one person said they'd kill him if he ever set foot on the Rez. Definitely more than one person wanted revenge against him."

"Any names attached to the rumors?" asked Zeb.

"So far all I've got is rumors. No one is saying who started the allegations or who stated they would kill Sun Rey," replied Rambler.

"Does Senator Russell have a bone to pick with you or one of the power players on the Rez?"

"Curious question," replied Rambler. "Not that I know of. Do you know something I don't?"

"No," said Zeb. "Just a thought running through my head."

"Seems to be a habit of yours, speaking your thoughts out loud I mean," said Rambler.

"The best revenge is revenge." Zeb said it aloud, pondering its meaning.

"Come again?" said Rambler. "I'm not following you, Zeb. You're not making sense. And you're speaking your thoughts out loud again."

"This is about revenge," said Zeb. "R-E-V-E-N-G-E."

"Revenge against Senator Russell?"

"And likely revenge against me," replied Zeb. "Maybe even revenge against you."

Zeb reached over and picked up the note from the floor. He read it aloud to Rambler. "The Best Revenge Is Revenge. This Isn't Over. We Will Meet Again."

"What the hell is that supposed to mean?" asked Rambler. "What on earth are you talking about?"

"It was in a note left behind for me shortly after Helen and I were assaulted. The attackers may have left it behind, but really it could have been anyone. Kate found it in the doorjamb but not when she first came in. She found it later when she was leaving the office."

"Do you think you're next on the killer's list?" asked Rambler. "Or do you think it's something else entirely?"

"I'm on someone's list. I just don't know for certain whose list it is or where on the list I sit," replied Zeb. "Or, for that matter, what the list is all about."

"If the person or persons who attacked Helen and you today wanted to kill you, it seems to me you would already be dead," said Rambler. "Obviously you're not number one on the killer's hit list."

"But I must be on it. Why else would someone leave that note? I'm thinking whoever is behind this just wants to make me sweat a little first."

"Beware the fury of a patient man."

Rambler's words struck a nerve.

"We know the killer is more than a little twisted in the mind and unflappable."

"Unflappable?" asked Rambler.

"Who else would risk shooting someone with a loud shotgun and then take the time to walk a few hundred yards and fire a second shot when there could have easily been campers, fishermen, neighbors or people out for a night stroll? The shooter had to have brass balls or a damn good reason to do what they did."

Any idea on what the killer's motive might be?"

"I'm afraid to say I just might understand it all too perfectly," replied Zeb.

"The murder of Sun Rey reeks of revenge," said Rambler. "And it is nothing if not cold blooded and riddled with anger."

"Rambler, anyone linked to Senator Russell, myself and maybe even you could be next on the list."

"Why me?"

"You don't think it was an accident that the murder was committed on the Rez, do you?"

"Probably not, but a killer might believe it would be easier to get away with murder on the Rez. It's a common misconception that murders on Indian reservations don't get solved."

"We've got to whittle down our list of suspects," said Zeb. "You work on it from the reservation angle, and I'll work on it through a potential enemies' list that Sun Rey might have."

"Don't forget his father might have more than a few local enemies. Men in his position can piss people off."

"We both need to stand back and think of why someone would want to make sure both you and I were involved in the murder investigation of Sun Rey."

"In the past Senator Russell has done me more than a few solid favors," said Rambler. "I owe him. You want me to give him the bad news? I'm less personally linked to him than you are. It might be easier coming from me."

"Thanks, but no thanks. I'll break the news to him myself. I owe him that much."

"Okay, your call," said Rambler.

"We've got some real history between us," said Zeb.

"A bromance with a United States Senator? Never took you for the type. But, hey, you never can tell these days, can you?"

"Knock off the funny business. It's just history, history that I really can't share with you."

"Must have something to do with what happened down ol' Mexico way, eh, compadre blanco?"

"What makes you say that?" asked Zeb, stunned by the fact that Rambler would know anything at all about Mexico or, for that matter, say anything about it.

"I hear things," said Rambler. "We redskins have our special ways that the White man doesn't understand. We can hear on the wind what is whispered miles away and we can close our eyes and see what can never be seen."

"Don't believe a tenth of what you hear and only half of what you see," said Zeb.

"Sounds like I hit a nerve," said Rambler. "To paraphrase the great Nez-Pierce Chief Joseph, 'I shall speak of it no more forever'...except maybe to you, if necessary."

"I'd say that's a good idea. Now let's get back to business. You said Song Bird and a returning military guy found the body?"

"No, I said Song Bird and a returning military veteran found the body," said Rambler.

"You make it sound like it was a woman who was with Song Bird."

"It was. One of our finest. In fact, she is the first Native American woman to serve side-by-side in combat with the Army Special Forces in Afghanistan. She served with the Army Rangers for three consecutive tours. She is highly decorated to boot," said Rambler. "Not only the first Native American to serve in that capacity but one of the first five women ever to do a complete twelve-month tour in a combat zone with Army Special Forces. She's quite a woman and has one of the most powerful spirits I have ever witnessed."

"What's her name?"

"Echo Skysong," replied Rambler. "You may have read about her in the *Native American News* or the *Courier*. Both papers gave her a significant amount of ink after her second tour of duty. I don't think she was too happy about that. She's a very private person. She was really ticked when *Stars and Stripes* wrote her up."

"I read the local articles. I didn't know about the one in *Stars and Stripes*. In fact, I met her once, briefly, at Song Bird's house. We chatted for a few moments, but this was before all of the publicity. The one odd thing I remember is that even though she was on leave she wore her military uniform boots with a stunningly beautiful, handmade Apache dress. I asked her about wearing boots and a traditional dress, sort of in a joking manner. She said they were the most comfortable shoes she had ever owned. I didn't go into it any further than that, but I had a strong suspicion that her family was poor."

"Damn near everybody on the Rez is poor, Zeb. Poverty and Apache Indian are practically synonymous. But her family was nearly destitute, even by Rez standards. The family was poor monetarily, but wealthy in the ways that really matter. All that being said, she's a beautifully spiritual woman and one hell of a looker to boot."

"I couldn't help but notice that," said Zeb.

"You ever date one of the girls from our team?" asked Rambler.

"Just one, Maya Song Bird, back in high school. It was really more just hanging out than serious dating. Outside of Doreen I never really dated much at all, much less Native American girls," replied Zeb. "I believe you just asked me a question you already knew the answer to."

"I did," said Rambler. "You don't need to be so politically correct about it. Let me cut to the chase. You should ask her out on a date. I know for a fact she's not seeing anyone. She'd be a hell of a catch. She's younger than you, but I also know she has a thing for older guys. You should think about it, seriously think about it. Hell, if I wasn't married, I'd ask her out in a heartbeat."

Zeb stammered out something that Rambler clearly understood to be an excuse. Zeb mumbled something about Doreen, who had been dead for well over a year now.

"Maybe later," said Zeb. "I just don't know if I'm ready to date yet."

"What the hell are you talking about? You know Doreen wouldn't want you to be alone, and the whole town knows you are lonely. Want me to set it up?" asked Rambler. "I would be glad to do you the favor."

"No." This time Zeb's voice was firm and resolute. His heart was still on the mend, of that he was certain. To go out on an actual date would feel like he was being unfaithful.

"I didn't say you should marry her. I merely suggested some female companionship might do you some good. You like motorcycles and so does she. In fact, she bought a Harley with her re-enlistment bonus between her first and second tours. It's a Harley Davidson Iron 883. It's the only one I've ever seen up close. Very cool bike. With your love for bikes, you would really dig it."

Zeb's mind flipped to Doreen's grave marker. Doreen had it written into her will that her Harley Davidson Electra Glide should be preserved in hardened plastic and used for her headstone. Then Zeb thought about his own Harley. He hadn't ridden it; hell he hadn't even turned the engine over since he and Doreen took a weekend getaway out in Yuma shortly before she was murdered in the coldest of blood by a sword through her heart.

Zeb could clearly see the icon etched into the sword that had killed Doreen, two serpents, snakes, entwined on a staff and mounted by a devil. The sword's logo formed an image in his mind as though the evil spirit from hell was looking directly at the freshly dead body of his deceased wife. With all the will power he could muster Zeb forced the horrible picture from his mind. Rambler's voice came echoing at him from what seemed like a distant empty cavern.

"Hey, hey cowboy. You hear me or have you gone deaf?" asked Rambler.

"What did you say again?" asked Zeb.

The overwhelming sadness in Zeb's voice told Rambler all he needed to know about the journey Zeb's mind had just taken him on.

"My brother, my cowpoke, my White brethren," said Rambler, "I know there is suffering in your heart. Anyone can see the gate to your spirit has been slammed shut and wired tightly with heart strings from your past. But you need to move forward with your life. You can do that and not betray your love for Doreen."

Rambler's words were hard to hear, but they were both sound and true. Zeb had to move off the dime at some point and take a step forward with his life. But every time he thought about momentum moving him toward change, a painful or a loving thought or image of Doreen came blasting into his brain.

"I know. I know that at some point I have to get on with that part of my life. Thanks for your concern. I just don't know if now is the right time," said Zeb.

"There's never going to be a *right* time," said Rambler. "If you are waiting for the *right* time, you will carry that moment right into your grave. I hate to sound so harsh, but you know I thought the world of Doreen."

"I know you cared for Doreen. I promise you that I will think about what you're saying," said Zeb, knowing that Rambler would be relentless until he conceded at least the possibility of thinking about dating the local Native American war hero.

"Great. Think about it, but if you need an idea for a date, take her to Ted's Shooting Range and see if you can outshoot her. I'll bet you dollars to donuts you can't. She can toss a half dollar coin in the air and shoot a hole in the center of it using her .22 rifle or her .22 pistol. Hand her a service revolver, and she'll blow that same coin to kingdom come."

"Bullshit," said Zeb. "That only happens in the movies."

"Echo is an expert markswoman and has the looks of a young movie star. I'll bet you she can do it. What are you afraid of? That you might actually enjoy yourself? That it might actually be fun? That she might actually be able to outshoot the legendary Zeb Hanks?"

Rambler's chiding was fair play. Zeb had been a superior marksman since he first picked up a gun. Both Song Bird and Jake had schooled him with just about every handgun and long gun legally available and a few more that weren't available to law abiding citizens. On the rifle range as kids he and Rambler were by far the best student shooters. Both of them had made the finals in the state clay pigeon shooting contest. Some rich kid from Tucson with his own personal rifle range had beaten them. Zeb and Rambler finished tied for second.

"No, I'm not afraid of having some fun," said Zeb. "I am not afraid to enjoy myself. Deep down inside I'm a fun loving guy."

"Yeah, right. You are a regular hell raising fun factory. Anyone with eyes can see that."

Rambler's mocking works were fair game, and Zeb knew them to be true.

"Gimme a break," said Zeb. "You know I used to be a fun guy. Look at all the good times you and I had back in the day."

"That was back in the day, a lifetime maybe two lifetimes ago. It looks to me like you have been holding yourself back from the joy of living for quite a while. I am not saying that you should not mourn properly. I do believe you should. I also believe that as long as you are breathing in air and taking nourishment you should be enjoying life as well."

"I suppose," lamented Zeb.

Zeb's mind wandered to the possibility of getting outgunned by a woman. Even though she had Army Special Forces training it seemed pretty unlikely she could outshoot him. The shooting challenge seemed like an easy way to get back on a horse he had put away in the barn for over a year.

"Is she your cousin or something? Why are you so interested in me dating her?" asked Zeb.

"You want to know something?" asked Rambler.

"Not really, but I'd bet you're going to tell me anyway."

"You carry that sad expression on your face when it comes to women, hell you have a long face when it comes to anything but work. You look as forlorn as W.C Fields on the cover of the Beatles album, *Sargent Pepper's Lonely Hearts Club Band*. I think some female interaction would do you a world of good. I speak as your long-time friend and as someone who knows your meager dating history. In fact, I think it is about time you dated a Native American woman...again."

"I'll think about it," said Zeb. "No promises, but I will give it some serious thought."

"If you drive out here right now, you can meet Echo. She and Song Bird are waiting here with me. They're standing about thirty feet from me, right next to Sun Rey's body," said Rambler. "You have the opportunity to kill two birds with one stone. You have to come and see Sun Rey's body anyway. Why not meet Echo in the process?"

It smacked of a set-up. However, the dead body was real and Zeb had an obligation to Senator Russell and the law. Rambler wouldn't be fooling around when it came to murder.

"I'll be there in twenty minutes," said Zeb.

"Good," replied Rambler. "That way, even at this time of year, you can arrive before darkness. You'll get a better look at all the things you should want to see."

6

INSIDE ZEB'S HEAD

Zeb grabbed his gun and badge for his trip to the Rez. He walked to the kitchen to refill his tea for the drive. As he waited for the water to come to a boil, a multitude of strange contemplations passed through his mind. He thought of the note left behind at the time of the attack at his office. He ruminated on what it had said: *The best revenge is revenge. This isn't over. We will meet again.* Zeb was certain the note had been a direct warning to him from Rodriguez. Was this, the death site of Sun Rey Russell, the next meeting place the note spoke of?

Deductive reasoning told the sheriff that the tattoo Helen had seen on the intruder's arm was a reasonable, but not conclusive, confirmation that Rodriguez was one of the attackers. Rodriguez didn't quite fit Helen's description. He was larger than the intruder she described, but he did have a high, squeaky voice. However, considering the stress of the situation, the voice being muffled by the mask and Helen's state of mind, she could have mixed things up.

Zeb had long assumed Rodriguez had figured out that Senator Russell was responsible for him being sent to Alaska. Somehow Rodriguez had also figured out he had been sent away at Zeb's request. Rodriguez's subsequent mental breakdown likely pushed the agent far over the edge. Zeb reckoned Rodriguez had a rather large axe to grind against both Senator Russell and him. Killing the senator's son would get retribution against the senator. Murdering Sun Rey near but just off of Zeb's turf on the Rez would quite literally create a triple shit storm for Zeb and crush the senator in one fell swoop. The location also brought Rambler into the equation. What that meant was a conundrum. In Zeb's mind Rodriguez was enough of a deviant to create a complexly nefarious plan with many working parts.

Zeb nodded in agreement with himself as he continued to try and put the pieces together so they made sense. If one of the intruders at the sheriff's office had been Rodriguez, the former Army Ranger/sniper and FBI agent easily had the skill to have killed Zeb, Helen and anyone else who might have been there. However, if it was Rodriguez, he chose not to. His deliberate actions were obviously meant to terrify Helen and threaten Zeb. The invaders at the sheriff's office had a dark plan. It flashed through Zeb's mind that the killer was truly seeking revenge, a slowly cooked and well plotted out vengeance. Then again, considering the number of people who may have had it in for Sun Rey, he couldn't discount the possibility of numerous other suspects. Still, Rodriguez loomed ever large in his mind.

Zeb's link to Sun Rey could be best defined by several degrees of separation. Zeb was a long term acquaintance but by no means tight with Sun Rey's father, Senator Russell. However, there were several dangerous links between the men. In the past he had quietly done Senator Russell a few 'under the radar' favors. The senator in turn had backchannel financed Zeb's expedition to Mexico that led to the killing of Doreen's murderer, Carmelita Montouyez. Zeb considered that part of his relationship with the senator to be strictly business. Zeb assumed Senator Russell viewed it the same way. Of course, to Zeb it was as personal as personal could ever get.

The possibility of Rodriguez being involved with El Coyote's drug cartel from his days in the Tucson FBI was not out of the question either. It seemed obvious that if Rodriguez had murdered Sun Rey, the pound of flesh he sought to exact from Senator Russell had been wholly consumed. Zeb was certain Rodriguez blamed his mental breakdown and subsequent temporary medical discharge from the FBI directly on Senator Russell. It was at Senator Russell's request that Rodriguez was shipped north to Alaska. Why Senator Russell had pulled strings to help Rodriguez get his badge back along with his Arizona duty had an unexplained and foul odor hanging over it.

If the mentally ill agent was out of control, he was definitely going to be difficult to contend with given the vast experience Rodriguez had as an FBI field operative coupled with his military background. That is, if as Zeb was assuming, the demon behind Sun Rey's death, Helen's broken arm and collarbone and Zeb's crack on the head were indeed one and the same person. Everything in his gut clearly pointed the proverbial finger directly at Rodriguez. Then again, Zeb was an experienced and adept law man to recognize his own prejudice.

Zeb was aware that Rambler had acted as a middle man for Senator Russell on the Rez for years. Exactly what that entailed had been a well-kept secret by Rambler. Since the senator held an important position on funding the BIA and had the power to direct contracts on the Rez, Zeb could only assume a fair amount of money and numerous deals had gone down between the men. He had no trouble with the politics of that. Such things were simply business as usual.

Rodriguez's dark attitude toward Zeb was a horse of a different color. For some reason the former FBI agent carried a deep-seated hatred for Zeb. The reasoning behind that animosity was nothing the sheriff could directly put his finger on and certainly nothing he could prove beyond a shadow of a doubt. It passed through his mind that if Rodriguez was somehow linked to the cartel, he was also linked to Carmelita. That, however, was mere speculation, and Zeb had no idea of how he could prove such a relationship. If Rodriguez were linked to the cartel and Carmelita, was there the possibility he knew Zeb had killed Carmelita?

Zeb finally redirected his train of thought. He has getting way ahead of himself. Such thoughts were far too random. He took a sip of the chamomile tea. It helped slow his thinking. A calmer mind quickly led Zeb to the conclusion there was really nothing outside of his vague suspicions and a fairly common military tattoo that linked Rodriguez to any of this. The more thought he gave it the more Zeb felt the light touch of paranoia mix into his thoughts. Yet he couldn't free himself from the idea that Rodriguez was Sun Rey's killer. Zeb shook his head to clear his mind of the paranoid path it was headed down. He stepped into his truck and rolled down the window just as an owl made repeated trilling sounds. Zeb counted eight of them. Song Bird had taught him as a youth that the owl was a night creature he should avoid all contact with. Song Bird had many times mentioned that if an owl calls out nearby in the evening it was a bad omen. If one called out near you during daylight hours, it prophesied an even more malicious warning. At this moment twilight was approaching. Zeb considered that he might be caught between the devil and the deep blue sea.

Zeb looked out the truck window to his left. On the longest branch of a gnarly, dying, white oak tree the yellow eyes of a whiskered screech owl glowered at him. The entire skin of his body erupted in gooseflesh. He rubbed his arms and blinked once. He looked a second time in the direction of the owl. It had disappeared as though it had never existed. Had he imagined the creature? In the distance he heard eight more calls from the bird of prey. From a further distance the quavering warble from the screech owl sounded more like a whistle than a hoot. Zeb searched his mind to remember exactly what Song Bird had taught him about the owl. Be aware when you hear the evening owl, Song Bird had said, because the hand of evil approaches stealthily from an unexpected place.

Sheriff Zeb Hanks may have been a White man, but Song Bird had taught him enough of the Apache ways to recognize a malevolent omen when it crossed his path. Experience had taught him such a strong and obvious presence indicated the hand of evil was fast approaching. Life had taught him it was time to keep up his guard.

7

MEETING

A few miles down the road, after trying to put the eeriness of the owl's ominous warning into proper perspective, Zeb placed a call to Safford's ambulance service.

"This is Sheriff Hanks. How long before you can send an ambulance to pick up a dead body?"

"Where is it?"

"At the edge of San Carlos Lake," Zeb replied.

"Not exactly our turf. I don't want to step on anyone's toes."

"You won't be. We've been asked to pick it up by the local authorities.

"Drowning?"

"No. Not a drowning. A dead body. I don't know the exact cause of death," replied Zeb.

"The crew is picking up an acute asthma attack in Thatcher. They should be able to be there in an hour, maybe a bit longer."

"That works," said Zeb. "I will be at the scene."

"Okay. Where exactly are we going to send the ambulance and crew?"

Zeb gave them the location as Rambler had described. Knowing it would be dark by the time they arrived, he detailed the directions and asked the person to read them back for the sake of clarification.

A quick trip north on State Highway 70 brought Zeb to the southern border of the San Carlos Reservation. He exited the main state highway and traveled slowly down a poorly maintained gravel and dirt road that led to his destination, San Carlos Lake.

Arriving at the scene, Zeb saw Rambler, Song Bird and Echo Skysong standing in a small circle just to the east of the dead body. Zeb knew immediately they had placed themselves there so as not to interfere with the movement of the spirit of the dead man should it be headed toward the dying light of the setting sun. The passage of the spirit of the newly deceased was yet another piece of invaluable information regarding Native American customs about which Song Bird had tutored him.

Zeb immediately noticed the remains had been covered with a traditional, handmade blanket. Rambler, as tribal police chief, always carried one or two in his truck for occasions just like this one, covering the newly dead. The blanket was filled with the handiwork of multiple Apache women and contained the traditional symbols required for passing from this life to the next. Though the dead man was not a member of the Apache Nation, his spirit nevertheless needed proper attending. Since tribal Medicine Man Jimmy Song Bird was present, it was his hallowed obligation to see that the ritual was correctly performed. The gathered group glanced toward the serenity of a setting sun. The purple, blue and pink desert sky darkly juxtaposed with the quiet repose of the dead body lying on the sandy shoreline of San Carlos Lake.

Song Bird greeted Zeb in the traditional Apache way.

"Dagot'e."

"Dant'e," replied Zeb.

They gave each other a long arm embrace, each gripping the other's elbow as their forearms rested firmly against each other. Eye contact was deep as their friendship was long. Song Bird could immediately see something more than the death of the senator's son was on Zeb's mind. In turn, Zeb witnessed how easily Song Bird read him. Such was the depth of their bond.

Circling Zeb from the southerly direction, Rambler noticed the large lump and small white bandage on the back of his friend's head. Zeb's attempt to cover the injury with his hat was pointless when it came to Rambler's keen eye.

"Looks worse than I'd heard it was," Rambler said, softly touching Zeb's injury.

"Somebody got the jump on me," replied Zeb. "Sort of embarrassing."

"Shit happens," replied Rambler. "At least you've still got a head to hang your hat on."

"Thank the good Lord for small favors," replied Zeb. "Everyone can use a hat rack now and again."

Song Bird interrupted the friends' kidding interaction. He discreetly tipped his head in Echo's direction.

"This is Echo Skysong, Sargent Echo Skysong. She is home on leave and about to be discharged from the United States Army. Zeb, of course you remember meeting her at my house a few years ago." Song Bird's words were spoken with great pride, as though she were of his own flesh and blood.

Zeb tipped his cap to Echo. She quickly thrust a hand in his direction. At once he noticed her grip was strong, firm and soft. More than her handshake he noticed she carried the faint odor of Arizona desert sage. It seemed to waft from her hair and skin. Zeb had always found desert sage to be intoxicating as well as memory provoking. Her eyes, dark as the night sky rising in the east, fixed a gaze on him, entrapping him for the briefest of moments. Realizing the intensity of her inspection, Echo glanced away ever so briefly. She was not embarrassed by her actions. She was merely doing what three tours with the Army Rangers in Afghanistan had taught her to do—read people instantly, make a snap judgement and act accordingly. Echo immediately saw into the heart of an injured soul. It was a look she had seen on many of the faces of the women, children and men in Afghanistan who had lost family members to what they called the 'eternal war with the infidels'. She looked into Zeb's eyes and spoke directly, factually.

"Good to see you again," said Zeb.

"Likewise, Sheriff Hanks. I respect your work."

"Thank you." A brief moment of awkward silence ensued before Zeb asked the obvious. "How did you discover the body?"

"Song Bird and I were walking the rim of the lake when I noticed the body from back there, by that large rock," said Echo.

As she spoke to him, even from five feet away he smelled another faint herbal odor. He thought about how Helen had described the smell of herbs and sage on her attacker. Zeb slipped the connection into memory. Many people used herbal remedies and cooked with them. Now was not the time to let his imagination run amok and start putting together pieces of an illusory puzzle.

Echo pointed a few hundred yards behind them. Spotting the body in shallow water while looking into an early evening sun from such a distance would require extraordinary vision.

"Echo spotted it long before I could tell exactly what it was," said Song Bird.

"Actually, I felt it first..." said Echo.

Song Bird knew exactly what she was talking about. Zeb and Rambler looked at each other. Rambler raised his eyebrows in acknowledgement while Zeb stared back blankly. Perhaps it was military instinct that caused her to have such an unusual ability.

"...and then the distinctly malicious odor of death flared my nostrils," said Echo.

Zeb was familiar with the smell of death but likely not as habituated to the stench as a three-tour combat veteran. This time of year the stagnant water of San Carlos Lake hid the scent of the dead body from Zeb's senses, even as he stood only feet away from it. But it was the fact that Echo noted she *felt* the presence of the deceased man that aroused his curiosity.

"Felt it?" asked Zeb. "How so?"

"She has the power of Lozen," said Song Bird. The fact that Song Bird interrupted and answered a question directed at Echo told Zeb that was all the answer he was going to get.

Echo remained stoic as Song Bird's remark left Zeb at a loss for words. What did the power of Lozen mean? He was caught off balance by something perhaps unique to Apache culture, maybe even to Echo specifically. Because of Song Bird's reaction, it didn't seem like the right moment to discuss with Echo what it meant to have *felt* death from such a distance. Zeb made a mental note to ask Echo what it meant to have the power of Lozen. Both matters would be good reasons to have a cup of coffee with her.

"I think it is best if you identify the body, that is, if you can," said Rambler. "He's pretty messed up from the shotgun blasts."

Before reverently pulling back the sanctified Apache blanket that covered the dead man, Zeb noticed two stones by the dead man's head. Before he could ask, Song Bird spoke.

"The stones are blue goldstone and white calcite," said Song Bird.

Once again, as so many times in the past, Zeb gratefully became the student of Apache beliefs. Song Bird, the perpetual teacher, obliged without even being asked.

"Blue goldstone provides a pathway for connecting us to the Divine. It is the stone of wisdom. Blue goldstone teaches us that no matter what happens there will always be light within the darkness. The spirit of the deceased must be led to the light. The white calcite is the center of the spiritual ritual regarding the tending of the soul of the deceased. We performed that sacred rite before you arrived," explained Song Bird.

Zeb committed the knowledge to memory then took a flashlight from his belt and shined the beam on the face of the dead man. Even though half of his neck and most of his lower jaw had been blown away, he instantly recognized the dead man as Sun Rey. Kneeling near the body, Zeb removed a ring from the dead man's finger. The flashlight provided light enough to read the inscription, *SRR-to a bright future my son-CJR.* It was a private inscription to Sun Rey Russell from Senator Clinton Jefferson Russell. The message was clear. Senator Russell had fully accepted his wayward son as his offspring. The weight of the phone call Zeb would have to make to Senator Russell hit him like a fast moving freight train. He took a long moment to collect his thoughts and consider his course of action. Although Zeb was one hundred percent certain the dead man was Sun Rey, he decided he would wait until he matched the fingerprints before calling the senator. A few hours would make no difference now. Choosing his words to the dead man's father likely would be exceedingly impactful. Respect for the dead and the living made him want to do this right.

Driving slowly down the gravel road toward the dead body and the gathered few, the Safford ambulance lights bounced erratically on the rutted road sending headlight beams into the bare trees and shadowy night. Upon arrival a man stepped out from the passenger's side, a woman from the driver's side. With great efficiency they opened the back of the ambulance, removed a gurney, flipped down its wheels and trudged it over the rough terrain. When they reached the body, they removed the traditional Apache blanket in order to transfer the body to the gurney. The woman from the ambulance began to fold it, eyeing the dead man and his wounds with great interest. Her partner brought a regulation county morgue bag and blanket from the back of the ambulance to encase and cover the deceased.

"Please place the traditional Apache blanket directly atop the body and then place the county blanket on top of that," Song Bird commanded.

"Sure, whatever," said the woman. "That's cool. I dig the Indian thing."

The ambulance team loaded the body onto the gurney and half-pushed, half-carried the body over the rugged ground and placed it into the back of the ambulance. Shutting the back doors of the ambulance, they headed back toward the others.

"Do you want Doc Yackley to have a look at him tonight, or can it wait until tomorrow?" asked the ambulance driver.

"I'll call him and ask him to have a look tonight," said Zeb. "Please take the body directly to the hospital morgue."

"Please burn the Apache blanket that is covering him when you are done with it," requested Song Bird. "Please do not merely throw it into the dumpster."

The woman nodded respectfully at the medicine man.

"I couldn't help but notice that this man, even with parts missing, looks a lot like that dude who used to run the 322 Coffee Bistro. Is it him?" asked the ambulance driver.

"I don't know for sure," replied Zeb. "At this point I'm not absolutely certain of who it is."

"It looks like he took a point blank shot to his junk. I know a half dozen women who wouldn't mind it one bit if his private parts were blown straight to hell," said the woman.

"Why would they think that way?" asked Zeb.

"I hate to be crass, being that he's dead and all. Let's just say he was one rotten asshole. I'd say he was a real pervert who didn't have a frickin' clue that no means no, at least when it came to his sexual advances toward women," said the woman. "From what I can see it looks like he reaped what he sowed."

"Are you one of those women whom he was aggressive toward?" asked Zeb.

"Hell no. I don't dance that way, if you catch my drift, Sheriff Hanks. But it won't take much effort to find the women he molested and raped. Everyone knows about him. If it's who I think it is, he was a creep of the worst kind, a major league sex perv and the lowest common denominator of human being."

"I take it you didn't care for him?"

"The world is a better place with some people not in it."

"You'll probably get little argument from most people about that," said Zeb. "As far as this one goes, do you have names?"

"I'll give you names of some women who might want to see him dead," said the woman.

The woman from the ambulance took a piece of paper from a small notebook she carried in her pocket and wrote down five names for Zeb. After a moment she asked for the paper back and added a few more names. As she wrote, the man from the ambulance chimed in.

"The dude was a real dickhead, if you know what I mean. He thought his shit didn't stink and everyone else's did. Catch my drift?"

"Got you loud and clear," replied Zeb. The woman from the ambulance handed the paper back to Zeb.

"Those are just the ones I can think of off the top of my head," she said. "There are more. I guarantee it. Just ask around at any of the bars or at that strip joint he used to own over in Tucson. I can only imagine how he treated the women out at that commune he ran."

"There's a special red-hot flame in hell for assholes like him," said the man from the ambulance.

"Can I get both of your cards, just in case I need to follow-up with either of you."

Zeb took their cards, thanked them and watched the taillights disappear as the ambulance slowly headed down the dirt road back to the main highway. He turned to Rambler, Song Bird and Echo Skysong.

"Good to know we have such compassionate ambulance drivers," said Zeb.

"Guess those two didn't care much for him," said Rambler.

"Did he have the same kind of reputation on the Rez?"

"Yes, sir, Sheriff Hanks, he did," replied Echo. "Since I've been back on leave this time, I've personally heard of at least three women who say he raped them. But none of them are going to talk to any of you."

Rambler, Song Bird and Zeb all knew exactly how that story went. Rape was all too common of a crime on the Rez. Most often a family member was involved, making it a crime of incest. Women on the Rez had long learned to keep their mouths shut, knowing to rat out a family member would mean becoming ostracized by other family members and maybe even the community itself. As dysfunctional as that seemed it was a fact of life on the Rez.

"Will they talk to you?" asked Zeb.

"Perhaps," replied Echo. "But if they did, I couldn't share it with you, Rambler or even Song Bird. That would be as taboo as them talking to you."

"Even though he's dead?' asked Zeb.

"He has a powerful father, a White leader who could make things far more miserable for them than their families ever could," explained Echo. "Same thing happens in the military. You never shake the branches of tree. You just might get a big stick dropped on your head."

"Don't the women want justice?" asked Zeb.

"We've been seeking justice for hundreds of years from the White government and even from our own. Look what it's got us," said Echo.

"What's it gotten you?" asked Zeb.

"Just more of the same shit," replied Echo.

This time her voice carried genuine anger. She had a point, a damn good one. Zeb looked at Song Bird and Rambler. There was no doubt where they stood on the subject.

"If they don't cooperate, there is little I can do," said Rambler.

"He's dead," said Echo. "It seems like he got his due. What more can be done? Let God sort it out."

The sun dipped below the horizon. Desert life began to move about, even in the presence of the human beings. Some of the night animals formed a sort of a circle a distance from where the dead body had been laying. Other animals peered in from the shadows through the oncoming night. Zeb flipped on his flashlight. The beam shot directly at Echo's military boots. For a woman she had fairly large feet. As he raised the light, it flashed on Echo's right forearm. He caught site of a tattoo similar to the one Helen had described. Her fingernails shone in the light as though they had been recently coated with clear finish. He thought of the whiff of herbs he had caught from Echo's breath earlier. Instinct told him to get close enough to smell her breath. There was no way to do that without attracting the wrong kind of attention.

On the ride back into Safford he pondered about how he would ask her about the tattoo, the herbs and maybe even her shoe size. Helen had implied the person in the boots was a man, but she also noted she had told him that the intruder whispered in a rather high voice. Echo's boots might have been as large as the ones Helen described. Zeb had felt something good when he thought of Echo. His immediate reaction was to scratch her off the long list of suspects he was putting together in his head. How many people with that exact tattoo wearing military boots were wandering around between Safford and the Rez? Then he thought of what she had said. 'It seems like he got his due. What more can be done? Let God sort it out.' He shook his head. Could she have killed Sun Rey? She certainly had the skills that matched up with the facts of the killing.

That night in Zeb's dreams Doreen repeatedly appeared to him, as she often did, on her motorcycle. As usual she was smiling and laughing, only this time she pointed to a tattoo on her right forearm. It was exactly the same one Agent Rodriguez and Echo Skysong had on their arms.

8

TOO MANY SUSPECTS

"Can I have a word with Zeb?"

In his usual, abrupt manner Doc spoke before the person answering the phone at the sheriff's office had a chance to say hello.

"Of course," replied Helen. "Is this Doc? If so, where are your manners? Perhaps you need a bit of a refresher course in phone etiquette?"

"Helen, is that you?" Before she could utter a reply Doc Yackley started up again. "I thought I told you to stay home for a few days and let that collarbone of yours start to mend up. I knew you'd go back to work. That's why I said a few days instead of a few weeks. What do you think you're doing anyway? You're not going to heal up unless you give your shoulder and arm some time to get better."

"Mind if I get a word in edgewise, Doctor Yackley?"

"Be my guest. After all, even though you don't act like it, you are the patient."

"I am only using my left hand and arm. That is what you prescribed, is it not?"

"That was part of it," replied Doc.

This time Helen was the one who did the cutting off. "I have followed every one of your orders except the one about returning to work. We've got a lot on our plate right now. If I'm not here, chaos will reign supreme."

"Hmm," said Doc. "Do you even know who Chaos was?"

"No, but I bet you're going to tell me."

"I am," said Doc. "Chaos was the primeval god of primordial nothingness that all Creation came from."

"That's a lot of hooey," said Helen. "God created the universe in seven days. That's the story of Creation. I do, however, know what chaos is. Chaos is me not being here."

"I believe we are mixing our beliefs..."

"Hush up, Doc. All this time I thought you were a good Christian man. What's with all this talk of ancient gods and this Chaos malarkey?"

"Ancient belief systems are just a hobby of mine. I am quite certain you know I'm a good Christian man, or you wouldn't trust me with your health and that of your family."

"I was keeping you honest, Doc," said Helen. "Someone has to put you in your place every now and then. Ever since your wife passed you got no one holding the reins in on you."

"I appreciate your desire to see that I don't run wild," said Doc. "On the other hand, I'm certain everyone at the office is well qualified, and the county sheriff's department won't have to shut down if you find the good sense to take a few days off."

Helen leaned forward in her chair and tapped her pencil repeatedly against her day planner.

"I remember back when you rolled your fancy new red Cadillac three times and smacked it into an open culvert..."

"...four times..."

"...four times. You didn't miss seeing one single patient. If I remember correctly, and I'm certain I do, you broke your wrist and got one heck of a bad whiplash that time. You had a cast on your arm for over a month and your neck in a brace for the better part of two weeks. If that didn't stop you, why should this stop me? I'm not hurt half as badly now as you were then."

"I was younger back then, quite a bit younger than you are now," replied Doc.

"Bah," replied Helen. "Us old timers know how highly overrated youth is."

"Too bad it's wasted on the young."

"Such is the way of life."

"Helen, you were one of my very first patients when I moved to town..."

"I was your third. My youngest children were your first two patients," said Helen. "As I remember you were still a little wet behind the ears in those days. Seems as though old Doctor DeRusha had to live a couple of extra years just to set you straight about healing."

"Time has marched on for both of us and my ears are drier than desert dust, but I'd hate to think I gave you anything other than the best medical advice my years of experience, which you don't hesitate to mention, have given me. So, that being said, please be careful," said Doc. "Setting a broken collarbone is one thing, but re-setting a broken collarbone ain't exactly what you'd describe as fun."

"I will exercise extreme caution when it comes to my shoulder and arm," said Helen.

"Thanks for listening to me," replied Doc. "Didn't think you would. Don't know if you really are paying attention to me, but that's your privilege."

"I suppose you want to talk with Zeb about the autopsy on the dead body that was brought in last night from San Carlos Lake?"

"I do."

"Is the dead man Senator Russell's son?"

"It is."

"Senator Russell is going to be heartbroken. He only recently made amends with his son. This is just terrible," said Helen.

"Indeed it is," said Doc Yackley.

"God's will, I suppose," said Helen.

"Don't know about that," replied Doc. "Sometimes chaos rules the day."

Helen pretended not to hear Doc's jab.

"I feel so bad for Senator Russell. I voted for him five times. I'll vote for him in next year's election too."

"I'm sure you will," replied Doc. "Mind if I talk to the sheriff?"

Helen buzzed Zeb.

"I've got Doctor Yackley on line one for you. It's about the autopsy," said Helen.

"Thanks, Helen. I've got it."

Zeb picked up the phone and waited for a few seconds until he heard Helen hanging up on her end. Helen was not only his secretary and his aunt but also the epicenter of a large portion of the town's gossip. Once she got word of something it spread like a flu bug at the grade school.

"Doc."

"Zeb."

"Mornin'."

"Backatcha."

"What've you got for me, Doc? Was it as we suspected?"

"Yup," said Doc. "Lock, stock and double barrel. I was able to positively identify the body as that of Sun Rey Russell. The slug to his neck was from a twelve-gauge shotgun. It was what killed him. On the autopsy report you'll see exsanguination as the cause of death."

"He bled to death?"

"Right. Didn't figure you'd know the fancy medical term for it, so I thought I'd tell you, but I guess I would have been wasting my breath," said Doc.

"It was just a guess based on what I saw," replied Zeb. "Deduction, that's all."

"The shot to the neck blew the left carotid artery right out of his neck."

"Would death be instant?" asked Zeb.

"He would have bled like a stuck hog. I doubt the shock of it all would have allowed him to even reflexively reach up to his neck to try and stop the bleeding. Death itself would have zoomed in on him like a stealth bomber," replied Doc. "For sure he didn't suffer the pains of the tortured damned."

"Do you think he was still alive when he got his manliness blown off?" asked Zeb.

"Doubt it. Shock, panic and fear probably got the better of him. I don't think he would have lived long enough for someone to walk a couple hundred yards to his body," replied Doc. "If he was alive, he would have been in a deep state of shock and wouldn't have felt much."

"Your best guess is that he didn't feel the second shot?"

"The second shot was bird shot. As you know, bird shot has lots of pellets meant to cover a wide area. If he hadn't already been dead from the twelve-gauge slug, which I believe he probably was, I don't think the bird shot to his groin would have killed him, nor do I believe he would have felt it. But it would, and it did, remove his male organs rather effectively."

"It's painful to even think about it."

"Only ever seen a man's privates removed so violently one other time. They got caught up in a hydraulic auger during cotton picking season when a farm hand was playing with himself a little too close to dangerous equipment. Strange deal, that one was."

"Indeed," replied a cringing Zeb, trying unsuccessfully to remove the image from his mind.

"I can confirm with almost one hundred percent certainty that the shot to the neck was from a distance of roughly two hundred yards. The shot to the groin, I have to believe, was very personal. It looks as though the killer simply slipped the gun down Sun Rey's pants before pulling the trigger. I know that because Sun Rey still had his belt on. So after the killer shot Sun Rey in the neck and head, the murderer walked or ran up to the body, reloaded with bird shot and gave Sun Rey a dismembering of the worst kind."

"You said killer, not he. Any reason to believe the murderer might have been a woman?" asked Zeb.

"Instinct tells me things. An angry woman or a jealous lover would not be out of the question, but who the hell knows when it's this kind of thing? There's no need to hurt a man once he's dead," said Doc. "You sure as hell can't kill someone twice."

"Maybe there were two killers, each taking their own revenge," said Zeb.

"Hmm," replied Doc. "I guess that's why you're the sheriff and I'm just an old country doctor."

"If the shot to the privates wasn't to make certain he was dead, in your esteemed opinion what was it all about?"

"Sending a message of anger," replied Doc. "Or a warning."

"Not following you entirely, Doc. A warning?" questioned Zeb.

"The shot that blew his penis and testicles off could be a warning to anyone who might have been working with Sun Rey. Maybe he had a rape buddy? I'd be checking to see if any of the victims were gang raped."

"As far as we know, Sun Rey always acted alone. But we don't really know that much because we've never had any rape charges brought up against him."

"Could be just about anything, I guess. But what I do know is that you've got a calm and angry murderer out there walking the streets. It takes a whole lot of cool to kill someone from a distance, walk up to the body and make a statement with a second shot. Whoever did this thought it out very well."

"Or had a whole lot of experience," added Zeb.

"Meaning?" pondered Doc.

"Military or police background," replied Zeb. "Or maybe prior murder experience."

"I guess any of those could be the case," said Doc. "But I hope none of them are. If the killer is cool, calm, angry and experienced all rolled into one, you've got the worst of all worlds on your hands."

"You're profiling a hit man," said Zeb.

"Or a hit woman," added Doc.

"You have someone in mind?" asked Zeb.

"No, not really. Just seems like these days it could be anybody. Considering that it is Sun Rey laying in the morgue, I could see a woman doing the killing or hiring someone to do it," said Doc.

Zeb's quieted his mind in order to focus clearly on two very specific women—Kate and Echo. Kate hated Sun Rey. He knew she had the ability to kill without remorse. She had killed a man in the line of duty, and yet she carried none of the usual angst of a first kill. On the other hand, maybe one of the women who was raped by Sun Rey hired Echo. She certainly was capable of making the shot. Then again, maybe one of the women who were raped had the skills needed to do the job. He shook the thought from his head in order to empty it of high speed thinking. His imagination was running wild with too many suspects.

On the other end of the line Doc listened to the silence. He knew what Zeb was thinking. "I can almost hear your mind ticking," said Doc. "You've got someone in mind, don't you?"

"I've got no shortage of suspects," said Zeb. "I'll use your information to help build a stronger profile of the actual perp."

"My suspicion is that Sun Rey was a serial rapist," said Doc. "Only met the man a few times, but there was definitely something wrong with him both mentally and spiritually. He talked like a sadist. After this many years of doin' what I do, it's not that hard to spot someone with a sick mind who is still somehow well enough to function in society. He ain't exactly the only one around here that you should keep an eye on. More than a couple of crazies running around the area, especially with the mine hiring like they have been and the casino doubling in size. Crime follows casinos like dust follows a wagon train, and a man stuck in a hole all day digging copper has too much time to think."

"I can't do a thing until someone acts on their craziness," replied Zeb. "I don't have the manpower to look into the background of every new person in the county. What I can do on the Rez is limited to whatever Rambler can and will help me with."

"I know," said Doc. "I know. Your job is no piece of cake."

"I'm hearing that Sun Rey sexually assaulted a fairly large number of women, both in town and out on the Rez," said Zeb. "Kate was suspicious of that a long time ago."

"This may sound crazy," said Doc. "But is there any chance Kate might be involved? As in...she might be the one who pulled the trigger?"

"Funny question coming from you. Any particular reason that you ask?" said Zeb.

"Just a thought," said Doc.

"Why don't I believe you?" asked Zeb.

"Well, you've got me there. It's just that after she fired the bullet that put Jimmy Joe Walker down for good, I had a little talk with her?"

"And..."

"And she had the least amount of remorse of any person I've ever known who had killed someone. To her it seemed no different than putting down a rabid dog or killing a buck deer to put meat on the table. She felt nothing that I could discern anyway, that came close to guilt or misgiving or sorrow. It was almost like she was glad to get that first kill notched on her belt," replied Doc.

"She hated Jimmy Joe for all the evil things he'd done," said Zeb. "But it was a clean kill and there was really no option. It was kill or be killed."

"Still you'd think she would have had some emotional reaction. For the love of God, that's only normal. Kate's impassive response is what worries me. My guess is that she didn't feel much different toward Sun Rey than she did toward Jimmy Joe," argued Doc.

"She had a brewing hatred for Sun Rey," said Zeb. "I know that for a fact. But I doubt she would have taken it this far unless there is something that happened to her or someone very close to her. I think I would have heard about it if that were the case."

"In any case, think about it," said Doc.

"I'll keep it on my radar," replied Zeb.

"My God, I hope she didn't do it," said Doc.

"Me too," added Zeb. "Doc, any rape victims or potential rape victims in your files that you would care to add to the mix?"

"Since this is a murder investigation, I don't think I am crossing HIPPA boundaries. That being said, I can probably add a few names to the list. When Sun Rey was living in the area, I had more than a couple of women who came to me after having contact with him who appeared to have sexually related injuries. None of them would direct any complaint in his direction, so I had nothing but my suspicions to go on and nothing to report. Maybe I should have trusted my instincts. It might have saved a life and allowed justice to be properly served," said Doc. "I'll give you their names if you have some corroborating evidence. Screw HIPPA."

Zeb pulled a list of names from his pocket and read it to Doc Yackley.

"You don't have to say anything, just grunt if you think I'm on the right track."

Doc's reaction told him all he needed to know.

"Thanks, Doc. I don't think any HIPPA boundaries have been crossed."

"Glad to help in the course of righteousness."

"Justice is sometimes hard to figure and even harder to come by, Doc. Maybe he got what was coming to him," said Zeb.

"Zeb, never forget you are the sheriff of Graham County. You are the one who sets the example for proper enforcement of the law. Even though it's me you're talking to, in the future you better think twice about your words before they leave your mouth," cautioned Doc.

"I'm not saying he was guilty or that the proper punishment was served by a shotgun slug to the neck and shotgun pellets to his manliness. What I'm saying is that he might have gotten away with horrible crimes forever if someone hadn't done this. I'm not saying it's right. I'm saying it's what happened. I've been doing this job long enough to know that sometimes that's the way things go."

"I suppose you've got to make a call to Senator Russell?"

"I do."

"Delivering bad news is never an easy thing to do," lamented Doc.

"I'm certainly not looking forward to letting a personal acquaintance and a politically powerful man like him know his son has been murdered."

"I've delivered bad news way too many times," said Doc. "I wish you good luck, if that's what you need."

"Thanks. I do think it's what I'll need, but with formidable people you just never know how they will react."

"For your sake I hope Senator Russell doesn't blame the messenger," said Doc.

"I am more than a little suspicious he might do just that." Zeb hesitated. Doc knew his friend all too well. He waited for what Zeb would say next. "Or not."

Zeb hung up the phone. He thought about the conversation with Doc. He assumed Doc had no understanding that sometimes it was best that certain criminals were dealt with outside the normal means provided by the legal system. It was an assumption he shouldn't have been so quick to make. Zeb felt no guilt about his comments. The world was no worse without Sun Rey in it. Zeb was also acutely aware that no man or woman possessed the sole right to pass judgement and play the role of God. There was no easy answer in this kind of situation. Zeb could wax philosophic all day and justify any action he might take. Even then, he might never know if he was right or wrong. In his job, the decisions he had to make never seemed to be black and white. He buzzed Helen. It was time to deliver the bad news to Senator Russell.

9

BAD NEWS DELIVERED

"Helen, could you get Senator Russell on the line for me?"

"Yes, I can," replied Helen. "But before I do, I think you should know you have a visitor who is waiting impatiently for you."

"Who?"

"Agent Rodriguez."

The day had just dropped off the edge of a steep cliff and deteriorated from bad to worse. Rodriguez's presence meant only one thing to Zeb...trouble.

"Hold the call to Senator Russell. No, wait. Put the call through. Tell Rodriguez it will be a few minutes," said Zeb. "That SOB can wait."

"Zeb, watch your tongue. Cursing does not honor the Lord," rebuked Helen.

"Please tell Agent Rodriguez that I will be a few minutes longer," said Zeb. "If he asks, tell him he's been outranked."

"Yes, Sheriff, I can do that," replied Helen.

Helen turned to Agent Rodriguez. "Sheriff Hanks has one pressing matter, and then he will see you."

Rodriguez grunted, not bothering to look up from the ancient *Field and Stream* magazine he was perusing.

The pleading tension in Senator Russell's voice made it clear he was anxiously waiting to hear what Zeb had to report.

"Zeb, have you got anything? Did my son show up on your radar?" Senator Russell's voice cracked like a man who feared what the truth might be. "I've been worried sick about him. He's not a well young man. You know that. I am so afraid, afraid something horrible has happened. I actually feel sick to my stomach."

"I do have something, Senator Russell."

"Good. I was just as afraid you might have nothing to report to me."

"I'm afraid your gut is telling you the truth," said Zeb.

"Oh, dear lord," replied the senator. "Did he hurt someone...again?"

"No, not that I know of," replied Zeb.

"Thank God. I was worried half out of my mind that he was acting out on his violent tendencies again," said Senator Russell. "So, what do you have for me? Tell it to me straight. No matter what it is, it can't be worse than the anticipation of not knowing."

Zeb sought the right words. He knew it was as much what he had to say as how he said it that might have the greatest effect on the concerned father.

"Tell me. I can handle the truth," said Senator Russell. "It seems like I've had a lifetime of tough news regarding Sun Rey."

"I'm afraid it is bad news, Senator. Very bad news."

Palpable fear and angst, along with an emotion Zeb couldn't quite put his finger on, shot right down the telephone line.

"He's dead, isn't he, Zeb?"

"I'm afraid so, sir," replied Zeb. "Yes, sir, Sun Rey Russell is deceased."

"What happened?"

"We don't know yet for sure."

"Is there anything you can tell me?" asked the senator.

"Your son was shot...twice."

"Did he suffer?" asked the senator.

"I don't believe he did," replied Zeb.

Zeb waited out an uncomfortable silence. Senator Russell was obviously mulling over what to do next.

"Is there a crematorium in town?"

"Yes."

"Could you have the funeral director contact me?"

"I can," said Zeb.

"Please do that."

The senator's voice choked and cracked with pain as he talked. Zeb gave him a moment before speaking.

"Do you want a copy of the autopsy report?"

"Please," replied Senator Russell.

"Is there anything else you want from my end right now?"

"What?"

"Is there anything else I can do for you at the moment?" repeated Zeb.

"I'm sorry, Zeb, I can't think straight. I don't even know what I'm thinking right now. I'll be in touch when my head clears. Thanks again," said Senator Russell.

"Please feel free to contact me any time," said Zeb. "I'll personally handle anything you need done on this end."

"Thank you, Zeb. I appreciate your kind offer more than I can say. Pardon me, but I have to go now. I have things to attend to."

"I understand. Goodbye, Senator. I will keep you apprised as things come up."

"Goodbye, Zeb."

The senator's phone went dead. Zeb took a deep breath. The story of Sun Rey Russell was a cruel narrative with a rotten ending.

The intercom buzzed. Helen had obviously noticed the phone call with Senator Russell had ended.

"Zeb, do you want a few minutes before you see Agent Rodriguez?"

"No, Helen. Send him in."

Helen politely opened the door for Agent Rodriguez who brusquely forged his way past her and entered the office of Sheriff Zeb Hanks. Zeb simply stared hard at Rodriguez as he settled all too comfortably into the chair across from the sheriff's desk.

"Looks like you got away with another one," said Rodriguez.

"Another what?" asked Zeb.

"Murder."

The men locked eyes. Arrows of hatred zinged between them. How dare Rodriguez sit across from him in his very own office and accuse him of murder?

"You actually have the audacity to believe I killed Sun Rey?" asked Zeb.

"Or had him killed," replied Rodriguez. "There is very little I would put past you."

Zeb clenched his fists in righteous anger.

"Care to elaborate on your theory?" asked Zeb. "It ought to be a real dandy."

"Don't get smug with me, Sheriff Hanks. We both know you killed Carmelita Montouyez in cold blood. I am halfway to proving it. If I have anything to say about it, your evil deed is going to put you in a Mexican prison where you can rot for the rest of your life," said Rodriguez.

"What sort of medical leave are you on?" asked Zeb. "Physical or mental?"

The question was uncalled for, but Rodriguez had burrowed far too deeply under Zeb's skin for him not to throw a counterpunch. Rodriguez rose quickly to his feet making anvils of his fists.

The thunderous power of Rodriguez's clenched hands pounding Zeb's desk vibrated the glass in the hundred-year old windows of the sheriff's office, knocked over a cup full of pencils and sent motes of dust flying from every corner of the room. As Rodriguez stepped back and expanded his full height by throwing back his shoulders, his jacket flipped open. Zeb zeroed in on the double shoulder holster he was wearing. Each side held a Springfield 1911 compact .45. Zeb thought it to be a good choice of weapon except for its two-pound weight. The 1911 was deadly accurate and could stop a bad guy dead in his tracks.

Zeb dropped his right hand by his side and pulled a .45 caliber Kimber Ultra-Carry II from a hidden holster screwed to the inside wall of his desk. Two could play this game. Keeping a powerful weapon hidden close at hand was just part of the business. It was exactly the sort of self-defensive weapon a sheriff just never knew when or if he was going to need. His thumb switched the safety off, and he held the gun between his legs. Zeb slowly lifted the barrel of the Kimber and pointed it directly at Rodriguez's heart. If the FBI agent was going to throw some lead in his direction, Zeb was sure as hell going to go down swingin'.

"Sheriff Zeb Hanks, let me put it this way. My time in Alaska, thanks to you, was not good to me. I lost my family. My career, or what's left of it, is in the shitter. In general, I am not feeling like a happy man. Every last bit of my pain has to do with your bullshit connections with Senator Russell and things you are personally responsible for. Now his son is dead, and I believe you are the one person to whom I can connect all the dots for Sun Rey's death and the death of Carmelita."

"Somewhere in that twisted mind of yours you have come to the conclusion that I am somehow responsible for Sun Rey's death," snarled Zeb. "And this person you call Carmelita."

"I don't think you're involved, Sheriff Hanks, I know you are," said Rodriguez through gritted teeth.

"Sun Rey was a real piece of work," said Zeb. "Death was his ultimate destiny."

"Death is everyone's ultimate destiny. Isn't that how you see it, Sheriff Hanks?"

"That's the first intelligent thing that has come out of your mouth."

"That little peckerwood's death doesn't bother me one way or another. But since you're the one who likely put an end to his life on earth, or at least had your fingers in the nefarious deed, I feel it's my duty to see that true justice is done," said Rodriguez.

"Not that it matters to you, but just for the record, I didn't kill Sun Rey or this person whom you seem stuck on, Carmelita Montouyez," said Zeb. The calmness in Zeb's voice at the mention of Carmelita clearly irritated Rodriguez.

"I've read Sun Rey's file. He was an A-number one asshole," said Rodriguez. "I don't know exactly why you killed him, but I sure as hell am going to find out so I can put the final nail in your coffin."

"You're out of your freaking mind, Rodriguez. First of all, I'm telling you for the last time, I had nothing to do with Sun Rey's death. Secondly, I've never heard of anyone by the name of Carmelita Montouyez, much less killed her."

"Bullshit," sneered Rodriguez. "Your lies are going to send you straight to hell."

"Believe what you will about someone I've never heard of..."

Rodriguez was steaming. "You had sex with here, but I made love with her. She never loved you. She loved me. She was just using you, you fucking stupid asshole."

Zeb eyed Rodriguez up and down. His words were a smack down sucker punch aimed directly at the Sheriff of Graham County. If Rodriguez truly was Carmelita's lover, then Rodriguez had definitely been in bed with El Coyote's drug cartel. In his wildest imagination Zeb had not seen that. Finally, it was clear to Zeb why Rodriguez wanted so badly to get him. Revenge. Revenge for killing one's lover was something Zeb understood all too well. He knew Rodriguez would not rest until he had Zeb put away for good, or killed him. One option that quickly occurred to Zeb was ridding the planet of Rodriguez. Whatever would ultimately happen between the men was anyone's guess. The more Zeb thought about it, the more it seemed that Rodriguez's claim to be Carmelita's lover made no sense. Something was dreadfully wrong with that story. Whatever it was, Zeb would have to figure it out, but for now Sun Rey's death was priority one.

"What on earth would possess me to kill the senator's son?" asked Zeb.

"I don't know what motivates you, Sheriff Zebulon Hanks. I only know that you operate outside of the law and on your own terms when it serves you. You're a cold blooded murderer and a pathological liar. What's a little more blood on the hands of a psychopath like you? Your time has come and gone, and your old west cowboy style of justice is about to come to an end."

Rodriguez spewed venomously as he spoke. Zeb could only wonder if maybe Rodriguez truly had been Carmelita's lover. Or maybe he was one hell of an actor using his inside information to wear away at Zeb?

"God has ordained it your fate to bring me down? Is that it?" asked Zeb.

"Somebody has to put a stop to your lawlessness. I figure it might as well be me."

Helen had left the door slightly ajar. This time it paid off in spades. She had heard every word of the ugly conversation between the men. Fearing that Rodriguez might start shooting any moment, she called Jake and Kate to her desk and hurriedly advised them of the situation. They bolted into Zeb's office.

"Jake, Kate, what's up?" asked Zeb.

"Rambler wants to see you ASAP. It's a matter of life and death," said Jake. "Any chance you could finish your meeting with Agent Rodriguez at a later date?"

If Rodriguez was going to try something, anything, now would be a very bad time. Rodriguez turned and looked at Jake and Kate. The agent's training made it instantly recognizable they had positioned themselves defensively. Any intention he had of killing Zeb would have to be put on hold. Rodriguez recognized he was outmanned and outgunned. If he had any intentions of acting violently, at this moment it would be nothing short of suicide. He had too many reasons to live, millions of them to be exact, some from his dealings with the cartel and some from Senator Russell's coffers.

"I don't know how you called in backup, Sheriff Hanks, but you are as clever as a fox, I will hand you that much. You can bet your bottom dollar I won't forget how you do business."

Rodriguez stood up, picking up the coffee cup full of pens that had tipped over when he pounded Zeb's desk. With a tip of the hat he politely excused himself to all present. Jake, hand on his gun grip, followed him out of the building to get a look at his vehicle. He noted it was a bright red Ford truck with four doors and a standard-sized bed with a black liner.

Zeb secured his weapon back into its hiding spot under his desk.

"What was that all about?" asked Kate.

"Rodriguez thinks I killed Sun Rey, and I think he might have."

"Did you?" asked Jake.

"Hell, no," replied Zeb. "He'd have been a waste of a bullet."

Jake turned to Kate and asked, "Did you blow his balls all to hell?"

"No, sorry to say I didn't have the pleasure," replied Kate.

"Do you think Rodriguez is a gun for hire?" asked Jake.

"I don't know. He certainly is capable of killing someone. I could see that in his eyes," said Zeb. "Rodriguez might be off his nut, but he has a bone to pick with me, a personal one. He might have had something against Sun Rey. He's mighty unstable. He might even kill for pleasure. Who knows?"

"Then Rodriguez is a problem in the sense you need to be constantly looking over your shoulder for him?" asked Kate.

"I wish it were that simple, Kate. I really wish it were."

Kate sat in the chair across from Zeb. The look on her face told Zeb it was clear she wasn't leaving until she knew more details. Kate was the ultimate team player. Zeb could always trust her to do the right thing, even if it was slightly or completely outside the law.

"What's the biggest problem, other than he seems to be out to get you for personal reasons?" asked Kate.

"He is out to get me for personal reasons," said Zeb.

"Okay. What's the biggest issue between you and Rodriguez?"

"He knows too much about Mexico," said Zeb. "He knows too much about Doreen's death because he was in on the case as an FBI agent. He knows too much about Doreen's killer. He knows too much about the cartel's operation. He knows too much of the political relationship between Senator Russell, Elaine Coburn and you."

"That's not good," said Kate.

"He has the power to put me away. It seems to be the primary goal of his existence," said Zeb.

"Why is he so intent on ruining you, Zeb?" asked Kate.

"It's complicated," replied Zeb. "And I don't have all the facts...yet."

"But I assume you will get them?" asked Kate.

"I don't really have any choice in the matter," replied Zeb. "It's quite literally do or die, when it comes down to me and Rodriguez."

10

SKULL SESSION

Senator Russell's private cellphone rang just once. He saw the name of the caller and answered before it had the chance to ring a second time.

"Agent Rodriguez, what have you done for me?"

"I have spread seeds of doubt, Senator Russell. Seeds of doubt that have been sown and are currently being watered and fertilized."

"Excellent," replied the senator. "Well done."

"Sheriff Hanks knows in no uncertain terms I am out to get his sorry ass and hang it out to dry. I made that abundantly clear. That will keep his level of attention to detail off the charts. He's paranoid about me enough as it is. This should be the proverbial icing on the cake," said Rodriguez.

"Does he suspect anything other than you are out to get him?"

"I fed him more than enough information to make him wonder what the hell I know and how I know it."

"Good. Keep him off balance."

"I can do that."

"By the way, he asked for your medical records," said Senator Russell.

"So what? Send him the dummy medical chart we set up."

"Just letting you know," replied the senator. "You need to be prepared just in case he comes after you with any of the false information we've planted."

"It might do me some good to have his records as well," said Rodriguez. "He and I are involved in deep psychological warfare. I need to have every advantage I can get. I can't stand the man, but he's no fool. I need everything you have on him that you haven't already given me."

"I know," said Senator Russell. "I'll send my notes on him to your phone within the hour," said Senator Russell. "Do you need anything else right now?"

"Untraceable dead presidents."

"Of course, you will need some cash."

"I am going to have to buy some information along the way. I will be as discrete as possible."

"How much?"

"Not much. One hundred grand for now. That ought to do it."

"You can pick it up at the office of State Representative Devon Dawbyns," said Senator Russell. "Spend it wisely."

"Like an owl," replied Rodriguez. "Dawbyns is new to the game. I know he used to work for Sheriff Hanks. You're certain he can be trusted?"

"I own him, lock, stock and barrel. He crosses me, and he knows he's a dead man. Don't give him one second of thought," said Senator Russell.

"Okay, if you say so. Regarding Sheriff Hanks and his team, I want to keep everything under the radar as much as possible. Expenses have been minimal, but they're likely to increase in the very near future."

"Absolutely. Be certain you leave no trail behind that could lead back to me or even vaguely point in my direction. My position in the Senate is tenuous at best. Any scandal with my name attached to it could be devastating. The next election is less than twelve months away. It will be a tight battle as it is. Too damn many liberals moving across the state line from California. I don't want to lose my seat, no matter the cost. That would be devastating for me as well as for you."

Rodriguez had built a career working around people just like Senator Russell. The agent was completely indifferent to party labels. He stood tall in the airy atmosphere high above the political fray. As far as he was concerned, the politicos all sprung from the seeds of the vast underbelly of an unscrupulous society. Why the voting public never caught onto politicians was one of life's greatest mysteries in his mind.

"Roger that, boss. You will be so far out of the loop no one will ever know to even glance in your direction."

"I'm paying you big money to keep it that way, Rodriguez. Just do your job and do it with excellence and discretion."

"I believe you once told me that you chose me because I operated off the grid with extreme discrimination. I can say that is a perfect description of how I do your bidding," assured Rodriguez.

Senator Russell chuckled. Indeed, those were his exact words. Rodriguez's conversation had just confirmed one important fact. If the former FBI agent screwed the pooch on his dealings with Russell, it would be his ego that would take him down. And, if Rodriguez's ego did get out of control, Senator Russell had people who would take care of him.

"That's why you make the big money, Agent Rodriguez. That's what makes you so valuable to a man in my position. I hold the key to the vault from which you will be able to become, or should I say, are becoming a wealthy man."

"Yes, sir. I do understand completely. I know precisely where and how my bread is buttered."

"One more thing."

"Yes, Senator Russell."

"Keep contact between yourself and Elaine Coburn to a minimum for the present time. I don't want Deputy Kate Steele to get any ideas that you and Elaine are still horse trading."

"Of course, Senator Russell. The circle of trust should remain as small and tight as possible."

"Well stated, Agent. With your understanding of how things actually work, your future just might be in politics."

"Definitely not my cup of tea. I shall leave those types of deeds to the experts. Good day, Senator."

"Good day, Agent Rodriguez. Keep everything on the down low, but stay in touch."

11

SHERIFF'S OFFICE

Zeb's office intercom buzzed from the outer office.

"Yes, Helen, what is it?"

"Curtis Lowe is here about the security cameras. Do you want to talk with him?"

"Yes, please send him right in. I'm just finishing some paperwork," said Zeb.

Curtis Lowe entered the partially opened door of the sheriff's office. He stood quietly at the rear of the room, looking down at the floor until Zeb gave him a nod of recognition. Young Curtis Lowe carried a thin, almost wispy frame. For a moment Zeb could see Curtis' father, Levi, in him. Back in high school some of the kids who picked on Curtis' old man called him Twig because of his slight frame. Somehow that disparaging moniker made Levi a fighter, a junkyard dog of sorts. The combative trait apparently hadn't been handed down to his son. Curtis' pale, white skin, soft features and hair pulled back into a ponytail gave him an asexual, almost womanish appearance. As Zeb looked the young man up and down, he couldn't help but notice the shoes he was wearing were dead ringers for those Helen had described as being worn by the second intruder.

"Nice tennis shoes," said Zeb. "Red Keds. I used to wear them myself when I was a kid. As I recall, your father did too."

"I got them on sale on the Internet. I've worn Keds for as long as I can remember. My dad used to get them for me all the time. He wore them too, black ones, until they jammed his feet into ill-fitting, state prison shoes."

Zeb smiled. Mentioning Curtis' jailed father right off provoked this puny boy-man into taking a jab at him. The shoe remark was a fairly unsubtle innuendo toward Zeb and his part in putting Levi Lowe behind bars. It boiled down to bad manners on Curtis' part, but it showed some spine as well. Maybe Curtis did have a touch of his old man's junkyard dog hidden away behind his scrawny facade. Zeb understood, maybe even envied, the boy's chutzpah. Zeb had hated his own father and never would have stood up for him had he been sent to prison. In fact, prison was a place he often hoped would be his own father's destiny. Zeb momentarily softened his stance toward the young man.

"Take a seat, Curtis. I'll be right with you."

Curtis tentatively looked around the room. He took a seat in a chair that sat against the back wall, about as far away from Zeb as possible while still being in the same room. After a few moments the sheriff motioned him with a wave of his hand to the chair directly across from his desk.

"You don't care much for me, do you, Curtis?"

"Sir?"

"I go way back to grade school with both of your parents."

"So?"

"So, I am friends with your dad and your mother."

"Yeah, right. Then why'd you nail him to the cross and help the feds put him in prison? You're some kind of friend. As they say, with friends like you who needs enemies."

"Your dad committed a crime. I assisted in arresting him. His crimes put him in federal prison..."

"His alleged crimes," interrupted Curtis.

"He pled guilty," said Zeb.

"Because he was set up by someone much more powerful than he was. He would have been stuck away for good if he hadn't agreed to a plea deal. You of all people understand that, Sheriff Hanks."

The shy young basement dweller was becoming more resolute with each sentence. As he spoke in anger a hue of color flushed the pall that shrouded the cheeks of his face.

"I know that's not why you're here, but if you want to talk about it I will be glad to discuss what I know about your father's case with you," said Zeb.

"No, thank you, Sheriff Hanks. I understand all too well how the system works. The cards are stacked against me, my dad and people like us. You know there is no justice for anyone but the wealthy, connected and powerful people in this country or in this county. We happen to be stuck in the middle class and, by virtue of that, we get screwed every time. C'est la vie."

The chip on the young man's shoulder was bigger than Zeb had time to deal with. A time might come when he could help the young man improve his views on the world, but today was not that day. Zeb shifted the subject.

"I know you are a self-taught computer expert," said Zeb.

"Not totally self-taught," said Curtis. "I took a class or two and my dad helped me. Actually, my dad helped me a lot. He's the one who's practically a computer genius."

"I was unaware that he possessed computer skills on that level," said Zeb. "He must have taught you well."

"My computer skills are the reason you hired me. That's why I'm sitting here facing your wrath. One of my systems, specifically the one I installed in your office, failed temporarily."

"Yes, let's talk about that. How long will it take you to get the security cameras in my office up and running again?" asked Zeb.

"They're already functioning at one hundred percent," replied Curtis.

"How did you find out something was wrong with them?"

"Helen called. She asked me to fix them. She mentioned something about a break-in here at the sheriff's office and that the cameras weren't functioning properly when it occurred. I would call that ironic, wouldn't you, Sheriff Hanks?"

He knew Curtis had been living in the basement of his mother's home since he graduated from high school. Zeb's eyes flashed once again to the young man's Keds. Zeb was no fashion bug, but he doubted red Keds on a twenty-year old computer nerd would make much of an impression on girls. Zeb also knew the money the county had paid Curtis for his work was at least enough to get him some decent clothes, a decent pair of cowboy boots and a small down payment on something other than the dying, old rust bucket of a car he'd parked just outside the sheriff's window. Most importantly, were the red Keds on Curtis' feet the same ones worn by one of the intruders?

"Ironic? How so?" asked Zeb.

"I mean, isn't the sheriff's office supposed to be the last place in town that a crime could possibly take place?"

Zeb considered letting the dig pass. Someone had failed to teach this young punk good manners or, for that matter, a greater understanding of how things fit together. He knew Curtis' parents well enough to know they would have taught him to be respectful. He eyed Curtis again. This time he saw a confused young man acting out his pain.

"You might say that. But as it happened, young man, the failure falls directly on your shoulders, does it not? It's your system that failed. I would like to know how and why the security system we paid you for didn't protect my staff, especially Helen."

Curtis stared blankly at Zeb. No confusion, no hatred, not much of anything showed what was happening behind his vacant, youthful eyes. Whatever was churning around in his brain was a mystery to Zeb.

"I know your mother and Helen serve together on several church committees. I have no doubt your mother will see Helen and ask her what happened. Your mother is a smart person. She will put one and one together and realize the reason no one has been put in jail for assaulting Helen is because we had nothing on our security cameras. She will understand that is your fault."

Curtis began jabbering, explaining what happened in what sounded like so much computer-ese double talk. Bullshit was bullshit. Even if Zeb didn't understand the technical language, the mendacity of a lie still carried an unmistakably foul odor. The young man's glaring weak spot also exposed itself. Curtis Lowe did not want his mother thinking poorly of him.

"Hold on one second. You're talking so fast and so furiously that I don't know what you are talking about. However, I do know the BLM has a computer expert from the federal government in town today. Maybe he can help me understand this better. Give me five minutes, and I will have him here."

"Fine," replied Curtis. "But I know my system."

"Obviously not as well as you think you do."

Zeb made a quick call and three minutes later the federal computer IT expert was sitting in Zeb's office next to Curtis. He was a she and her name was Shelly. She was young, good looking and wore a Call of Duty, Black Ops 2 T-shirt, a pair of tight fitting jeans and shoes that looked like they might cost a month's salary. She was hardly any older than Curtis, but they obviously were worlds apart in many ways. As Curtis began to explain to her what had happened, he broke into a nervous sweat.

"What you're telling us is not only unlikely but almost impossible based on the parameters you've laid out. Perhaps you want to start over again and tell the entire story this time," said Shelly.

Zeb sat back and watched an interrogation being done on a local IT expert by a much smarter, more experienced one. The more Curtis talked the more he dug himself into a hole. It wasn't long before only the top of Curtis' head was sticking out of the muck and mire he'd burrowed himself into. After ten minutes Shelly gave Zeb a nod. Zeb asked Curtis to wait outside in Helen's office. He carried a fearful face and hung his head low on rounded shoulders as he dragged his feet into the reception area.

"That young man is lying through his teeth," said Shelly. "If he's not lying, then he's completely incompetent. Not only is what he's saying out and out fiction, but I doubt he even covered his tracks. I think he assumed you'd choose to remain ignorant rather than look into the root cause of your problem."

"Bad assumption to make about a sheriff," said Zeb.

Shelly pointed to Zeb's computer. "May I?"

Zeb stood up from his chair and offered it to her.

"Be my guest."

A few keystrokes later the federal IT expert smiled, inhaled deeply and abruptly stopped keyboarding. She pointed to the computer screen which was full of numbers, letters and other computer symbols. It was Greek to Zeb but simple language to Shelly. Suddenly Helen burst into the room.

"Curtis just took off running. I couldn't stop him," said Helen, pointing to her right arm which was now in a sling.

"Damn it," said Zeb.

Zeb looked out the window. Curtis was fumbling with his keys trying to open a stuck door on his junker. Jake was slowly walking up behind him. A few seconds later Jake walked through Zeb's office door, pulling Curtis by the ear with the escapee on his tiptoes. This time Curtis' face was reddened for a number of reasons.

"What'd this one do?" asked Jake. "I figured anyone skedaddlin' at full speed out the front door of the sheriff's office couldn't be up to nuth'n good, so I collared him."

"He did something," said Zeb. "But I don't know exactly why."

"Actually, he ran smack dab into me. Dang near knocked me over," said Jake, rubbing his bruised chin.

Shelly stared cuttingly at Curtis. Curtis sheepishly hung his chin on his chest. Jake let go of his ear but stayed within arms-reach of the runner.

"Do you want to tell them or do you want me to?" she asked.

Curtis, fully ashamed, stared down at his feet. He rubbed the toe of the right Keds in a small circle. He'd been caught red handed.

"I heard over at the BLM that there was an incident here, at the sheriff's office, the other day," said Shelly. "By any chance was it between two and three in the afternoon?"

"Almost two-thirty on the button," said Zeb.

"Thought so," said Shelly.

"You can tell that from looking at that?" asked Zeb, pointing to the nonsensical symbols on the computer screen.

"Someone programmed your computer to shut down the security cameras, not only in your office but in the surrounding three square block area, between two and three in the afternoon on the day you and your secretary, Helen, were injured."

Zeb walked over to Curtis. Towering over the younger man he gently placed a hand on his shoulder and, without warning, harshly shoved him down into the chair.

"Your mother isn't going to like it if both her husband and her son end up behind bars at the same time, is she, Curtis?"

Curtis' humility returned in a heartbeat. "No, sir. I would do just about anything to see that didn't happen."

"Good. I'd rather not throw you behind bars while you make a phone call to your family attorney. Perhaps if you talk to me, off the record of course, then maybe we can make this thing go away, and your mother will never have to know what you have been up to. Are you game for saving your sorry ass?" asked Zeb.

The tension in Zeb's voice was as clear as the taut muscles on the back of his bulging neck. The sheriff's office had gone out of its way to do Curtis' mother a favor by giving her son some extra work,

work that might get him moved out of her basement and maybe even push him one step closer to manhood. Curtis knew the score. He had purposefully betrayed not only the sheriff's trust but had besmirched his mother in the process.

"You've deceived your mother. I'm sure your father would be ashamed of you..."

"My father wouldn't be in prison if it weren't for you," shouted Curtis.

"We've already been over that. Your father confessed to defrauding the United States government while doing local BIA subcontracting for the Department of the Interior. Worse yet, the money was defrauded from funds provided to the San Carlos Reservation from a committee that Senator Russell chairs, which makes it even more embarrassing. That's all there is to it," said Zeb.

"No that is not all there is to it," yelled Curtis.

"And what makes you believe that?" asked Zeb.

"I downloaded my father's file. He was covering for Sun Rey," said Curtis. "He took the fall and that's why he's in jail. Sun Rey is the real culprit here. At least, based on the fragments of information I was able to put together, I think he is."

Another suspect in the murder of Sun Rey Russell may have just exposed himself. If Curtis blamed Sun Rey for his father being in jail, he might have killed him. After all, Curtis' loyalty to his father was extreme. Zeb stared into the face of Curtis Lowe. Except for the emptiness in his eyes, he certainly didn't seem to have the appearance of a brutal killer.

From the corner of the room, Helen, who had slipped in, cleared her throat. Zeb's ire rose like fire.

"You could have killed Helen. Do you know that?"

Curtis turned toward the injured sheriff's secretary.

"I am so sorry, Helen. No one was supposed to get hurt. Can you find it in your heart to forgive me? I'm ashamed that you got injured. It just wasn't supposed to happen that way."

Helen looked into the young man's eyes. She could see he was suffering. She could see how weak and misguided he was. Even though she had been on the hurting end of things, she carried forgiveness in her heart for Curtis.

"Of course I forgive you," said Helen. "I forgave you right away. We are taught to hate the sin, but love the sinner."

"I guess I have to learn that lesson the hard way," said Curtis.

"But you must do penance of some sort, don't you agree?" asked Helen.

"I do," said Curtis, once again hanging his head low. "Somehow when you put it that way, I suspect the penance will find me."

"Perhaps it will," said Zeb. "For now I'd like you to tell us what else you were after when you and your partner broke into the office and downloaded everything from the main computer? Better yet, let's start off with who your partner was," said Zeb.

"I don't know," replied Curtis.

"Don't know or won't tell?" asked Zeb.

"Honestly, I don't know who it was," said Curtis.

"You don't really expect me to buy into that line of crap, do you? Really? Look it, you've done nothing but lie to me. How can you possibly expect me to believe you don't know who you were working with?"

"I don't know who my partner was, I swear. We only talked on the phone until the day we broke into your office and your computer," explained Curtis.

"Helen, please take Shelly with you and shut the door behind you," said Zeb.

"This was just getting to be fun," said Shelly as she departed with Helen.

Helen left the door slightly ajar. Zeb walked over and discreetly closed it before returning to his desk. This was definitely going to be a private conversation.

12

INTERROGATION

Zeb sat squarely at his desk, his elbows firmly planted on its surface. His jutting chin rested on the back of his intertwined fingers. He leaned forward, eyes transfixed on Curtis.

"You know what liars do, don't you, Curtis?"

Curtis returned Zeb's question with a blank and empty stare.

"They lie," Zeb said forcefully.

Zeb buzzed Jake three short buzzes, the signal to come to his office and enter without knocking. Knowing that Curtis was one of the culprits who had injured Helen shed a whole new light on everything. Experience told him that the young man, no matter how great the level of his anger toward Zeb for having helped put his father behind prison bars, was unlikely the brains behind the crime. Jake slipped in quietly and placed himself ominously in Curtis' blind spot. The sun streamed through the window, casting Jake's shadow across Curtis' Keds. Curtis jolted when he noticed it. Zeb and Jake were not about to play the good cop-bad cop routine on this punk. Two bad cops would work just fine.

"Do you want to talk, or do I need to give you a Graham County lie detector test?" asked Zeb.

Jake's ominous chuckle told Curtis that the Graham County lie detector test didn't involve hooking him up with wires to a machine. His flesh rippled with fear of unknown possibilities. He'd heard rumors. His mind created his worst fears, and his imagination took him to a shallow grave in a remote part of the desert. His forehead and neck burst into a horribly uncomfortable sweat. He gripped his hands together tightly and rested them on his lap. Curtis didn't want Zeb or Jake to see how quivering and damp they were. Something his father had told him during a prison visit popped into Curtis' head. His father's words pierced his mind like an Apache war arrow. 'Never cross a bad path with Sheriff Hanks. He's a good man, but he's got a dark streak that runs through him that will stop at nothing until he gets what he wants. Whatever you do, don't aggravate him. If you do, you will lose and lose badly.' Yet somehow, both father and son had managed to cross Sheriff Zeb Hanks. If ever there was a time to acquiesce to his father's warning, Curtis knew now was it.

"What do you want to know?' asked Curtis. "You've got me dead to rights. I'll tell you everything I can."

"Everything you can?" asked Jake. "Shouldn't that be everything you *know*?"

Curtis coughed into his hand and looked out the window toward some distant spot where the potential of freedom lay.

"Tell me about your partner in crime," said Zeb.

"We weren't partners."

Zeb admired the defiance in the young pipsqueak's voice.

"Okay, your cohort in crime. Let's not mince words. Let's be friends," said Zeb. "You seem to be a smart young man who doesn't want to make a bigger mess of his life than he already has. Curtis, I am certain you are someone who doesn't want to destroy his family any further than it already has been. Think about your mother."

"I told you, I don't know his name. I don't even know what he looks like. You've got to believe me," pleaded Curtis. "Oh, God, but this is going to kill my mother. Please don't tell her. Please!"

Zeb considered scaring Curtis by saying that whomever did this just might have designs on killing his mother. He refrained because Curtis had a special love for his mother and he was weak. Harsh words would only freak him out, even though it was quite possibly the truth. Zeb's gut told him Curtis was not a real criminal. Eventually he would give up all he knew. Zeb had done this often enough to know who crumbled and who didn't. Curtis was a cookie. If he had a backbone, he didn't show it. He would surrender what he knew.

"If you tell us the whole truth, your mother might not have to know about this. I can make that happen for you," said Zeb. "But you'd better start over again. This time don't leave anything out, or I will make your life a living hell."

Jake brought Curtis a glass of water and whispered in his ear. "Sheriff Hanks is not a man you want to trifle with. Trust me on that. Even I can't control him when he's angry."

Curtis' pupils widened with fear as he stared into Jake's leering smile. Somehow he mumbled a 'thank you' to Jake, not knowing if it was for the water or the warning. He took a sip of the cold water. It had the distinct taste of iron as it dribbled over his tremoring lips, some of it slipping down his gullet, more of it down his chin. Curtis wiped the spillage dry with the back of his sleeve. His head swooned as he searched for the right words, words that wouldn't enrage either of his interrogators. In his young life he had never so clearly understood the absolute power of fear. His words came out as a stammer.

"A f-f-few weeks ago, ri-right after you c-c-called me to put in a security camera system, this dude got a hold of me by phone…"

Jake pushed the glass of water closer. Curtis politely shook his head.

"Slow down. Take it easy. Do you still have the phone number in your phone's recent calls history?" asked Zeb.

"No. I don't."

"Did you erase his phone number?"

"No. I'm not stupid. Jesus…"

"Watch your language, son," said Jake.

"The call was blocked. My phone is set up to catch and store all incoming calls, even ones from blocked numbers. I have a special app on my phone that circumvents people who are trying to hide their phone number. I have to assume by the way it was blocked that the call came from a high end burner. For sure the person who called knew a lot about phone functions."

"How many times did you talk with this man?" asked Zeb.

"Three times, but I can't say with one hundred percent certainty it was a man I was talking to," said Curtis.

"What do you mean?" asked Zeb.

Jake loomed ever closer to Curtis. He leaned over and smelled a flowery cologne on Curtis.

"The voice was robotic. Whoever it was used a voice distortion app to disguise how they sound. It could have been a man, a smart kid or even a woman for all I know. But I don't know and I have no way of knowing or even guessing."

Zeb and Jake shrugged their shoulders. This was a twist they would have to deal with later. Neither had a clue as to what it meant, other than someone was disguising his or her voice. It could mean Curtis knew his cohort, but it could also mean it was a woman or a computer savvy teen.

"We will deal with that later," said Zeb. "Did this person use the voice distortion app every time?"

"Yes."

"How many times did you have conversations with this person."

"That time, a week later and the day of the break in," said Curtis.

Both Zeb and Jake were a little surprised by the absolute certainty with which he gave his answer. People that spoke with such exacting certainty were usually well-rehearsed liars. Curtis might be of that peculiar ilk, but it hardly fit his profile.

"You're sure about that?" asked Zeb.

"Absolutely certain," replied Curtis.

"Don't ever lie to me again, Curtis," warned Zeb.

"I won't."

"Okay. What did you talk about?"

Once again Curtis took no time in searching his memory. His response was as instant as it was certain.

"The first time he asked if I was an independent contractor. When I told him I was, he said he had some work for me installing security cameras. When I told him that was my specialty, he began asking a lot of questions about the system I was putting in for you," said Curtis.

"He brought it up, out of the blue, that you were installing security cameras for the sheriff's department?" asked Zeb.

"Didn't you find that a little odd?" asked Jake.

"No. I figured he had seen me in here working," replied Curtis. "I even imagined it was somebody who worked here or somebody you had talked to."

"What did you tell him?" asked Zeb.

"My answers were fairly generic. Now that I think about it, I suspect I was being probed in order to see what I knew, who I was and what kind of system you were installing."

"And you told him?" asked Jake.

Curtis turned toward Jake and nodded. When Jake didn't backhand him, he turned around and looked toward Zeb.

"The conversation was short. He said he would be getting back to me. I remember him asking when I would be done with the job here, at the sheriff's office. I told him. I realize now that I probably shouldn't have given him as many details as I did, but that's all water under the bridge at this point, isn't it?"

"Did he call back when you were done with installing the security cameras here?" asked Zeb.

"Oddly, he called back almost immediately after I was finished. I had no longer walked in the door of my house, right after I completed the job here at the sheriff's office, when the phone rang. It was the same distorted voice."

"And again there is no phone history of that call either?" asked Zeb.

"None. I checked. Believe me I checked," replied Curtis. "I checked and re-checked. I don't like it when my systems fail."

"What did this person have you call him or her?"

"What?" asked Curtis, nervously looking over his shoulder at Jake who had shifted his feet, moving in a step closer to the young culprit and enlarging the shadow his body projected.

"His name. What name did you call him by?" repeated Zeb.

"He said his name was Jude."

"Just Jude? No last name?" asked Zeb.

"No. Just Jude. Nothing else. No last name."

"What did he want?" asked Zeb.

"He said he wanted exactly the same set-up as I had just installed here," said Curtis.

"Identical?"

"That's what he said he wanted."

"Where were you to install this identical system?" asked Zeb.

"He said he'd let me know. Then Jude started talking about my dad. Jude said he knew him back in the day."

"Did Jude say where he knew your dad from?" asked Zeb.

"No, but Jude knew everything about my dad, all kinds of personal stuff. The more he talked the more I realized that my theory that my dad had been set up by Sun Rey was true. Jude even sent me some encrypted files that proved it."

"Do you know Sun Rey?" asked Zeb.

"Just from getting coffee at the 322 Bistro," answered Curtis.

"Have you talked to him lately?"

"I don't get out much," replied Curtis. "But now that you bring it up I haven't seen him in the 322 lately. I've been sort of looking for him. I figured if I talked with him he might let something slip that could help me free my dad. He owes me that much."

"Do you have it in for Sun Rey?" asked Zeb.

Curtis suddenly became alive with fire.

"Hell, yes. I'd do just about anything to get that rat bastard."

"Would you kill him?" asked Zeb.

Curtis gulped heavily. Hot sweat dripped from his brow into his eyes. His hands became so damp they slipped off the arms of the chair.

"I've fantasized about it, especially when I'm playing video games," replied Curtis.

"Do you own any guns?" asked Zeb.

"We have guns at home. They are my mom's now that my dad is in prison. They are locked up in a gun safe."

"Do you have the combination to the gun safe?"

"Of course," said Curtis. "My dad taught me to shoot when I was six."

"Are you a good shot?" asked Zeb.

"Excellent. I won the county shotgun shooting contest by freshman year," said Curtis.

"Impressive," said Zeb. "What kind of guns are in the cabinet?"

"Three or four shotguns, a 30.06, a .22 rifle and a couple handguns. Not a lot," said Curtis.

"Shells?"

"All kinds. You name it. Shotgun slugs, bird shot, .22 long and short shells, bullets for my .38 and my dad's .45. My dad and I liked to buy shells on sale and keep stocked up. You never know when big brother is going to take away your guns and ammo," replied Curtis.

Zeb looked past Curtis at Jake.

"When was the last time any of the guns were fired?" asked Zeb.

"Before all this crap went down with my dad, a couple of years I guess. Unless my mom shoots them, but I doubt that."

"I'll look into it," said Jake.

"Look into what?" asked Curtis.

Zeb ignored Curtis' question.

"Were you able to ultimately download those encrypted files Jude sent you?" asked Jake.

"No. They were read only files. When I tried to reformat them so I could save and print them, they disappeared. Jude put some serious work into the security system, very professional. I was still on the phone with Jude when I looked at my father's files. Jude told me he would allow me to download those files to my computer and help set my father free if I did him a favor."

Once again Curtis hung his head.

"Let me guess. He wanted you to break into my files?" asked Zeb.

"Yes, sir. That is correct. He said my father could be out of prison in no time if I had the information from your files."

"Any particular files?" asked Zeb.

"He wanted all files from a specific time frame," said Curtis.

"What time frame exactly?" asked Zeb.

"Everything on your computer starting twenty months ago to eight months ago. He was very precise on the dates."

Zeb looked over at Jake. They both knew exactly what that meant. A smart person could extrapolate enough information to realize that Zeb was in Mexico, and if they could dig deep enough into the information, they could figure out that Zeb had killed the woman who had murdered his wife.

"Did he say anything about specifics he was looking for?"

"No. He wanted everything on your computer, but he made special note of that specific time frame. When I began to ask why that time period, he shut me down quickly."

"How much did he pay you?" asked Zeb.

"I asked for twenty grand," said Curtis.

"That was pretty ballsy of you," interjected Jake.

"It was how much I thought I needed. He offered ten. We eventually agreed on fifteen thousand dollars. Cash money. I needed the money for a lawyer to get my dad out of prison. It was my family's only chance, my dad's only chance. Don't you see? Wouldn't either of you have done exactly the same thing?"

Both Zeb and Jake let Curtis' question pass.

"Did he pay you?" asked Zeb.

"Some of it. Actually he paid me almost half. He said he'd give me the rest when the files from your office had been gone through with a fine-tooth comb. He also promised me everything from your computer that related to my dad and to Sun Rey."

"Have you received those files yet?"

"No. I think I was conned."

"You were," said Jake. "You're the perfect dupe."

Curtis shot a sneer in Jake's direction. Jake, arms folded across his chest, responded with a chortle.

"Tell me how the theft of information from my computer went down," said Zeb.

"It was simple. I used a flash drive. Your system is so antiquated it took only a few keystrokes to get everything I wanted. You need someone to bring your security up to date," said Curtis. "It's terribly outdated."

"It ain't gonna be you that does the work," snarled Jake.

"I understand our security needs to be updated," said Zeb. "What I need to know is what happened the day of the incident. I want to know everything from start to finish."

"Everything?" asked Curtis.

"Everything."

Curtis inhaled deeply and exhaled a forlorn sigh. He was backed up against a hard wall. Zeb was grateful Curtis feared the sheriff's department as much as he feared his partner in crime.

"I slept in. I had been up all night playing *Assassins Creed: Rogue* with a dude in the Czech Republic. I kicked his sorry Communist ass," said Curtis.

"There hasn't been Communism in the Czech Republic for almost thirty years," said Jake.

"You know what I mean," said Curtis.

"Actually, I don't," said Jake. "What is the game about? Revenge?"

"In a manner of speaking it's about revenge," replied Curtis. "Mostly it's about the Seven Years' War. You probably know it as the French and Indian War," said Curtis.

"We called it the first real world war," replied Jake, a history buff who would not to be outdone by a smart-ass young punk when it came to war knowledge.

"We can discuss all of that later," said Zeb. "Go on, Curtis. Tell us what happened that day."

"I had my cellphone under my pillow. I had it set on vibrate. My mother doesn't like it if my phone rings and disturbs her. Anyway, when my phone began to vibrate, I answered it and it was Jude. I looked at the clock. It was ten minutes to two. I was groggy but when I heard Jude's voice, it woke me up quickly," said Curtis.

"What about his voice woke you up so fast?" asked Zeb.

"Money. He said it was time for me to get to work so I could earn the money I needed to get my dad out of prison. When I heard that, I paid extra close attention."

"What sort of plan did he have set up?" asked Zeb.

"You know that row of three abandoned houses on First Street a few blocks down from the BLM?" asked Curtis.

Zeb nodded. They were a perennial eyesore and hangout for low-end drug addicts, meth users and glue sniffers. The city had been fighting with the property owner for years to tear them down.

"There's an alley that runs behind them. There's a deep drainage ditch behind the second house."

Zeb and Jake both knew the ditch as the First Avenue gully washer. It had been there since before they were kids, a leftover project of the Depression era WPA.

"He told me to park down in there and make sure no one saw me. If anyone did see me he told me to drive around for a few minutes and then come back. No one saw me. He told me he'd be sitting behind the wheel of a blue Ford F-10 with tinted windows. I'm pretty sure it was a 2003 or 2004. He told me not to be alarmed because he'd have a stocking cap covering his face. He said he was bringing one for me as well."

Curtis took a deep drink of water. The truth seemed to be drying him up.

"Go on," urged Zeb. "What happened next?

"I pulled in next to the truck. I mean to tell you I was scared. When he looked over at me with his face covered by that stocking cap, I thought he might pull a gun and kill me. But I knew I had to put that feeling aside for the money to get my dad out of prison.

Then he signaled me to get in his truck. I put out my hand to shake his, but he didn't shake hands. He had latex gloves on. He handed me a black stocking cap, the kind with holes for the eyes. Then he made some remark about the color of my shoes. He said I should never wear anything distinctive that someone might remember. I felt stupid. He really sounded like he knew what he was talking about. I got the feeling this wasn't his first rodeo."

"I don't imagine it was," said Jake.

"Go on, Curtis. Then what happened?" asked Zeb.

"He told me to put on the stocking cap to cover my face. It was new, and it smelled funny, like mothballs and chemicals. There were eyeholes, but there were no holes for my nose or mouth. I felt like I couldn't breathe because I have allergies to chemicals. I have all kinds of allergies, had them since I was a kid."

"Stick to the facts," said Zeb. "Your allergies don't concern us."

"Right. Then Jude told me to scrunch down in the car, and he ordered me not to look at him. In fact, he told me to stare at the floor of the truck."

"Did you see anything remarkable on the floor?" asked Jake.

"A cigar butt and a screwdriver. Other than that it was clean, unusually clean. I picked up the cigar butt and put it in the ashtray without looking at Jude. Then I handed him the screwdriver. He told me to put it on the seat. He said thanks. Funny thing was he laughed when he said thanks. Then he handed me a pair of latex gloves."

"I bet he did," said Jake.

"What do you mean?" asked Curtis. "All I did was hand him the screwdriver."

"He gave you the latex gloves after you picked up the cigar butt and screwdriver. Before you put them on you gave him fingerprints and enough DNA to frame you."

"Shit," said Curtis. "I'm such an idiot. I never even thought of that."

"You make a solid argument about being an idiot," said Jake.

"Let's just say that you could have made much better choices," said Zeb. "Continue."

"We sat there with the windows slightly open. He went over his plan with me repeatedly. He kept asking me if I understood exactly what was going to happen. Then he asked me for my cellphone and..."

"And what?" asked Zeb.

"I guess maybe I should have told you this before. When I put in your security cameras, I put additional micro-cameras just to the left of the lens of each of the security cameras."

"For what purpose?" asked Zeb.

"So when we shut down the regular security cameras we could monitor your every move and see exactly where everyone else in the office was. We needed to know that Helen would be alone at the front desk, that you'd be in the bathroom, and, hopefully, the rest of the office would be empty. Jude knew you'd take an afternoon bathroom break that would take at least five minutes. He had me rig your official security cameras so he could shut them off from my phone. I thought the whole thing was rather ingenious," said Curtis. "I mean this whole thing took some real expert planning on his part."

"You're wasting your admiration on the wrong guy," growled Jake.

Curtis blushed a deep shade of red. Indeed, he had chosen poorly. He was in shit up to his eyeballs and could see no way out.

"Zeb, how do you figure he knew you would be in the bathroom around two-thirty?" asked Jake.

Curtis gulped loudly.

"I guess I told him that one."

"How on earth did you know I might be in the bathroom at that time?" asked Zeb, more than a tad creeped out that anyone knew such a private part of his daily life.

"Helen was visiting my mother one day, and they were joking around about work. Helen said you were one of the most 'regular' people she ever knew. When I overheard them talking, I thought she meant regular as in normal. But when they kept chuckling about it, I figured out they were talking about something else. I asked my mom about it, and she told me the story Helen had told her. I guess you'd say it was a private joke of sorts. Then I verified it on the hidden camera."

Jake laughed out loud. "How many criminals have we caught over the years because of their routines, Zeb? Hundreds? Thousands?"

"Shit," said Zeb. "No pun intended."

"Okay, you disabled the security system so you could go in and out of the sheriff's office without being noticed," said Jake.

"Disabling it would also make it so there was no recording of anything at that time. Yes, that's how I planted the micro-cameras linked to my cellphone," said Curtis.

"Clever," Jake retorted. "Crooks with a back-up system aren't generally rookies."

Zeb nodded at Jake's comment and made a few quick notes. Curtis waited until the sheriff was done jotting before he spoke again.

"We were watching you and Helen and grabbed a lucky break when Helen accidentally knocked her stapler to the floor," said Curtis. "That allowed us to sneak in and surprise her. It was an accident that my associate called a gift from God."

"More like the devil's work if you ask me," said Jake.

"Then he hogtied Helen and taped her mouth shut. I thought that was really mean. I was really hoping he wouldn't harm her in any way," continued Curtis. "I wanted to run away and forget the whole thing, but I was in way too deep."

"Your best bet to have kept Helen safe would have been to not get your sorry ass involved in the first place," said Jake.

"I know. Helen's a friend of my mom's and mine. I mean I know her, not a lot, but some. She is always so nice to me. I watched things happen from where she couldn't see me. I didn't want her to recognize me," said Curtis. "I'd have been so ashamed if she had seen me that I don't know what I would have done."

"Your partner in crime, if he'd noticed that Helen recognized you, he just might have put a bullet in your brain," said Jake.

Curtis rubbed his sweaty forehead.

"I'd suggest you burn your Keds," said Zeb.

"I will burn them today. Thank you," said Curtis.

"Proof that you're not a complete idiot," added Jake.

Curtis knew he had every jab Jake was tossing in his direction coming but was angry and embarrassed enough to toss a hard stare in Jake's direction. Jake chuckled so hard he had to wipe a tear away from the corner of his eye.

"Go on," urged Zeb.

"When you came out of the bathroom, I had just about finished getting everything off of your computer and onto the flash drive," continued Curtis. "If we had had one more minute, all you would have found would have been Helen all bound up. Instead you ended up taking a nasty clunk on the back of your head. How does it feel? You got hit pretty hard, I mean it made a nasty sound. Maybe Jude knows you and is pissed off at you? I didn't think that was nice, I mean how hard he hit you, but what could I do?"

"The pain is gone. Physical pain is always temporary, but the fact that it happened irritates me at every waking moment," said Zeb. "So, you had better hope we catch your associate."

"From what I can tell, you will," said Curtis. "You guys seem to know what you're doing."

"Do you know why Jude didn't kill me right then and there?" asked Zeb.

"No. Frankly I was scared to death he was going to. I didn't want to see that. If he had shot you, I don't think I'd have ever slept again. If he had killed you, I think I would have turned him in, but that would be like signing my own death warrant. I think Jude really is a bad ass, just like in the movies."

"He didn't say anything about wanting to kill me or Helen?" asked Zeb.

"Now that you mention it, he did say 'That damn sheriff is going to have to pay sooner or later for what he's done. Just not now. He's got to suffer first.' I wanted to ask him what he meant, but thought better of it. I was just glad I didn't have to witness a murder."

"Then what happened?" asked Zeb.

"Jude told me to remove the mini-cameras. I did that in about two seconds flat. Then we slowly walked to the car, which he'd parked just outside the south side door. When we got in the car, he slowly pulled out. When we got a few blocks away, he reached under his seat and handed me an envelope that contained six grand in one hundred dollar bills. Then Jude drove me to within a block of my car and dropped me off. But before he let me out of the truck, he had me remotely switch the security cameras back on. As I watched him pull away, he took a left on Seventh Avenue. It was then I think I saw him remove his stocking cap. I can't say for sure but it seemed like he had darker, thick hair. It was hard to tell, and I didn't want to stare in case he was looking back at me. Then he just more or less disappeared. I haven't heard from him yet about the other nine thousand he owes me," said Curtis. "I don't suppose I'm going to, do you?"

"Nope," said Jake. "I don't suppose you are."

"You're going to have to give us the sixty, one hundred dollar bills he gave you. It's evidence from a major crime," said Zeb.

"Really?" asked Curtis. "Even though I helped you out? Come on, man. I earned that money the hard way."

"You're lucky you're going home rather than to a jail cell," said Zeb. "But just in case your partner in crime tries to use your fingerprints to set you up, I want to fingerprint you for your own safety. Jake, get his fingerprints."

Jake led a shame drenched Curtis Lowe to the fingerprint room. One by one his ten digits were recorded for posterity. When he was done, Jake offered him a cloth to wipe the ink from his hands. Curtis dropped his head into his hands and broke into a blubbering moan. Jake let him bawl it out, like a newborn calf. Each had, in their own way, hit bottom at one time or another and fully understood the pain young Curtis was suffering. When he found his voice, he spoke.

"I may not be going to jail, but if my mama gets wind of it, I'm going straight to hell for what I've done."

"Then it's a good time to tuck a little religion under your belt. I hear the Lord forgives, but we won't forget. Go," said Jake, holding the door open. "Get the hell out of here."

Curtis departed disgracefully, followed only by a shadow of dread.

13

THE GHOST OF DOREEN

Kate watched Curtis and Jake leave the sheriff's office and head into the fingerprint room.

"What did you find out from Curtis?" asked Kate.

"That kid got caught up in a fantasy," said Zeb. "He actually believed that abetting in a crime would get him money to help set his dad free from prison. Idealism gone awry."

"He's a scared, inexperienced, young kid who didn't think through the consequences," said Kate. "Then again, I would venture to guess that we've all done dumb things in our lives that could have gotten us into big trouble. But, on the other hand, he's a millennial."

"Meaning?" asked Zeb.

"Meaning he's used to having everything his way and having it right now. He may act and sound like a wimp, but remember he was brought up by the TV and the belief that participation and winning are the same thing. He could be acting. For all we know he could be a mass murderer. In some ways he fits the profile. His actions could have gotten Helen killed," said Kate. "Or you."

"...or me. I guess I hadn't thought all that much about myself getting killed. But if Helen had died because of my failure to protect her, I couldn't have lived with myself."

Zeb eyes drifted off toward the distant peaks of Mount Graham. It wouldn't be long before they would be covered in snow. Seasons changed, times changed, but young men acting irrationally was one thing that never changed. A young man with a poorly thought out cause would always be the world's most dangerous weapon.

Kate stood silently by. She assumed Zeb was thinking about Doreen. It was clear that even though more than a year had passed Zeb still burned the torch for his dead wife. Kate could clearly see the loss of Doreen was eroding something deep inside Zeb. Kate also knew the pain of the loss of his wife might keep him stuck in a single moment for the rest of his life. His life could easily become as murky and dead as a pool of stagnant water.

Kate had been good friends with Doreen. They had been close enough for Doreen to instruct her on what to do if she died before Zeb. She had told Kate 'Don't let Zeb wallow in pain and, for God's sake don't allow him to be lonely. Do whatever it takes so he doesn't rot on the vine.' Kate quietly took a seat in the old beat up chair across from Zeb. She watched his eyes and waited. It was quite apparent he was so lost in thought that her presence was not even on his radar. For ten minutes a sad silence shrouded the room. Eventually Zeb turned and met eyes with Kate.

"I guess I was lost in thought," said Zeb.

"I saw that."

"How long was I zoned out?"

"A while," replied Kate.

"Oh. Sorry."

"You looked reflective. Where did your mind go?"

Zeb pointed toward Mount Graham.

Kate noticed his hands had aged. They still looked strong but somehow older. Tracing an invisible line from his fingertip she saw that he was pointing toward Ladybug Saddle, a favorite spot of Doreen's and Zeb's. It was where they collected wildflowers and picnicked. It was where Zeb had found the courage to woo Doreen. Kate retraced her gaze from Ladybug Saddle back to Zeb's fingertip and followed the line up to his eyes. A pronounced foggy sadness rested there, like a mother bird sitting on an empty nest. She recognized she had not done her part to fulfill Doreen's wishes.

"Can we talk...frankly talk?" asked Kate. "Without judgment?"

Almost absentmindedly Zeb responded, "Sure, but you sound awful serious."

"I am serious, Zeb. We need to talk about Doreen."

Zeb turned away. A solitary tear fell to the back of his hand. He let it just sit there for a brief moment before covering it with his hand. He shivered when he noticed how cold the tear felt as it landed. The tears from his eyes were definitely less abundant than they had been, but the pain in his heart was as plentiful as ever.

"We need to talk about you, Zeb," said Kate. "About your feelings for Doreen."

He didn't look up at his deputy as he spoke. "Why? She's gone. Talking won't bring her back. Talking about me won't change anything. I did what I had to do. It's over."

Though there was a tacit understanding of what Zeb had done in Mexico to revenge Doreen's murder, this was the first time he had spoken the words that confirmed what he did. Kate made no judgment. Who was she to judge? This discussion wasn't about anything he'd done in the past. They were talking about the here and now and what the future might bring.

"And not living your life won't honor her memory," replied Kate.

Zeb stared right through Kate. Her words had seemed to come out of nowhere. All this time he believed he had an ally in his only female deputy, someone who would never cross the threshold of his feelings regarding Doreen. Her words seemed caustic. It took all he had to quell the anger that rose as naturally as a summer thunderhead.

"Would you like to talk?" asked Kate.

Zeb turned away again. Doreen's face appeared in his mind, not in some ghostly fashion but almost literally. She was soft, beautiful and radiant. She was as he remembered her on their wedding day, the day they had vowed to love, honor, obey and protect. The word 'protect' stuck in his craw like a deadly chicken bone. He coughed hard, nearly losing his breath. His failure to protect Doreen had caused her death. It was an obstacle on the road to normality he could never circumvent.

"Are you okay?" asked Kate.

Zeb put his hand over his mouth as he continued to half choke through his coughing fit. At the same time, he was silently reciting his and Doreen's wedding vows in his head. At the end when the words 'til death do us part' came to his mind, he quit thinking. He quit coughing as well. He turned to Kate.

"Yes, I guess maybe I would like to talk. I think that might be a good idea."

"Do you want to start or would you prefer that I speak first," said Kate.

Doreen had taught him that when a woman had something to say it was best to let her say it. He smiled. Letting a woman speak first was one of Doreen's ten commandments of love. He kept all ten in his wallet written on a small piece of paper.

"You go ahead. I think I need to listen," said Zeb.

Kate cleared her throat. She knew Zeb. Her words must be carefully chosen or they might not be heard at all.

"Doreen did not want you to be alone in case something ever happened to her. She told me her heart would break all the way from heaven if you were sad and lonely when she was gone from your life."

"When did you two talk about this?" asked Zeb.

"Not even a week before she was murdered."

Zeb gulped. He never felt right when someone else called Doreen's death murder. He felt he had exclusive rights to that territory. Suddenly the importance of that particular issue melted away.

"Was she having a premonition? She had lots of them, you know," said Zeb.

"Perhaps," replied Kate. "She was talking to me over a cup of coffee about the horrible car accident that took the life of her first husband and their child.

The mere mention of the accident twisted Zeb's mind into a jumble of unbreakable, snarled knots.

"She told me that she never felt it was right that they died and she lived. That is, until she met you. Loving you gave her the ability to feel like she could live again. Then she began to worry every day that something would happen to you. And if something didn't happen to you, she was certain it was going to happen to her."

"She was right," interjected Zeb. "Something did happen to her."

Once again Zeb turned away from Kate's voice. His sights and thoughts loitered up on Mount Graham. A lone eagle floated on the updraft between his office and Ladybug Saddle. It was joined shortly by a second eagle. Zeb knew they mated for life and imagined them to be companions, lifelong companions.

"What am I supposed to do with my life, Kate? I feel lost. I've felt lost since Doreen was killed. Only the other day I had a glimmer of hope, but that led to me being bonked on the head. I'm trapped in a world not of my own making."

"Doreen wanted you to go on with your life...to find love again."

"I, I can't do that. It wouldn't be right. It would just be so wrong," said Zeb. "No, I don't even want to consider the possibility of loving a woman ever again."

"Wouldn't you do anything that Doreen asked of you? Didn't you do everything she asked of you when you were together?"

"Yes, of course, I did," replied Zeb.

Kate reached into her jacket pocket and withdrew a letter. It was addressed to Zeb in Doreen's handwriting. Puzzled, Zeb looked at Kate.

"She left this for you. She gave it to me to give to you in case she died before you did. She asked that I wait one year or until you were ready before I handed it over. I think you're ready now," said Kate.

Zeb ran the envelope through his fingers, turning it to every angle possible. It seemed to weigh pounds rather than ounces. In his hands he held Doreen's words. Words that came from beyond the grave. Words that came out of the past. Zeb squeezed his fingers together to keep his hands from trembling. Something very much alive radiated from the envelope.

"What makes you think I'm ready? And ready for what?" asked Zeb, his mind shooting in a thousand directions. "Doreen must have trusted you deeply to leave this responsibility in your hands."

"She did have faith that I would do the right thing," replied Kate.

Kate reached back into her pocket and pulled out a shiny piece of black obsidian. It was a stone known to everyone as an Apache tear. She slid it across Zeb's desk. He looked at it without touching it. He cupped his hands around it, still not allowing them to make physical contact with the Apache tear. He let the power of the stone emanate in a linear fashion through his hands, up his arms, around his brain and down his spine until its energy cloaked him completely. Song Bird had given him several black obsidians over the years. The medicine man had always presented them to Zeb in times of trouble. Song Bird had also taught Zeb how to pay exacting attention to the power of the obsidian. Kate then removed her phone from her pocket. She pressed on the photos app.

"Many years ago, when I first met Doreen, she gave me a dreamcatcher. It was handmade by an elderly Apache woman. Last night I took these pictures. I know that only because they are time stamped on my phone. I have no recollection of taking them. It was during the middle of the night."

Kate turned her cellphone toward Zeb. In the center of the dreamcatcher that hung above her bed was the outline of a winged angel. The angel was holding her hands in front of her. On her ring finger was the ring Zeb had given Doreen on the day of their wedding. It was unmistakable. Zeb did a double take. Kate slid her finger across the face of the cellphone and the next picture appeared. It was identical to the first only the wedding ring was on a necklace around the neck of the winged angel.

"I also had a dream last night. In the dream Doreen came to me and told me to show you these photographs, and you would know what they meant," said Kate.

Zeb could no longer hold back his emotions. Inside he was falling to pieces. This was a sign, a sign Zeb and Doreen had talked about many times. If one should die before the other, they had agreed to send a message. The first to die would free the other from suffering and pain by taking off their wedding ring and wearing it on a gold chain around their neck.

Zeb felt as though he were going to have a stroke. In the next instant he felt as light as a feather. The confusion and tightness in his mind changed from pain to joy. The internal confusion that wrested all strength from his body dissipated like a dying dust devil. When he looked up to thank Kate, she was gone. It was like she had never been there.

Zeb waited and waited before opening the letter. As he read it, he began to feel stronger, free of the bondage that kept him from moving forward, free of the hate that too often rested in his heart.

The letter from Doreen was simple and complete. It said, 'Zeb, I love you eternally. Now that I am gone you should share your love with another.' She signed her name and had drawn a heart with an arrow through it.

14

EVIDENCE

Zeb's cellphone rang. It was Rambler's ring tone.

"Good news, Zeb," said Rambler.

"I can always use some of that," replied Zeb.

"I think I've got Sun Rey's murder weapon," said Rambler. "We will have to match the ballistics, but we've got a .12 gauge and one spent cartridge and one spent small game shell."

"Where did you find them?" asked Zeb.

"We dragged San Carlos Lake. Everything was sitting in three feet of water at the north end of the lake. It was weird how close everything was together..."

"Almost like someone planted it there?" asked Zeb.

"You read my mind, my white-eyed amigo. Just like it was put there for us to find."

"I don't know if that's good or bad," said Zeb.

"It's better than nothing, wouldn't you say?"

"The million-dollar question is why someone would plant them for us to find?" asked Zeb.

"The million-dollar answer is, drum roll please, to lead the investigation astray."

"When did you ever have a murder case where the evidence was as easy to find as the back of your hand?" asked Zeb.

"Exactly never," replied Rambler.

"Right. Can you do me a favor and bring the gun, cartridge and shell into town? We have the ability to check the ballistics here. It would be a great help."

"It's going to cost you coffee and donuts," said Rambler.

"Sure, why not?"

"See you in fifteen minutes. You want the serial number off the gun?" asked Rambler.

"It wasn't filed off?"

"No siree," said Rambler. "It's all there. Clear as a bell. Gun looks almost new."

"This has to be a set-up. A gun that's easy to trace found in shallow water near the scene of the crime? Seriously, have you ever even heard of that happening?"

"I've seen it on *CSI*. Maybe this is the one in a million times when it actually happens in real life," said Rambler.

"Wanna bet that this isn't a set up?" asked Zeb.

"Indians aren't gamblers. We own the casinos," said Rambler. "Less risk, more reward. So I don't think I'll be taking your bet."

"Didn't think you would," replied Zeb. "The serial number please?"

Rambler rattled off the serial number from the potential murder weapon. Zeb jotted it down.

"Did you check it for prints?" asked Zeb.

"Do you think we have the specialized kind of equipment that can read prints that are on something that has been underwater for a while, even a short while?"

Zeb chuckled. That kind of specialty product was the exclusive purview of the FBI, the DIA or even higher up the food chain.

"Doesn't hurt to ask. You never know what kind of extras the government throws your way," said Zeb.

"What they throw our way is usually garbage."

"See you in fifteen minutes for coffee and donuts."

"I'm working on expanding my belly so it's going to cost you," said Rambler.

Zeb knew Rambler was a workout fanatic and that he carried almost zero body fat on his lithe frame.

"You're the one donut eating cop I can afford to feed," said Zeb.

Zeb hung up and immediately called Josh Diamond, Kate's fiancé, at his shop, Diamond Guns and Ammo. The owner answered on the first ring.

"How goes it, Sheriff Hanks?"

"Why so formal? Is the ATF Bureau listening in on you again?" asked Zeb.

"You never know. Somehow I can't seem to keep off their radar. Ever since the fire at my business I sense their ever suspicious eye checking me out."

"If it were anyone but you, I'd call it paranoia," said Zeb.

The night Josh's business and apartment were destroyed was the night Doreen was murdered. Josh stopped short of saying anything else, especially considering it was all entangled with their trip to Mexico.

"How are things in your line of work?" asked Josh.

"If you want to know the truth, it's as busy as a one legged man in an ass kicking contest," replied Zeb.

"I think I already know most of it. If you keep making my best gal work overtime, you might just ruin my relationship. As it is it's already eating into my love life."

"I'm truly sorry about that," said Zeb. "It's just that I haven't gotten around to hiring anyone to take my former deputy and newly elected State Senator Devon Dawbyns' place yet. You still not interested in the job?"

"Nope, not interested. It would be a conflict of interest with Kate working there. Plus, I don't know if our relationship could take that," replied Josh. "Besides, I hear the son of one of Jake's old buddies is up for consideration. I hear the dude's name is Sawyer Black Bear."

"I barely know the half of it myself. I guess there are no secrets in this town," replied Zeb. "His application is on my desk. I've only glanced at it."

"Helen gave everyone a copy of his background information. I assume you know that?"

"I do. I suppose you discussed it with Kate?"

"Of course I did. Goes with the relationship thing, you know that," said Josh.

"Save me some time. What do you think of him, on paper anyway?"

"Sounds like a good guy, hell of a good guy. How much you want to know?"

"Not much. Not nearly as much as I should. Give me a synopsis."

"Okay. You already know his father is a friend of Jake's."

"Right. Jake mentioned they were both called in during the Wounded Knee confrontation on the Pine Ridge Reservation back in 1973. Jake was a pup working his way into the U.S. Marshal service."

"Hard to believe Jake was ever a pup," chuckled Josh. "Might just have to name my next dog Jake."

"He might like that, or he might take offense. Depends on the dog. I'm fairly certain Jake was working on being the alpha pup."

"Anyway, Black Bear is part Swede and part Lakota. His old man was a U.S. Marshal, Jake's direct supervisor. His mom is Lakota and was an American Indian Movement activist. She was, probably still is, a major league radical."

"Sounds like oil and water," said Zeb. "I don't imagine Wounded Knee made for peace in the family household."

"Probably not, but they're still married. Either because of his background or in spite of it, Black Bear is an expert in understanding cross-cultural stuff. He probably heard about Wounded Knee and the AIM movement every day of his childhood."

"Kids like that usually end up torn and troubled," said Zeb.

"He has a history of minor legal scrapes as a kid and split to be on his own at seventeen. He joined the Marines, got busted for punching a small town Montana cop in the nose when he asked for his fishing license. He wants to move here so he can someday retire and fish the Sea of Cortez," explained Josh.

"How old is he?"

"Early forties," answered Josh.

"He's been a deputy sheriff on the Pine Ridge Reservation ever since he got discharged from the military. I'd say he's uniquely positioned to understand scams that get pulled on the Rez and how the politics of the Rez works."

"Should I hire him?" asked Zeb. "In your opinion, that is."

"The times they are a changing, Zeb. It would be good to have someone with that deep of a Native American background on your team. The Rez and the county are getting more intertwined all the time."

"I'll take that as a qualified yes," said Zeb.

"Check him out. Based on the number of times you've asked me about the job, you must need someone. Enough of that. So why the pleasure of your call?"

"Can you track down a gun for me?"

"Why don't you do it yourself?"

"Paperwork in triplicate to all kinds of state and federal agencies, other bullshit red tape the city just added, not to mention that you can do it faster and better than I can. Are those reasons enough? You'd really be doing me a huge favor."

"Gotcha. Okay, give me the serial number," said Josh.

Zeb rattled it off. Josh immediately said, "I can already tell you that it's a military issued weapon."

"Based on the serial number, can you tell where the gun came from, what base or what branch of the military?"

"Do you actually believe the military is that organized?" asked Josh. "The military is part of the government and runs like a big, fat, bloated tick of a bureaucracy. They have more fools and jackasses running their day-to-day operations than just about any branch of government, including the State Department, Department of the Interior, the IRS, etcetera."

"I hear you, loud and clear," said Zeb.

"Not only is the boondoggle of the military industrial complex squishier than a bloated tick, they routinely move weapons from place to place. Having been at war for over a decade has only complicated the issue. In the military Peter is always robbing to pay Paul and Paul steals it right back. However, I can tell from the middle two numbers it was originally issued to an armory in Arizona. So it's a local weapon, or it was a local weapon at one time."

"It's also a murder weapon," said Zeb.

"Sun Rey's?"

"You've been talking to Kate, haven't you?"

"It's the only recent murder in the area. It's not exactly rocket science putting a few facts together," said Josh.

"Are you sure you're not looking for gainful employment?" asked Zeb. "I can put you to work today, tomorrow at the latest, with a bonus starting last month, if you'd like."

"Sorry old pal, but I've got plenty to do around here," replied Josh.

"Any chance you can learn anything more about the gun?" asked Zeb.

"Did you check the national data base to see if it was stolen or merely lost in the bureaucratic jungle?" asked Josh.

"Not yet. It's next on my list."

"Who are you sending it to for latent prints? FBI or DIA?"

"Any idea on who's a better bet to actually get me the timeliest answer?" asked Zeb.

"If you know someone you can trust on the inside of either the FBI or the DIA, then go with them," replied Josh. "Remember, almost everyone in that system is always trying to move up the ladder, and most don't give a shit whose toes they step on."

"I know the Special Agent in Charge at the FBI Field Office in Phoenix."

"Lieutenant Colonel Jensen?"

"You know him?"

"He's a customer, and he's done all he can to keep the FBI out of my shit. He's a righteous man. He could have stayed in DC and been an Army General Officer, but instead, he joined the FBI and was offered the move to Phoenix as the field office SAC. He's a good man. He moved to help take care of his aging parents, but it didn't hurt his son is about to be called up by the Arizona Diamondbacks and his daughter is on a soccer scholarship at ASU. I believe he can be trusted."

"Thanks for the inside dope. I'll ask him. I really appreciate it."

"Any time."

"Coffee sometime soon?" asked Zeb. "It's time we caught up."

"Just so we're clear, I'm not going to be bribed into taking the job as one of your deputies for a couple of reasons," replied Josh.

"And those reasons being?"

"One, Kate would outrank me..."

"I never thought of you as being sexist," joked Zeb.

"I'm not. It just might lead to trouble if we had completely different ideas on how to do something at work."

"Got it," replied Zeb.

"Second, I like the freedom of self-employment. I can work as much as I want and get away if I need to," said Josh.

"Your point is well taken. Still, the offer remains open."

"I appreciate it, but take my advice and hire Sawyer Black Bear. Bye."

Zeb punched the numbers into the federal data base of stolen guns. Josh's gut instinct and information had been correct. The gun was stolen or had gone missing from the Tucson National Guard Armory less than one month earlier. He called Josh back.

"When you were in the National Guard, would it have been easy to steal a weapon, specifically a weapon like this one?" asked Zeb.

"Hell, no and hell, yes."

"Don't know that I follow your logic, Josh."

"If you had someone doing the paperwork who understood the rules and regs of administrative paper shuffling and could make paperwork disappear, you could get it done in a heartbeat. Otherwise, you have to sign your life away for anything and everything involved with weaponry. But, like I said, if you are the one handling the red tape, doing the paperwork, or if you knew someone who would take a bribe, you could have your own private arsenal," replied Josh. "You could have automatic weapons, bazookas, hell, even old fashioned flame throwers, Humvees and maybe a tank or two if you knew the right person."

"How often do you think that kind of thing happens?" asked Zeb.

"Way too often," replied Josh. "There are more than a few folks who sign up for the military specifically to build a personal arsenal. Extremist groups of all kinds find their way into the military. I would venture a guess that sort of nonsense has been going on since the Revolutionary War."

"I guess I shouldn't be surprised that there are people who want a huge cache of private weapons. I'm not a military vet, but it seems to me these folks in charge would want to keep a close eye on things," said Zeb.

"Think again," said Josh. "If they're the crooked ones, they gain the most. More than one supply sergeant has retired a multi-millionaire on an E-8 salary."

"Thanks, Josh. It's been a real eye opener," said Zeb. "Adiós."

"Good luck," said Josh. "You'll never track that weapon down even if you access all the military paperwork. If someone is stealing guns, even something as simple as a .12-gauge shotgun, you can bet they are covering their asses up to their eyeballs. Ciao for now."

Helen buzzed Zeb. Senator Russell was on the other line. Zeb immediately took the call.

"Senator Russell," said Zeb.

"Sheriff Hanks," replied the senator. "What have you got for me?"

"I think we have the gun that killed your son."

"I know. A deputy from the San Carlos police force called me. He owed me a favor and decided it was time to even things up," said Senator Russell.

"I only heard about it a half an hour ago myself," said Zeb. "I've got it tracked down to the National Guard Armory in Tucson. It was likely stolen from there a month or so ago. It looks as though tracking down the paperwork is going to be tough. Any chance you could help me out on that?"

"I doubt it. Government thieves are experts in losing paperwork in a trail that is made difficult to follow by its very being," said Senator Russell. "I'll make a phone call. Don't expect much of anything especially if someone was planning from the beginning to use the shotgun as a murder weapon."

"Right."

"Get back to me the minute you know anything. I'll do the same," said the senator. "Good-bye."

Zeb hung up the phone. Senator Russell's tone sounded quite unlike his normal self. Strangely, the senator sounded distant, almost uncaring. Zeb figured the death of his son must be having a profoundly confusing effect on him. On the other hand, Zeb thought the senator would have done anything possible to help track down the paperwork as opposed to brushing that possible trail to the killer off as all but impossible.

Helen buzzed him again on the intercom. "Police Chief Rambler Braing to see you."

"Send him in."

Rambler, with a big smile on his face, entered with his usual casual manner.

"What's up, my big White bro? Rambler asked. "You look puzzled."

"Which one of your deputies owes Senator Russell a favor?" asked Zeb.

Rambler handed over the plastic wrapped .12-gauge shotgun. A zipped baggie held the spent casing and shell. As quick as a wink he plopped down in the big chair across from Zeb's desk and flipped one leg over the arm, crossing the other over his knee. He pulled a hand rolled cigarette from his pocket, put fire to it with an ancient Zippo lighter and took a drag.

"All of them. Don't us poor Indians with big important, well-paying jobs with good benefits have the White Chiefs in Washington to thank for everything we have? The first thing I do every morning is light a bundle of sage, get on my knees and say a prayer to the great White leader in Washington that he keeps me on the payroll."

"You're about as funny as a crutch and half as decorative all flopped out in that chair," said Zeb.

"It's my laid back Indian look. Chicks dig it. What do you think? Say, is it okay to smoke in here?"

"Nope," said Zeb.

Rambler flipped the cigarette around inside his mouth, appearing to put it out on his tongue in the process. Rambler watched Zeb's stunned look.

"It's an old Injun magic trick," Rambler said sarcastically.

"Nice trick, but I'm serious," said Zeb.

"You think it's easy learning to put out a cigarette that way. I burned my tongue a hundred times before I got it right," said Rambler.

"Is that why you speak with forked tongue?" asked Zeb.

"Now you're catching on," said Rambler. "A little humor is good for the soul. Now what has one of my deputies been up to?"

"One of your guys called Senator Russell about the .12-gauge you found in San Carlos Lake. The senator called me right after you hung up."

"I guess it could have been any one of them. They all know about it. They were all within earshot when I read you the serial number. You sure one of my guys did it?"

"Who else?"

"You."

Rambler's nonchalance was disarming.

"Me?" asked Zeb.

"You heard me," replied Rambler.

"Why would you suspect me?"

"Is your phone bugged?" asked Rambler.

"Shit," said Zeb. "It might be. Give me your cell phone."

Zeb grabbed the phone book as Rambler slid his phone across the desk. He quickly looked up Levi Lowe's home number. He was hoping Sheri wouldn't answer. He wanted to have a private chat with Curtis without having to go through his mother. Luckily, Curtis answered.

"Curtis, this is Sheriff Hanks."

"What do you want? I thought we were cool," said Curtis.

"We are...sort of," replied Zeb.

"Make it quick, I'm number two out of thirty gamers in a marathon of *Grand Theft Auto Five*. I've got a chance to win this thing and take home some serious coinage."

"Isn't that the game where all of the bad guys are law enforcement?" asked Zeb.

"Sheriff, I didn't know you were a gamer? Cool."

"I'm not. Our monthly professional magazine advised us that young men who play that particular game are three times as likely to be antagonistic toward authority figures," said Zeb.

"Sounds like some government social psychologist has too much time on his or her hands," said Curtis.

"I've got one question for you."

"Shoot."

"Did you bug my phone?"

The hesitation on the other end of the line was a shade too long.

"Uh, no." More hesitation. "But I think Jude, the dude I was working with, might have. I mean it seems like something he would do."

"Did he mention anything about it?"

"Indirectly," replied Curtis. "He said we had to know everything that went on in your office. So I suppose he might have bugged the phone lines. Seems like the natural thing to do."

"How can I tell if it's bugged?"

"It's so simple to figure out I think I can even teach you," said Curtis. Zeb let the snide remark go in one ear and out the other.

"Are you on the phone in your office right now?" asked Curtis.

"No," replied Zeb.

"Good. Take a look at the mouthpiece, you know the end you talk into. If there is a short red wire that doesn't look as old as the other wires, is clean and not dusty, he bugged you. If it were me, I'd check all the office phones."

"Thanks. Get a hold of me if your partner contacts you."

"I will."

"And Curtis..."

"Yes?"

"You're beginning to sound like a criminal," said Zeb.

"Hmmm. Those days are behind me. My future is in video gaming," replied Curtis. "But, I am a man of my word. I will call you if he gets in touch with me."

Zeb opened the handset of his phone and removed a wire that looked exactly like what Curtis had just described. He let out a small curse. Rambler was all eyes and ears. Zeb buzzed Helen to come into his office. He showed her what he'd found and asked her to check all the phones. They were all bugged.

"Looks and sounds like trouble to me," said Rambler. "Who wants to listen in on you?"

"If I knew, I'd know," said Zeb. "But I don't."

"Any idea at all?"

"I can think of a few people," replied Zeb. "But I don't have any evidence."

"I'll check all the outgoing calls from my office and see if anyone called the senator's office," said Rambler. "But I doubt I'll find anything. You still owe me a cup of coffee and a pair of donuts." Rambler tapped his flat stomach and smiled.

Before leaving the office Zeb gave the evidence Rambler had brought in to Kate. He asked her to take it to Josh to verify that the cartridge and the empty shell casing were fired from the gun. Helen had already told her about the phones being bugged. With that Rambler and Zeb headed to the Town Talk Diner.

"Any decent suspects?" asked Rambler.

"I've got a whole line up of people who might have had murdering Sun Rey pretty high up on their bucket list," replied Zeb.

"There are more than a few from the Rez, too. One of them is close to Echo Skysong," said Rambler. "Her best friend, actually."

"Do you think Echo had her fingers in this?" asked Zeb.

"I didn't say that," replied Rambler. "I didn't even imply it."

"But she certainly has the skill set to pull it off," said Zeb.

"Sure she does," replied Rambler. "She most certainly does, but so do a lot of other people. I hope that doesn't affect the possibility of you dating her. Innocent until proven guilty applies to everyone."

"I had a long talk with Kate yesterday about dating again," said Zeb.

"She's a woman, she's part Apache and she was Doreen's closest confidant," said Rambler.

"And how do you know that?" asked Zeb.

"The tom-tom drums send many messages my way," replied Rambler. "But I knew that by watching them interact. They chatted it up like only girlfriends can and do."

"I somehow missed that," said Zeb.

"Shit happens," said Rambler. "Sometimes we are just too close to see things."

Zeb reached into his pocket and pulled out the note written by Doreen that Kate had given him. He repeatedly folded it over in his hands.

"What's that?" asked Rambler. "My guess is that you want to share it with me."

"I do and I don't know if I should. It's very personal. However, in light of our conversation, I think you should see it," said Zeb.

Rambler reached over, plucked it from Zeb's fingers and read it.

"Well?" asked Zeb.

"If you really, really loved Doreen as you say you did, then you should honor her wishes. When I give it a gut check, I think she is pointing you directly at Echo Skysong, but that's just a feeling I get."

Zeb sipped his chamomile tea. His eyes traced a beeline to the end of the counter where he and Doreen had had so many private, whispered conversations. It took no imagination for him to see the shadowed images of the past when he and Doreen shared their love over the luncheonette counter.

"I should pay attention to all things visible and invisible," said Zeb.

"Indah and Indeh...both the living and the dead," added Rambler.

"I really should pay attention."

Rambler handed Zeb the letter from Doreen. "Dude, she loved you, she really loved you. Finding love again will not diminish what the two of you had."

"I think I need just one more sign, and then I will know what to do," said Zeb.

"Pay attention, amigo. It just might be coming sooner than you think," replied Rambler.

Zeb looked up from his tea. Rambler's eyes were twinkling just as Doreen's once did.

15

AN OFFER OF MAGIC

Zeb viewed the crisp morning sunshine on a cloudless fall day as a good omen. The desert always spoke the truth. However, the day began with a rather odd phone call from Song Bird.

"Sheriff," said Song Bird.

"Why so formal? Am I in some kind of trouble?" asked Zeb.

"Quite the opposite," replied Song Bird. "I have an offer, an invitation of sorts. You might think of it as unusual."

It was unlike Song Bird to be so discreet that the medicine man's words took Zeb by surprise. He played along, but got right to the point.

"The suspense is killing me. What's up?"

"I would like to help you in a new way."

"Song Bird, you've been helping me all of my life. What new way can there possibly be for you to do something for me?"

"I would like you to participate in a ceremony."

"A Native American ritual?" asked Zeb.

Song Bird's vague reply was as strikingly strange as his original request.

"Yes and no."

"Can you tell me what the ceremony is?" asked Zeb.

"Yes and no."

Again, the medicine man was oddly evasive.

"Can you tell me why you want me to perform the ritual?" asked Zeb.

"You need it."

"Fair enough. What is the ceremony called?"

"Interference clearing."

Song Bird's response was nothing if not elusive

"Song Bird, you've known me and I've known you most of my life. I've never heard you even mention this. What was it again, interference clearing?"

Song Bird chuckled a knowing kind of laughter. He understood Zeb well enough to know that his response would be skeptical at best, confused at the least.

"Interference clearing," reiterated Song Bird. "The way you say it makes it sound like something from a football game or a Ouija board."

"Isn't interference clearing some sort of mumbo-jumbo those hippies out in Eden do?" asked Zeb. "I think I read about it in a pamphlet that was making its way around town a few years back."

Eden was a small town between Safford and the San Carlos Reservation. It had a strange and interesting history of drawing the unusual and the extraordinary to its confines. Not only had the Rolling Stones rented the old Maxwell mansion a dozen times as a place to decompress after tours, but just outside the township limits was a spiritual healing center. Zeb knew of the place mostly by the persistent rumor that drug parties were often part of the scene. Oddly, the sheriff's department had never had a complaint, not even as much as a single call to the Maxwell mansion or any of the hippie-dippy gatherings.

"A great teacher of this discipline, interference clearing, taught there many years ago when the Rolling Stones used to go to the Maxwell mansion to relax between tours," said Song Bird.

"You're a Stones fan?" asked Zeb. Zeb's head reeled at the thought of Song Bird being a fan of the group that was frequently referred to as 'The World's Greatest Rock and Roll Band.'

"I'm a Beatles fan too," replied Song Bird. "Big, huge fan of Ringo, ever since they appeared on the *Ed Sullivan Show* way back in February of 1964. It changed my life. It made me want to be a great medicine man and incorporate new drumming techniques into healing."

"I have to ask, Beatles or Stones? Your favorite?" asked a stunned Zeb.

"Stones, but really only because I know everyone in the band and most of the crew. I only know Paul and Ringo from the Beatles," said Song Bird.

"What are you talking about?" asked Zeb. "You're pulling my leg, right?"

"Sir Paul McCartney, or Paulie as he asked me to call him, has a place in Tanique Verde, over by Casa Grande. Way back when, Jags and I spent an afternoon over there. Jags hates it when strangers or friend call him Mick, says it makes him sound Irish, which he isn't. He's got a thing about that."

"You're yanking my chain," said Zeb. "You know the two living members of the Beatles and all of the Rolling Stones? Personally?"

"No big deal," said Song Bird. "Just one of those things that happened."

"How?" asked an incredulous Zeb. "That kind of thing doesn't just happen."

"I once took the band, the Rolling Stones, on a spiritual transformation journey. It was quite by accident. It's a long story for another time. Because of that I ended up with back stage passes to their Voodoo Lounge tour and hit a dozen or so of the shows on the tour. That must be twenty years ago now. One night, in Las Vegas if I remember correctly, they did my favorite rock and roll song of all time, *Not Fade Away*, for the encore. Many times they opened with it."

"How on earth did you get to know them in the first place?"

"They were brought to me by Eskadi Black Robes. He was just a kid, but he was a huge fan of the band. Somehow he finagled his way into their scene. He seemed to fit right in. They donated money to update the equipment at the reservation radio station. Even as a youngster Eskadi was a mover and shaker."

"Rest his soul," said Zeb.

"He is at peace," replied Song Bird. "He has worldly troubles no more."

"Wish I could say the same," said Zeb.

"Every man will have worldly woes. That goes with being human. But, Zeb, you may be carrying a heavier load than you need to. Maybe I can help you. I want to do an interference clearing for you. However, there's a catch," said Song Bird.

Zeb silently waited to hear what the catch was. Song Bird continued.

"I was taught a unique technique by the master on how to do a clearing on two people simultaneously, but the two people have to be of the opposite sex. I know that you need it, and I know that Echo Skysong needs it also. I was wondering if you'd be open to doing the ceremony with her?"

"Whoa, let's back up one second. I never had you pegged for a Stones or even a rock and roll fan for that matter. I certainly am surprised that *Not Fade Away* is your favorite song," said Zeb.

"Long live Buddy Holly," said Song Bird with a grin that flowed right through the telephone line.

"Right," said Zeb. "Long live Buddy Holly. What I guess I need to know is who are you, Song Bird? I really thought I knew you."

"I have spent one lifetime living many different lives. I have not only been a medicine man, but I like to think of myself as an eclectic man of the world."

Zeb's head was spinning. He had known Song Bird since he was a boy. Never had he heard as much as a whisper of this side of the man. Zeb realized the irony in thinking he could know everything about someone, yet in reality know far less than he thought. Gaping holes in his perception could appear right out of nowhere.

"You're kidding me, right?" said Zeb. "Just like back when I was a teenager and you and Jake used to play with my mind to teach me things. You two played some damn good practical jokes on me. This feels like one of them."

Song Bird was stone silent. Zeb knew the medicine man was serious.

"I re-iterate my offer. Would you like to go through an interference clearing ceremony with Echo Skysong?"

Zeb thought back to yesterday. He and Rambler had talked at length about Echo over coffee and donuts. Actually Rambler had done most of the talking and even mentioned an imminent sign could be on the near horizon, if Zeb paid attention. If this was a setup, Rambler and Song Bird were in on it together. In all the years he'd known them, neither man had ever done him a bad turn. Yet Zeb's immediate reaction was one of reticence.

"What does Echo say?" asked Zeb.

"I haven't asked her yet, but I know that she knows she needs what the ceremony has to offer," said Song Bird.

"Echo Skysong knows what interference clearing is all about?" asked Zeb.

"I don't have any idea if she knows anything about it," replied Song Bird.

"Then how can she possibly know she needs it?" asked Zeb.

"She is a smart Native American woman. She intuitively understands that after serving three tours in Afghanistan and doing what she had to do she needs to break down some barriers that are holding her back from being herself," said Song Bird. "War steals from the warrior and builds walls around her or him."

Though Zeb imagined that to be the case, he was no authority on the subject and found himself agreeing with something he knew little about.

"Plus," said Song Bird. "The power of Lozen has been gifted to her from the Great Spirit."

"What does that mean? The power of Lozen?" asked Zeb.

"If you partake in this opportunity, you will learn. If you choose not to become involved, there is no need for you to be bothered with such matters of the Great Spirit."

"Why me?" asked Zeb.

"I don't think you really need to ask that, do you, Zeb?"

There were so many things that created an artificial wall around Zeb. But of all the things that needed clearing in his mind, at least as far as he could see, the most prevalent was the loss of Doreen. Ever since her death and his subsequent mission to end the life of Carmelita Montouyez, Zeb had felt as though a part of himself had gone AWOL.

"I have chosen to ask you because you are much like Victorio, the great Apache Chief," said Song Bird.

Zeb was instantly humbled. Although he knew very little of Victorio, he did know Song Bird spoke with great reverence every time he mentioned the name of the legendary Apache Chief.

"You are spiritually akin to Chief Victorio. Like Echo Skysong, who is a twin through time of Lozen, it is my belief you are a twin through time with Victorio, brother of Lozen. In essence, you and Echo have a great many similar traits. You share many things in this lifetime."

Zeb had only heard the name of Lozen but knew little else and was most certainly intrigued. This whole spiritual thing, the interference clearing, somehow for some unspoken reason felt exactly right. Yet it was so far out of Zeb's comfort zone he really didn't know what to say or how to respond. And what on earth could Song Bird mean when he said that Echo was a twin through time with Lozen? Or for that matter that he and Echo shared a great number of similar traits? What kind of traits? What did it mean? How did it all link together and make sense to Song Bird?

"Think about it," said Song Bird. "Let me know when you know if interference clearing is right for your heart and your spirit."

"Can you tell me something more about it?" asked Zeb. "Can you tell me what I might be getting myself into? I feel as though I am standing on the ledge of an eternal abyss about to take a leap into the unknown."

Song Bird chuckled, but his message was succinct. Zeb had the distinct feeling Song Bird's presence was passing right through him and pushing him through time and space.

"It's more about what you are getting yourself out of than it is about something you are diving into," said Song Bird. "It is time for you to let go of the weight of all things that keep you bound to your sinful nature. It is time to quit holding so tightly onto earthly failings and weaknesses."

Zeb rolled his tongue around the inside of his teeth. It was an old habit that popped up when his brain began to delve into the unknown and possibly unknowable. He'd been doing the tongue rolling since childhood. Somehow it cleared his mind. His first reaction was to say no for a number of what he considered to be valid reasons. To begin with he was smack dab in the middle of Sun Rey's murder investigation. Not only was the search for Sun Rey's killer complicated, it had personal and political implications. On top of that he was hip deep in potential murder suspects. Plus, Agent Rodriguez was so far up Zeb's ass, at times he couldn't think straight. Then there was the note left behind when he and Helen were attacked indicating someone was seeking revenge on him.

"Think about it. I suspect you already know you are ready and that you should move forward with this," said Song Bird. "It is totally your decision. No one can make it for you. I don't want you to feel as though I am trying to influence you one way or the other."

Zeb's thoughts turned to Echo. Even though he knew little about her and less of the ceremony, he felt certain this sort of ritual would force him to bare his soul. He didn't know if he was ready for that. He certainly didn't feel ready to reveal his innermost thoughts and feelings around a woman he barely knew, a woman who could possibly be directly related to Sun Rey's killing. As to what Song Bird called Zeb's 'sinful nature', God only knew the depths of what that might provoke. Zeb had lived with fear and hate as part of his nature for as long as he could remember. Those terrible emotions had only dissipated for periods of time when Doreen stood with him as his partner and slept by his side as his wife. Only Lord, God above knew how much he missed her.

"Call me," said Song Bird. "I'll be waiting to hear from you."

Zeb hung up the phone and stared off into space. His sensed his life was once again about to change forever.

16

BREAKFAST WITH ECHO

Zeb showered, dressed and headed to the Town Talk diner for a bite of breakfast. He took his usual seat. While glancing through the upcoming week's football games on the sports page of the *Arizona Daily Star*, someone slid in on the bench across from him. The movement was so smooth and quiet he barely noticed. If the springs beneath the ancient leather hadn't groaned ever so slightly, he might not have noticed at all. Zeb looked up to see Echo Skysong's radiantly beautiful face.

"Sheriff Hanks."

"Sergeant Skysong."

"Call me Zeb."

"Call me Echo,"

"Did you talk with Rambler about me?" asked Echo.

Zeb saw Echo was a woman who got right to her point.

"Yes...some...a little I guess. Mostly he did the talking when it came to you. If we crossed a line, I'm sorry, but I don't think we did."

"You didn't," replied Echo. "It's all good. Who do the Cards play Sunday?"

"Packers," replied Zeb.

"Want to bet on the game?"

"Not a gambling man," replied Zeb.

Their conversation was interrupted by a waitress who asked for their order.

Zeb and Skysong both ordered breakfast. Echo ate heartily and spoke very little until she had finished. Zeb ate little and sipped tea as he watched her eat. Her mannerisms were firm yet graceful. She barely moved her lips when she chewed. He could find no words to describe the color of her soft brown skin. Echo's eyes were a strange combination of brown backlit by a blue-green hue. They were the kind of eyes he could get lost in and not even know it. Very quickly Zeb found himself captivated by her every action, no matter how slight or subtle.

"Didn't your mother teach you it's very bad manners to watch another person eat?" asked Echo without looking at Zeb.

"Gosh, I am so sorry. I was staring, wasn't I? I didn't mean to. I don't know why I was. Please forgive me. I meant no harm. It's just, well, you are, I mean seem so different from anyone I know."

"I'm just flesh and blood, like everyone else," said Echo.

"I doubt that," Zeb managed to reply before once again finding himself rambling on as he sought the right words to say to this compelling woman, someone he barely knew.

"Forget it," replied Skysong. "No harm, no foul. I hadn't been told you were such a sensitive guy. My informants tell me you can be one tough hombre, a real hard-nosed, old-fashioned, western sheriff."

"I'm not. I mean, I am. I mean...."

Zeb shook his head. He could practically hear rocks rattling around inside what felt like an empty skull. It was best not to dig the hole any deeper. He shut his mouth.

Echo shoved the empty plate away and slid her coffee cup to the edge of the table. She wrapped her fingers around the cup as if to warm them. Zeb couldn't help but notice her strikingly painted fingernails as they gripped the ceramic mug. They were all painted the same color blue, but each carried a small design at the center. It was something he had never seen before.

"You like my nails?" she asked straightforwardly.

Nothing missed this woman's eye. She'd caught him staring again. Embarrassed, Zeb fumbled for a reply.

"Yes. Yes, ma'am, I mean Echo. I noticed they are different from what I've seen before. They are very eye-catching...to me, that is. I mean I like them very much. They're different. Very nice, but not like anything I've ever seen."

Zeb fumbled along, twisting his words like a teenage boy on a first date. Skysong's laughter put him at ease.

"I just had them painted for the first time the other day. Sonja Trees painted them. She's my cousin, best friend and a beautician to boot. She knows you. She told me a lot about you."

"Is Sonja Trees Beulah Tree's granddaughter?"

"She is. She thinks you're cute. If I had to venture a guess, I'd say she has a crush on you," said Echo.

"Beulah and I go way back. I've see Sonja hanging around her grandmother's since she was a baby."

"She's not a baby anymore. She's twenty-six and has a little daughter of her own. Her husband was killed in a trucking accident last year."

"Sorry."

"She'll be all right. She's a survivor, and it doesn't hurt to have Beulah's blood running through your veins."

Echo clicked her fingernails on the coffee cup. Zeb's eyes studied them. Echo took notice and commented.

"I always kept my nails clear, dirty actually, when I was active in the military. I used to look at them in the Afghan moonlight and wonder if they'd ever look beautiful again. Weird, isn't it, worrying about fingernails when you are in a combat zone?"

"No. We all have private thoughts that become habits. I suppose a woman would want to look nice even in a time of war."

"Maybe. I hadn't thought about it quite like that, but I suppose we all have some vanity, don't we, Sheriff Hanks?"

Whatever veiled reference she was hinting at buzzed right past him.

"Tell me about your nails," said Zeb. As he said the words he caught himself. He was having girl talk with a special forces soldier who had just spent three years inside a dangerous war zone. Had he lost his mind?

"They are painted blue for the sky. Each fingernail carries a symbol of one of the many blessings I have had in my life." She held out her little finger. "This is the symbol of being born an Apache woman. The first of my earthly blessings."

Zeb reached forward and awkwardly put her hand into his, examining the image. Her hand was both soft like a woman's and strong like a soldier's. It was also almost as large as a man's hand. Zeb gently ran his first finger over to Echo's next fingernail. He saw a moon with the shadow of a second moon. He peered closer.

"Two moons?"

"September twenty-ninth is the date of my birth. The season of two moons. You would call it the season of the harvest moon. The moons remind me of the time and season my body came to be on this earth. A very specific blessing."

"It's unique," said Zeb. His response evoked a soft smile. He wanted to say more but couldn't find the words.

Skysong broke the uneasy silence that Zeb alone was feeling.

"What has Song Bird told you about this process of interference clearing that he wants to put us through?" she asked.

"Not much. Nothing really. What do you know about it?" asked Zeb.

"I know Song Bird, for some reason, likes to call the ceremony interference clearing. In reality interference clearing is nothing more than a silly new age name for an ancient Apache tradition. We call it the Teardrop Ceremony. It is an Apache ritual that uses black obsidian. You probably know the black obsidian as an Apache tear. He calls the process interference clearing because you're a White man. To bring a White Eye into the Teardrop ceremony would, technically speaking, be taboo."

"What am I getting myself into?" queried Zeb. "If you don't mind my asking?"

"Has Song Bird ever given you an Apache tear?"

"Yes, numerous times. He gave me one for..." Zeb stopped cold in his tracks. He barely knew Echo, yet he was about to discuss Doreen and his feelings about her.

"...someone you've lost?" said Echo, completing his sentence.

"How did you know that?"

"I know Song Bird and I know something about you," she said. "It doesn't exactly take a soothsayer or a highly experienced intelligence officer to put it all together. I am also Apache. I have been trained in many of the ancient ways. Since I was a child I have carried the spirit of an ancient warrior."

Echo held out another finger. She placed it in the palm of Zeb's hand. On it was painted a cloud and a hand holding a spear.

"What does that represent?" asked Zeb.

"Lozen, the warrior woman. I have been blessed to have received fragments of her spirit."

"Can you tell me what that means? I don't really have a basis for understanding it."

"It's complicated, but I can give you a few examples a White Eye might understand."

Zeb nodded. He was intrigued.

"Throughout all times the People have needed special protection. Lozen was one spirit that provided such security. I have been blessed with the power to know how to control horses. In times past when horses were like cars are now, it was a very important power. I was able to use my horse power during the war in Afghanistan."

"May I ask how?"

"Certainly. Afghani's ride horses in mountainous areas. Often they have hundreds of horses in one place. You know how horses get jittery at night when someone or something they don't expect enters their turf?"

"Of course. They snort, prance around and generally cause a ruckus," replied Zeb.

"Yes. From Lozen I received the gift of being able to walk into a group of hundreds of horses and move, steal in this case, as many as I wanted to without disrupting the drove. It came in very handy. If you have two hundred Afghan troops and less than one hundred horses, the battlefield situation changes immediately."

"So you're a horse thief?' joked Zeb.

"I prefer to call it by its more modern terminology, horse whisperer. But, yes, essentially I acted as a horse thief in the time of war. I saved lives by doing so. You may call it what you want. Would you like another example?"

"Heavens yes."

"Lozen's greatest power was the power to know where the enemy was. No adversary could hide from her."

"How did that work?"

"Like this."

Echo held her right hand, palm open, straight up in the air and above her head.

"I don't get it?"

"The power of Lozen receives a signal as to the location, distance and often the number of the enemy. The palm turns toward the opposing troops, then depending on which finger twitches, it tells me the number of troops and often, but not always because of the terrain, a cramping in the hand tells me distance."

Zeb ran his fingers through his dark hair which he had recently taken to wearing much longer than usual. Who was this woman sitting across from him at the Town Talk? Why had Rambler and Song Bird gone to such lengths to bring them together? What was this power of Lozen all about and did it affect him in some way? What the heck was going on?

A comfortable silence surrounded them. For a time, they were in world unto themselves. Zeb found only comfort, and it appeared Echo felt the same way. Eventually, although there was great comfort in their silence, Zeb felt obliged to talk.

"Can you at least tell me the purpose of the Teardrop ceremony?" asked Zeb.

Echo's face turned from natural beauty to lovely seriousness without really changing. It was as though she were instantly and unashamedly showing Zeb her heart, her spirit and her mind. His flesh rippled. For a flash of a second he was taken aback as something he couldn't define overcame him.

"Yes," she replied. "Are you ready to know it?"

"I don't know. I must be. I mean if Song Bird set this whole thing up he must know I am ready. Yes, I am ready."

"The obsidian stone, the Apache tear, is said to be calming in nature."

"Yes, I am aware of that. Song Bird taught me that many years ago."

"However, the history of the Apache tear is anything but calming. Once, not that long ago, there was a time when the Apaches had their land stolen by both the Mexicans and the White Eyes. We, the Apache People, could only raid and steal to live. Our land, our water, our crops had all been destroyed or taken over by those who wished to eliminate us from the face of the earth. Once, after a great cattle raid, the blue coats of the United States army trapped the People near Picacho Peak."

Zeb had learned from Song Bird long ago that the Apaches referred to themselves as 'the People'. Picacho Peak was not far from where he and Echo were sitting. He remembered Song Bird describing the distance between Mount Graham and Picacho Peak as a good day's ride on horseback.

"We had seventy-five great warriors who moved our cattle to save them from the White Eyes who wished to see us starve to death. But the American soldiers waited in ambush. Their first volley killed two out of every three of our best warriors. Fifty great warriors were massacred instantly. Their lives were taken in the blink of an eye. Those twenty-five warriors that remained were driven up the side trails toward Picacho Peak. There they had a choice. They could live as slaves under the White Eyes or die as brave warriors. They collectively decided that surrender was not an option. Instead of giving themselves over to the White soldiers, the final twenty-five brave warriors leapt to their deaths from the highest point of the peak. For decades after that the People found the bleached bones of our brave warriors in the cracks and crevices of the mountainside in many areas near where they leapt to their collective death. The Apache women and the lovers of the warriors gathered and wept one full moon for the dead. The women suffered the great pain of loss as nobly as they could. It was a terrible time in the history of the People. Not only had the warriors died, but the great fighting spirit of the People had also been squashed like a bug. The sadness of the women was so great that the Great Father imbedded the tears of the Apache women into the black obsidian. It was done so no one would ever forget the fighting spirit of the men who sacrificed their lives. If you hold a black obsidian stone to the light, you will see an embedded Apache tear. It was a gift from the Great Spirit to our people, the gift of remembering the spirit and sacrifice of brave warriors whom we might never know the names of and who could easily be forgotten with the passing of time."

"I never knew," said Zeb.

"It is also said that those who have been given an Apache tear in remembrance will never need to cry again because those Apache women had already shed their tears for them. It is a saga of tragedy, mystery, love, spirit and magic."

"Yet, I still cry," admitted Zeb. Hearing his own admission of tears to Echo surprised Zeb as he spoke the simple explanation of the pain in his heart. The words came from nowhere and everywhere but mostly from his soul.

"My guess is that is why Song Bird knows you need the ceremony. The Apache tears will balance your emotional nature and protect you from ever being taken advantage of again. You may be able to let go of the burden of hatred that your heart must carry from your losses. The stone can also produce clear vision and increase psychic powers."

"I have no psychic powers to increase," said Zeb.

"I do," said Echo. "I think Song Bird sees us as a pair. You need clear vision and I need to increase my psychic power. I need to use the blessing of Lozen that I have been given more effectively."

"Hmm." Zeb needed a few seconds to think about what Echo was saying to him. It was difficult to understand the complexity of it all in just an instant.

"The purpose of the stone is to bring light that is hidden from the conscious mind. The Apache tear dissolves negative patterns and purifies them. It can help us rid ourselves of recurrent negative, egocentric patterns," said Echo. "It removes our sinful ways. It destroys our hatred and opens our minds."

"I could use that," said Zeb.

"Couldn't we all?" added Echo.

Each quietly took a moment to reflect. This was new turf. This was a new place and a new concept that could help them both.

"I'm willing to give it a shot," said Zeb.

Echo reached across the table with both hands. Zeb slid his hands into hers. Once again Zeb felt her softness and her strength. Most of all the faint odor of Arizona sage permeated the area. An invisible but significant bond was spontaneously formed. Zeb had no idea what it meant. Echo had her suspicions.

"I will set up a meeting with Song Bird," said Echo, as she stood to leave.

"Just let me know when and where, and I will be there," replied Zeb.

Echo rose from her seat. As she passed Zeb on her way to the door, she momentarily placed a hand on his shoulder. He glanced at the images on her fingernails. When he looked up into her eyes, he could see the same images reflected as living things.

17

PRIVATE INVESTIGATOR

Zeb recognized the rap on his office door as Kate's.

"Come in."

She began talking as she approached Zeb's desk.

"I heard you had coffee with Echo Skysong this morning."

"Not much chance at privacy when you're the sheriff," said Zeb.

"None, really."

"Did you get smoke signals?" asked Zeb.

Not being party to the inside joke between Rambler and the sheriff, Kate could only respond with a puzzled look.

"Word gets around pretty quickly," said Kate.

"Well, I guess it must."

"It does. I talked with three of Rambler's deputies. None of them think anybody on the Rez police force is in cahoots with Senator Russell," said Kate.

"I kind of figured that would be a dead end, but keep it on your radar. You never know," said Zeb.

"Will do. Jake and I have seventeen young women to talk to. They have all publicly stated that Sun Rey either physically or sexually forced himself on them. The word is that sometimes he plied them with alcohol, other times they claim he sneaked them roofies. On a few occasions he simply forced himself on them."

"Did they mention this to friends or family?"

"Yes."

"Anyone else? Anyone with any authority like a doctor, social work, psychologist?"

"I'm afraid not. No one has approached the authorities on the Rez, and certainly no one has approached our office, at least as far as I know."

"Do we have a Cosby situation on our hands?" asked Zeb.

"No one has shot off Cosby's genitalia yet, at least not that we've heard," replied Kate.

"I'm fairly certain that would have made the daytime talk show circuit," replied Zeb.

"The talk shows would have a heyday with that one," said Kate. "When you think about it, it's kind of odd someone hasn't sought physical revenge against him considering what he allegedly did."

"As law enforcement officials, we have to remind ourselves that allegedly isn't proof, and it's not funny to any man to even think of having his private parts blown off," said Zeb. "It makes us all cringe."

"How do you think rape or even the thought of it makes women feel?"

"Point well taken," said Zeb. "Do any of the women seem like they might be particularly handy with a gun?"

"I'm sure most of them can shoot. They're all local women. Pretty good chance they've all hunted and can handle a gun to some degree or another. Are any of them expert markswomen? I can't say, but four of them have military backgrounds," said Kate.

"Start with them," said Zeb.

"That group includes Echo Skysong's cousin and best friend," said Kate.

"Sonja Trees?"

"Yes. How would you know that?"

"I hear things."

"Okay."

"Sonja has to be checked out, and since Echo has the training she does, she has to be ruled out too," said Zeb.

"You want to look into her alibi?" asked Kate.

"No. I might have a conflict of interest," replied Zeb.

"Having a cup of coffee at breakfast with her is hardly what I'd call a conflict of interest."

"It's a long story. I'll tell you about it later," replied Zeb.

"I can't wait," said Kate.

"I'll leave it to you to check on her alibi," said Zeb. "Leave no stone unturned."

"Got it," replied Kate.

"About those other women?"

"Right. I can't say I would lay a whole lot of blame on whoever shot him, especially if he raped them," said Kate. "I think a jury with women on it might see it the same way."

"The law is the law. Keep that in mind. We need to find out who killed him, and you need to keep your personal feelings out of it," ordered Zeb.

"My emotions are out of it," said Kate. "That's why I don't blame anyone who might have shot him. He ruined many lives. What happened to Sun Rey is called karma.

"Be that as it may, do your job. Do it completely. Do it without prejudice. We need to find the killer. We simply have to do our job."

"Do you have any other leads?" asked Kate.

"Sun Rey had more than a few guys kicked out of his strip joint, excuse me, gentlemen's club, for inappropriately touching the dancers. The bouncers gave me a few names of people who might have had it in for him, but I haven't come across anyone who threatened him directly, at least not yet."

"He's been a sicko his whole life. We may have to broadly expand our investigation," said Kate. "God only knows how far back this could go."

Jake knocked on the door to Zeb's office.

"I've got something interesting on Sun Rey," he said, sticking his head through the door opening.

"Come in. We were just discussing him," said Zeb.

"I have a contact at the Sierra Vista FBI Resident Agency. He said they were looking at Sun Rey's past and found out they weren't alone. The Washington DC police were doing a background check on him, and a private investigator out of Virginia has been digging into his past. I talked with the PI, Mike Patterson. Patterson was pissed because he never got paid, so he gave up the name of the man who hired him. The guy that hired him to dig into Sun Rey was Luke Pearce," said Jake.

"Luke Pearce?" asked Zeb. "The name doesn't ring a bell."

"It probably shouldn't, but there is something somewhat odd about it. Luke Pearce is an assistant chief of staff to Senator Russell."

"Senator Russell was investigating his own son? What for?" asked Kate.

"He wouldn't give up that information, but he said if we paid Luke Pearce's bill, he'd hand over what he had," said Jake.

"I've got over a million dollars left from Doreen's estate. I think this would be a good way to spend part of it," said Zeb. "How much is he owed?"

"Roughly eight thousand dollars," said Jake. "Plus a few expenses that he hasn't tallied up yet."

"Call him and tell him I'll pay the eight grand, but first he has to give us something so we know he is legit," said Zeb.

"Are you sure you want to do that?" asked Kate. "He may know nothing more than we already do."

"But he may know a lot more," said Zeb. "I think it's worth the shot. Jake get on it."

Fifteen minutes later Jake walked back into Zeb's office. Kate and Zeb were still hashing out a plan for finding Sun Rey's murderer.

"You have something already?" asked Zeb.

"I do," replied Jake. "But I don't know exactly what it tells us about Sun Rey's murder."

"What is it?" asked Kate.

Jake took the chair across from Zeb's desk. He carried a file and a small notebook, which he immediately flipped open.

"Sun Rey was nothing but trouble," said Jake.

"No secret in that," said Kate.

"We know he had trouble staying within the lines of the law," said Jake.

"No doubt about that," said Zeb.

"His old man covered for him since he was twelve. That's when he committed his first felony."

"At the age of twelve?" asked Zeb.

"An armed robbery."

"That's hard to believe."

"The PI faxed this over to me just now. It's Sun Rey's juvenile record."

"It must be a myth that juvie records are expunged," said Kate.

"None of us are lawyers," said Zeb.

"I think he wants the eight grand because he didn't hesitate one second in sharing this much. I also had a rather informative little chat with him," said Jake.

Jake handed Sun Rey's juvenile record to Zeb. Kate stood behind him as he glanced through it. It was fifteen pages long. Jake held onto a piece of paper on which he had jotted some notes.

"A real model citizen," said Kate.

"With a record like this he likely has been making enemies every step of the way in his short life," said Jake.

"It doesn't help that he was an asshole on top of being a habitual criminal, a sociopath, an armed robber, a psychopath, a chronic liar, a rapist..."

"Okay, Kate, okay. We get that he sticks in your craw," said Zeb. "But we're trying to figure out who killed him. That's our goal here. We can criticize him all day long, but it won't change the fact that he's dead or that someone murdered him. Our main job is to find out who did the deed. It would be good to know exactly why as well."

"I think we should find out whoever did it and give them a medal," said Kate.

"Whoa, whoa. Hold on, Kate. If you can't keep this from being personal, I am going to have to take you off the case," said Zeb.

"Okay. Okay. I can do that," said Kate. "I guess I was letting him get a little too deeply under my skin."

Her act of contrition seemed less than genuine to both Zeb and Jake. Both had been around too long and seen too much to not catch a half-truth.

"Why does Sun Rey get to you so personally?" asked Zeb.

"I don't know. Yes, I do know. He reminds me of a guy I dated who ended up raping the woman he dated after I dumped him. Every run-in I had with Sun Rey triggered all kinds of hatred inside me. I can control it. It's just that I know what he was capable of. We all know what he did to women around here. Now when we see his juvenile record, it seems as though he's been hurting women for a long, long time. I knew from the first time I saw him he should be behind bars. I just wish I had done something earlier to put him away," said Kate.

"We did what we could," said Jake.

Kate's eyes honed in on Zeb. He understood what the dark glare was about. It was his deal with Senator Russell that got the ball rolling to keep Sun Rey out of jail and into treatment. Even though she knew why things had to be the way they were, the politics of it all irritated her. Senator Russell had control over Zeb because of Mexico and the revenge Zeb got on Doreen's killer. Kate played a major role in all of it because it was her former supervisor and mentor from the FBI, Elaine Coburn, who set the whole thing up as the political go-between. The hatred she had for Sun Rey, however, was totally on her own shoulders. Kate wasn't violent by nature, but something about the way Sun Rey was murdered felt good to her. Maybe too good.

"Kate, do I have to consider you as a possible suspect?" asked Zeb.

The silence that followed his question was uncomfortable for all of them. Zeb and Jake knew all too well that operating outside the law was sometimes the only way to finalize things once and for all. Both had done it. They'd done it together as well. It was a line neither carried any regret about crossing. Somehow it didn't seem right to them that Kate should ever consider crossing that same line. It wasn't because she was a woman. It was because the emotional impact continually lurked in the back of their minds, and they did not wish that upon her. Both men hoped she hadn't crossed the line. Both men would know if she lied when she answered them.

"No, I didn't kill that bastard," said Kate. "But given the right circumstances I wouldn't have hesitated one second to do so."

Her answer didn't completely satisfy either Zeb or Jake. They both wanted to believe she wouldn't have put him down in cold blood. Kate felt their doubt.

"Wait a second. When I say I didn't kill that son of a bitch, I didn't kill him," said Kate. "If you don't believe me, I will turn in my badge and gun right here and now."

Zeb motioned for Jake to close the door. This conversation was definitely not meant for Helen's ears.

"Look, Kate, no one is accusing you of anything. But theoretically speaking, if you knew who did kill him, it might save us a lot of leg work and time. Do you know anything that might help us? Whatever you say stays in this room, right Jake?"

Jake nodded. This was hardly new territory to these lawmen.

Kate sighed heavily before speaking. "Like I told you, I wouldn't have hesitated for one second to kill him had the situation called for it. But I never got a genuine, legal opportunity for lethal force. If I had, I would have put him down like the rabid dog he was. Somebody beat me to the punch. That's the whole truth. I hope you believe me," said Kate.

The men looked at each other. They had walked down the exact same path Kate was standing on. They understood where she was coming from. She could be trusted. However, that didn't mean she wasn't somehow involved and was keeping that a secret. Both men kept her on their short list of potential co-conspirators.

"We were talking about the information the PI from Virginia gave you, Jake," said Kate.

"Right. What reason did Senator Russell give for Sun Rey's early release from the treatment center?" asked Jake.

"Senator Russell told me that Sun Rey thought the treatment center was too confining. He hated taking the medications they prescribed him. Senator Russell told me personally that Sun Rey left of his own accord," said Zeb.

"Well, he lied to you," said Jake. "It turns out Sun Rey's stint at the treatment center didn't end the way Senator Russell told us it did," said Jake, glancing at his notes.

"Go on," said Zeb.

"He was escorted out of the treatment facility in handcuffs by the security staff. He was picked up by the Capitol police. He was taken to a semi-secretive police booking station in DC. It's one of those off the books places that is set up exclusively for politicos, their families and friends," said Jake.

"It's a totally different class of people and set of rules for the insiders, isn't it?" said Kate.

"There's more, a lot more," said Jake.

"Let's hear it," said Zeb.

"As he was being held in a waiting cell, the charges were suddenly dropped."

"Back up a step," said Zeb. "What was he being charged with?"

"You aren't going to be one bit surprised by this one," said Jake.

"Rape, by any chance?" asked Kate.

"Rape, sodomy, assault, battery and a few other lesser charges were what the arresting officer said Sun Rey was supposed to be charged with. I believe the PI's information because the arresting officer just happened to be a close, personal friend of his. The arresting officer works exclusively for anyone connected with the Senate or related to anyone who works in the building. He said this kind of shit goes down all the time," said Jake.

"Does Senator Russell wield that kind of ugly power?" asked Kate.

"According to the PI, the senator's hand, if involved, is totally unseen in any of the paperwork," said Jake. "I asked that very question in every way I could think of."

"Do you believe the PI?" asked Zeb.

"I believe that's what he believes, but he might believe it because he can't find any evidence to prove otherwise," said Jake.

"After talking with him, what's your take on it, Jake?" asked Zeb.

"I don't know what the hell to believe because the story gets even weirder."

"How so?" asked Zeb.

"Senator Russell has a re-election coming up next year," said Jake.

"Right, we all know that," said Kate. "He's a shoo-in, isn't he? I doubt any scandal with his illegitimate son would have much of an effect on that."

"No, he's not a shoo-in, and his opponent is known to be unscrupulous. It seems that his opponent planted a woman in the treatment center to spy on Sun Rey. The PI called her nothing more than a hired harlot. Apparently, she was paid to see what Sun Rey was up to, what the truth about him was, or, if you believe some of the people in the treatment center, to provoke him into a felony that would then be exposed in Washington newspapers and on the national news," said Jake.

"Thereby throwing a wrench into the works of Senator Russell's re-election campaign," said Kate.

"She was obviously looking to dig up some dirt the tabloids could kick around for a week or two around election time," said Zeb. "Politics at that level is a dirty, ugly business."

"It's worse than that," said Jake.

"Please don't tell me she was the one Sun Rey raped and sodomized," said Kate.

"She was," said Jake. "She also dropped the charges against Sun Rey. Or, more correctly stated, her attorney advised her to drop them. This all happened just as the charges were being presented in this special court set up for our elected officials and their families."

"Why would she do that?" asked Kate. "She was raped, sodomized and beaten. Since it wasn't spousal or boyfriend related, and we all know how many women don't press charges in those situations, what on earth did she do it for?"

"She did it for one hundred fifty grand," said Jake.

"Whew," said Zeb. "Money can make a lot of bad things go away."

"For God's sake," said Kate. "What on earth is wrong with that woman?"

"One hundred fifty thousand dollars was put into her bank account and taken out fifteen minutes later. The PI has the security tapes from the bank showing her taking the money, in cash."

"Where did the money come from?" asked Zeb.

"Some untraceable offshore account linked to multiple dummy corporations," said Jake.

"Was the corporation set up by Senator Russell?" asked Zeb.

"There is absolutely no proof of that," replied Jake.

"Well that's a pile of garbage," said Kate. "Who else would have put up that kind of money for Sun Rey?"

"Sun Rey made a lot of money at the gentleman's club he owned, and the coffee shop was a cash cow, not a large one, but I have no doubt it had a fairly good cash flow," said Jake. "God only knows with his criminal mind what other shenanigans he had going on that might have raked in illegal money."

"Maybe he was using his own money," said Zeb.

"You guys don't really believe that do you?" said Kate.

"No," said Zeb and Jake in unison.

"Just tossing it against the wall to see if stuck," said Jake.

"Where is she now, the woman Sun Rey brutalized at the treatment center?" asked Zeb. "Is she employed by Senator Russell's opponent?

"Maybe we can find her if she's still working for Senator Russell's opponent," offered Kate. "She could shed a whole lot of light on this entire thing."

"The PI checked that out. She's long gone from that gig."

"Then where is she?" asked Kate. "Six feet under ground?"

"She's in the wind. Her trail went cold the day she got her cash. Once she got the payoff she moved out of her apartment and skedaddled quicker than you can say Jack Robinson," said Jake.

"Did she live with someone, have close friends, anything?" asked Kate. "No one can leave without some sort of trail."

"She had a roommate. The roommate said the woman had no family she ever spoke of. All the bills, including the lease, were in the roommate's name. She left no forwarding information of any kind. Unfortunately, the only other bit of information the PI could dig up was an electric bill in her name from Toronto, Canada. It was from seven years ago. When that dead-ended, he didn't follow up any further. He did say he would dig around if we wanted to hire him at the right price. My guess is that the money she got came with a set of new IDs."

"She's gone," said Zeb. "I doubt she knows anything that will lead us anywhere except down a rabbit hole."

"She's dead," said Kate. "I'd bet on it."

"There's one more thing of interest," said Jake. "Levi Lowe, Curtis Lowe's dad who's doing time in federal prison here in Safford for defrauding the federal government."

"Yes," said Zeb.

"All of his personal information as well as most of his business dealings were found on the computer Sun Rey left behind at the treatment center. It seems when someone from Senator Russell's office came by to pick up Sun Rey's personal effects the computer was somehow overlooked. The PI went over it. He admitted he was no computer expert but, in his opinion, it looked as though Sun Rey had committed fraud using Levi Lowe's personal data. Levi might be doing time for a crime Sun Rey committed."

"Shit," said Zeb. "I helped put Levi away. I might have been set up like a bowling pin."

"I think the PI earned his money," said Jake. "Are you going to wire him the eight grand?"

"Hell yes," said Zeb. "Send him that and two grand extra if he hands over Sun Rey's computer. Have him overnight the computer. Let him know we can make it worth his while to keep everything between us on the down low. Tell him we are very likely going to be using his services in the future."

"Are you going to have Curtis help out with looking into what was on Sun Rey's computer?" asked Kate.

"Hell, yes. If anyone has a vested interested and maybe the talent to find how the fraud was set up, it's him. In fact, maybe he suspected Sun Rey set up his father and wanted to look at the case files I had on my computer. Maybe that was part of his deal with Jude."

"You think you can trust him?" asked Jake. "He played rabbit on us once."

"He won't screw with us," said Zeb. "We will always have someone looking over his shoulder. He only works here at the office, and he downloads nothing. Got it?"

"Right," said Kate and Jake.

"Who is going to be the babysitter?" asked Kate.

Zeb looked at Jake. Jake shrugged his shoulders. He knew less about computers than Zeb or Kate. Kate knew the most, but she wanted to get going on interviewing the women who were allegedly raped by Sun Rey.

"Kate, you and I will take turns. We'll set up a schedule. Let's say twice a week, two hours each. How does that sound?" asked Zeb.

"Good," said Kate. "I have the distinct impression young Mr. Lowe knows exactly what he's looking for. If he doesn't, he'll sure as hell know it when he sees it."

Zeb laid out three copies of the list of seventeen women who Sun Rey likely raped. Along with their names were their last known addresses and phone numbers. He handed one list to Kate and another to Jake.

"I'll take the first three on the list," said Zeb. "You two divide the remaining fourteen any way you want. Let's get right on it. The quicker we start ruling some of these women in or out, the better. Don't forget to talk to their boyfriends. Vengeance, honor and protection may be at play here."

"Since Zeb is taking the first three, I'll take the next seven, and you can handle the final seven on the list," said Kate. "Is that okay with you, Jake?"

Jake nodded. Kate walked out of the room, cellphone in hand, dialing the first woman on her list.

"You busy?" asked Jake.

"Same as you," replied Zeb.

"Mind telling me why you are only going to interview three of the seventeen women?

"Got some other shit that needs tending to," said Zeb.

"Regarding Sun Rey's murder?"

"No," replied Zeb.

"Mind sharing what it is you're up to?"

"It is truly none of your business," said Zeb.

"I take it that it's personal?" asked Jake.

"Yup, it's personal," answered Zeb.

"Okay, then," said Jake. "Good luck."

"It's not about luck," replied Zeb.

18

STRIP JOINT

Zeb put the pedal to the metal and zipped westerly toward the second biggest city in Arizona. He had a single stop to make, the iCandy Gentleman's Club. The strip joint Sun Rey had owned was located just outside of the Tucson city limits. The three women on Zeb's list all worked there and, fortunately, all of them were hard at work earning a living that afternoon. It was no coincidence they were the women Zeb had chosen to put on his list. He had a busy night ahead of him and had arranged the list so the most likely suspects were divided evenly between Jake and Kate.

His sheriff's badge impressed the bouncer just enough to get Zeb to the manager, a rough looking Hispanic man named Carlos.

"What was the exact date and times you were looking for?" asked Carlos.

Zeb told him.

"Easy, peasy. We keep ninety days of time-stamped video from the floor. Insurance purposes."

"Right," replied Zeb. "Insurance is important."

Carlos punched a few computer keys and pointed to a list of girls who were working during the night in question.

"There you go, Sheriff...Hanks, was it?"

"Right,"

"They were all working."

He stroked a few more keys and instantly a time-stamped and dated video of the night in question appeared. In just three minutes Carlos was able to point out the girls in question.

"Hard working gals, all three of 'em," said Carlos. "Crazy chicks. I think they dig each other. I doubt any of them has a steady man in their lives. But that's their business, isn't it?"

"Yup," said Zeb. "These days it most certainly is. Mind if I have a little chat with each of them?"

"It'll cost you the going rate," said Carlos. "Don't hog their time. These girls need to make a living."

Zeb nodded and asked Carlos to send over the one dressed like a nun. Her stage name was Gidget. It took Zeb all of a minute to realize he didn't know anyone like Gidget. She was as tough as she was soft and lovely smelling.

The stripper pushed back Zeb's hat. While straddling his lap her leg bumped against his badge. He handed her a crisp twenty-dollar bill.

"You a copper?"

"Sheriff."

"Good work if you can get elected," replied Gidget. "My grandfather was a sheriff back in the day. You here on official business?"

She deftly kept earning her twenty spot as she spoke.

"It's about Sun Rey," said Zeb.

Gidget responded with a beaming smile.

"I liked having sex with him," she said.

"Why?" asked Zeb.

"Because even though he thought he was being rough he was really kind of a pussy. I controlled him completely. He was so completely shallow and stupid he didn't even know he was being manipulated. He was just kinky enough to satisfy me. He was a bondage freak, and, he tipped big. I made a thousand bucks every time I had sex with him. Easiest money I ever made."

"So it was never rape?" asked Zeb.

"Hell, no," replied the woman. "I was always the master, and he was definitely the slave. In fact, you could say I took advantage of him. Want another dance? It's only twenty dollars."

Zeb thanked her, gave her a ten-dollar tip on top of the twenty-dollar lap dance charge and asked about the second woman on his list.

"The bottled blonde with the purchased tits." She nodded her head toward a woman walking the perimeter asking customers if they wanted a dance. "She's all right, just a little unsure of herself. Why else would she have laid down hard earned money for silicone and scars just to have big boobs?"

"Could you send her over?" asked Zeb.

"Sure you don't want me again. I'm a much better dancer," she cooed seductively. She ran a sweet smelling finger across Zeb's lips. "If I can't excite you until your little man points towards the sky, the dance is on the house."

"Thanks, but please send blondie over here, would you?" asked Zeb.

"It's your money, copper...and your loss."

Gidget slipped off Zeb's lap, shook her booty, and turned and winked as she approached the blonde with purchased breasts.

"I hear you want a dance," said blondie.

Zeb handed her a twenty-dollar bill and asked her to sit next to him. He showed her his badge.

"Am I in trouble?" she asked coyly. "Or is this your way of turning me on?"

"No, I have a few questions about the man who used to own this joint," said Zeb.

The blonde instantly turned pale.

"He can rot in hell, that bastard," she said.

"He may be doing that at this very minute," replied Zeb.

The shocked expression on her face told him that she knew nothing of his demise.

"What do you mean?"

"He's gone to meet his maker."

"What?"

"His judgement day has come," said Zeb.

"When?"

"A few days ago," replied Zeb.

"How?"

"He ended up on the wrong end of a shotgun," said Zeb.

"Can't say as it surprises me," said the second stripper.

"Do you know who might have pulled the trigger?" asked Zeb.

"No, but they should sing praises to whoever did it," she replied. "Sun Rey was a bad, bad guy. If you really want to know what I think, it seems like a fitting end to his life."

Zeb looked her up and down. She seemed so young, so pure and too innocent to be a stripper. However, she didn't sound as unsure of herself as her friend had implied.

"Why do you do this job?" asked Zeb as the music stopped.

"That's going to cost you another twenty," she said, holding out her hand.

"I don't think I really want to know," said Zeb.

"You're right, you probably don't," said the stripper.

Zeb mentioned the third name on the list.

"That's her," she said, pointing to the stage. "I gotta run. I'm next on the pole. If you want to spend some fives or tens, come on over to the stage. Don't be a tightwad. Nobody likes one dollar bills."

Zeb handed her an extra five and asked her to send the current pole dancer to his table. Two minutes later she arrived.

"I hear Sun Rey's having breakfast with the devil these days," she said.

"You've heard?" asked Zeb.

"I've known for about thirty seconds, and I can't say I'm sorry to hear it."

"Care to let me know why?" asked Zeb.

"Twenty bucks." The reply came with a smile, an upturned palm and a come-hither look.

Zeb slipped a pair of tens into her open hand, and dancer number three spread herself across his lap, leaned into him and whispered in his ear.

"Sun Rey was a real A-number one jerk," she said, pulling back to press her breasts into Zeb's face. "But then again I may have had it coming, at least a little bit."

"What happened?" asked Zeb.

The stripper turned around and did a grind number on Zeb's lap, laughing all the while.

"What happened?" repeated Zeb.

She spun around and landed face to face with the Sheriff of Graham County. She proceeded to rub her breasts provocatively against him.

"I'd have slept with him anyway because he could have made me a headliner, you know, a number one dancer. Top girls make twice as much as everyone else. They get their pictures in all the ads, and they get to make big money on personal appearances. Who wouldn't want that? Instead he chose to drug me with a roofie, you know, Rohypnol, the date-rape drug?"

"I know what it is," said Zeb.

"I don't remember what happened after that. We might have had sex. We might not have had sex. There weren't any telltale signs except that my panties were missing. Maybe he had a thing for girls' sweaty underthings? Who knows? He never made me a headliner, that's about all I can say. He was a real piece of shit. He used people. A genuine asshole, if you ask me," said stripper number three.

All three of the women knew Sun Rey claimed to be related to a standing senator, but all were just as surprised to hear he was actually Senator Russell's son. These three women had perfect alibis. Unless Zeb was missing something obvious, they weren't guilty of killing Sun Rey. Zeb crossed them off the list of suspects. His evening held a second destination that was calling him.

19

CEREMONY PART 1

The trip back toward Safford and Graham County was interrupted by an important and secretive stop on the Rez. Curiously, Song Bird had given Zeb a hand drawn map to a place called Crazy Medicine Canyon. Zeb thought he knew even the most distant corners of the Rez, but Song Bird had insisted the place Zeb was headed to was far enough off the beaten path that directions were necessary.

The directions turned out to be a good thing. The location Song Bird had given him was not only unfamiliar, but parts of it were barely passable even with the high clearance of his truck. As he neared the destination, an almost full moon had risen in the eastern sky. The floor of the desert valley appeared lighted like early dusk while the surrounding area was lost in darkness. Zeb found himself entering a tight canyon through a dry riverbed. Though he believed he knew every square foot of the local area, he felt totally lost and more than a little disoriented.

A moment later Zeb was thankful to see a fire burning in the distance, marking the meeting place. Very quickly he found himself at the edge of a gently sloping hill. The geography was strangely beautiful, even in the darkness. Four jagged, stone bluffs dropped precipitously into a low-riding valley, forming a generally smooth canyon floor. The moonlight had risen high enough over the canyon bluffs to provide just enough light to guide him. As he pulled closer, the silhouettes of two people came into view. Both were dressed in traditional Native American clothing. Zeb flipped off his lights, got out of the truck and walked toward Song Bird and Echo Skysong.

The smell of Arizona desert sage rested on the quiet air. It mixed with the distinct aroma of jasmine. Song Bird approached him. Echo remained near the fire, her face glowing as she sat on the remains of an ancient downed tree. In Song Bird's right arm was a bundle of clothing. In his left hand the medicine man held an oil lantern. He handed Zeb the clothing, a plain, white cotton tunic shirt with heavy cotton pants, and a leather vest. Beaded knee length moccasins completed the outfit.

"Here," said Song Bird. "Put these on."

Zeb looked around. He hesitated and began to walk back toward his truck to change clothes.

"Change here," said Song Bird, pointing to the earth. "No one is looking at you but yourself."

Zeb looked down. He was standing in the middle of a fairly large circle. Song Bird held the lantern near the ground. Zeb could see sand paintings of a bear, a porcupine and a coyote. They had been drawn with colored sand on the desert floor.

"What are those?" he asked.

"The bear is the symbol for strength, solitude and humility. The porcupine for safety and protection. The coyote will help you recognize your mistakes and help you see the humor in them," explained Song Bird.

Zeb glanced up and over at Echo who seemed to be taking great interest in what the men were doing.

"Strip naked inside the circle," instructed Song Bird. "Bring the clothes you have on and throw them in the fire."

"It's my uniform," said Zeb.

"Then keep the badge. Burn the rest."

Song Bird's order was firm and carried a twist of humor. He spoke loudly enough that Echo could overhear. A lilt of genuine laughter from Echo carried on a light breeze that was beginning to rise from the south. Embarrassed about stripping naked in front of a beautiful woman, Zeb started slowly removing his clothes. When he was completely nude, he abruptly felt free enough to slow down the process and put on the ceremonial clothing without hurrying. Shame had left him. Echo watched the entire process without moving her eyes away from Zeb for a single moment. He wondered if Echo had stripped in front of Song Bird. If she had, Zeb was sorry he missed it. He quickly suppressed the thought. Nothing about this ceremony was intended to be sexual.

When he had changed into the Apache clothing, Zeb tossed his uniform into the fire. As he watched it go up in flames, Song Bird approached him from behind, placed a red headband over his forehead and tied it carefully in the back, making certain to avoid Zeb's recent injury. Together the men walked to the fire.

"You look like a warrior that I would be proud to fight alongside and die with," said Echo.

Song Bird began to hum and dance. Soon his humming turned into Athabaskan words that Zeb did not understand. He looked at Echo who seemed to recognize both the words and Song Bird's dance steps.

Song Bird danced for thirty minutes and then stopped. "That's enough of that," he said. "My legs are tired."

Echo smiled and threw something in the fire, causing the flames to sparkle in multiple colors. Song Bird sat at the southern end of the fire, Echo on the east and Zeb on the west.

Zeb eyed Echo. Dressed in a highly adorned calico dress, she also was ornamented with a red headband. Her hair was tied with hourglass-shaped embellishments Song Bird called nah-leens. The more Zeb looked at her the more timeless she became. He glanced at the dark canyon walls and the star-filled sky overhead. This entire moment had lost its sense of place and time. It carried only a sense of some unknown purpose. As his mind and spirit drifted away, he heard Song Bird's voice calling him back to reality.

"Listen closely. I will say what I have to say only one time. It is up to both of you to listen and remember." Song Bird sounded like a teacher scolding his students for something they might not do. "This Teardrop Ceremony will take place over three nights." Song Bird looked at Zeb. "For the next three nights you have within you the traits of an Apache." Then he turned to Echo. "You must hold your warrior spirit straight and true. Your hearts must be open."

Then Song Bird got up and began dancing, this time much more vigorously than before. His singing and dancing lasted long enough for Zeb to lose track of time altogether. By the time Song Bird stopped Zeb's body tingled with the loss of personal consciousness and the acceptance of a more universal mindfulness. Song Bird sat down and put his feet near the fire. It was then Zeb realized the medicine man was not wearing any shoes.

"Tonight I will sit with you. You will say nothing to each other until the sun rises over the canyon wall. You will eat and drink nothing because you will be neither hungry nor thirsty. Now sit on the ground and lean against each other's backs."

Zeb and Echo followed the medicine man's instructions without question. The night was cool, and Zeb found the warmth of Echo's body comforting. The smell of the sage she wore relaxed his mind and body. Her back was strong. She held her body firm and erect. Her spinal bones against his back, even through their clothing, felt symmetrically spaced. Instantly he sensed their bodies as though they were skin against skin.

Echo felt a man-sized strength as her back nestled up against Zeb. He smelled clean, something she wasn't used to in a man after three tours in Afghanistan. She had long gotten past the foul odors that men and women carry after being in the field for weeks at a time. However, cleanliness had a smell and nature all its own. She thought of how she had learned to trust the smell of bad odors. The stench of her fellow soldiers meant comfort and relative safety nearby. Zeb's lack of stench was a bit unsettling, but she vowed to get used to it. She was not in a war zone. She was not at war with the enemy. She was home. She was safe.

Song Bird bound them loosely together with broadcloth. It served to firm them up against each other and to make certain their bodies stayed connected. Then he placed a softened leather cover over their eyes.

"You have six hours until the sun breaks over the canyon wall. I want you to empty your minds of all that stops you from moving toward perfection. I want you to alleviate yourself from all the burdens that prevent you from becoming closer to the gods. I want you to examine yourself and each other without saying a single world," said Song Bird.

Song Bird started to chant and pound on a drum that he seemed to pull from thin air. After a few minutes he stopped, chuckled loudly and spoke sincerely.

"And I hope you were smart enough to empty your bladders, or you will be very uncomfortable and agitated."

Over the next six hours Song Bird kept the fire stoked to provide a small amount of additional warmth as the night grew progressively cooler. Periodically he would chant lowly in a humming monotone. Occasionally he would tell a story of traditional bravery, genuine love or terrible loss.

The time passed surprisingly quickly for Echo and Zeb. At the six-hour mark Song Bird unbound the broadcloth and removed their eye coverings. He offered them water. They drank. Song Bird then asked two questions.

"Did you empty your minds?"

"No," said Echo. "I tried but could not empty my mind."

Song Bird nodded and dropped a carnelian stone at her feet.

"The carnelian stone is meant to help conquer doubt, remove negative thoughts, increase self-confidence, create patience, establish peace and harmony within and assist in overcoming depression. Hold the stone next to your heart and after a while against your forehead. Feel the power of the carnelian stone. Feel its gifts."

Song Bird turned to Zeb.

"Did you empty your mind, Zeb?"

"No," said Zeb. "I periodically thought of nothing but mostly many things came into my mind. Gradually I focused on just a few of them, but I dwelled on them."

"What did you focus on, Zeb?" asked Song Bird.

"How Doreen's murder impacted my life and how that impact affected others."

"Yes, one action can produce many reactions," replied Song Bird. "Go on."

"I thought about what I had done. I wondered if my life had true purpose, true meaning. I wondered if it has any purpose or meaning at all."

"Does it?" asked Song Bird.

"Yes, I believe it does, but I don't always understand its purpose," replied Zeb.

"Do you want to?" asked Song Bird.

"Yes."

"Do you believe in the great Creator of all things?" asked Song Bird.

"Yes."

"Do you believe the Creator made you with a purpose in mind?"

"I don't know," replied Zeb. "I don't know if the Creator of all things made me with a purpose in mind or if he gave me free will and the ability to find my purpose."

"Maybe the answer is both," said Song Bird. "Maybe the answer is neither. Mostly you should not pass judgement on yourself."

He handed Zeb an Apache tear. "Here," he said. "I have given you Apache tears before. You did not pay attention as well as you could have. This time listen to the stone and hear what it has to say to you."

Song Bird handed Zeb a tin cup with warm water that had been brewing over two parallel sticks on the open fire.

"Sassafras tea," said Song Bird. "Take two sips and give the cup to Echo. Then drink some water, half a bottle." He handed Zeb a plastic water bottle. "Then give the bottle to Echo who will finish the water."

Song Bird then directed Echo and Zeb to stand. He placed them shoulder to shoulder facing east, the direction of the rising sun. Song Bird chanted once again. This time he circled the fire in a clockwise direction twelve times and then in a counter clockwise direction twelve times. He gently tapped Echo and Zeb by pressing the palm of his hand between their shoulder blades during each trip around the fire. Each pressing of the palm in their backs became lighter until the twelfth. The final touch was so light that his hand seemed to penetrate their skin. He then ordered them to sit. He spoke directly to Echo.

"Echo, what was it that could not be emptied from your mind?"

"A child. A young Afghan boy. He was ten or eleven years old. Because of our mission we dealt with the head of his clan on a regular basis. The clan leader gave us information in exchange for money and magazines with nude pictures of both men and women. He molested the boy on a regular basis. Our team spied on him continually. We knew he was harming the boy, but we could do nothing because of military orders. I wanted to kill him with my bare hands. I wanted him to suffer like I witnessed the boy suffering," said Echo. "No, I wanted him to suffer more than the boy suffered. I wanted to take his life."

"You personally witnessed the molesting?" asked Song Bird.

"I did on multiple occasions," replied Echo.

"Did you get the chance to kill this man?" asked Song Bird in a voice so soft as to be barely audible.

Echo's entire body began to tremble ever so faintly. She dropped her head into her hands. Not a single emotion did she exhibit. The story had greatly agitated Zeb, but he remained quiet and said nothing.

"I was given an off the books okay to execute him the day before we returned to our main base," said Echo. "But then those orders were rescinded at the last moment.

"Did you want to play the role of Usen and end his life?" asked Song Bird.

Zeb wanted to shout at Song Bird. His question was unfair. She had been given permission to execute him. It was war time. He was a child molester. He was evil. She had multiple, legitimate reasons to execute him.

When she didn't answer, Song Bird asked her again.

"Did you want to play the role of Usen and end his life?"

Echo lifted her head up and spoke softly.

"I don't know." Her words were hesitant. Song Bird stared into her eyes, reading her lie. Eventually, she spoke from her heart. "Yes, I wanted to."

"Do you think you hold the power of life over death?" asked Song Bird.

"It is not my power," she replied.

"Never forget that," said Song Bird. "Or you shall suffer mightily."

After a silence long enough to allow daylight to cover them, Song Bird asked one final question.

"What did you hear circling us when you were bound?"

"One man," answered Echo. "Moving stealthily, slowly. His movements were in a clockwise direction around us. He must have been on the move for twenty minutes."

Song Bird posed the same question to Zeb. His response was different.

"I heard a coyote, a single coyote."

"It was a wolf, a solitary wolf that carried the spirit of a man. He was studying both of you. He gave me a warning."

Song Bird stared intently into the hearts and minds of Echo and Zeb. One of them may not be right for the ceremony, but it was far too late to change what had already been set in motion.

Song Bird told Zeb and Echo to get into their vehicles and follow him back to the highway. From there Zeb headed home to pick up a new uniform and Echo headed home to think. They would meet again the following evening, just before dusk.

20

ECHO IS SUSPECT

"You look tired," said Helen. "Didn't you sleep well?"

Zeb stood in front of Helen's desk. Hands on his hips, the sheriff towered over her. She was his aunt and had known him since the day he was born. She was not about to be put off by any display of foolish masculinity.

"What are you doing here? You promised to take some time off to heal up, didn't you?" Zeb chided.

"I'm fine, hardly any pain. I'm more ticked off about what happened than anything. That's mostly why I'm here. I don't want to miss anything just in case something about the break-in of our office comes up. I'm the only real witness you've got."

"But..."

"No buts," interjected Helen. "I'm here and I'm working. If it gets to be too much, I'll go home and work from there."

Zeb knew better than to argue with someone, especially Helen, who had her mind already set in stone.

"Okay, but if you start to hurt, promise me you'll go home," said Zeb.

Under her desk Helen crossed her fingers and nodded affirmatively.

"Jake and Kate have both checked in by phone. They have talked to the other fourteen women who were possibly molested or raped by Sun Rey. They want to run everything by you."

"Good. Send them in the minute they arrive."

Jake arrived first. He brought some tea from the Town Talk for Zeb and carried two coffees for himself and Kate. He'd already given Helen a blueberry muffin and some tea.

"You look like you didn't sleep so well," said Jake.

"I was up all night," replied Zeb.

"Doing what?" asked Jake. "You have a new girlfriend or something?"

"We'll talk about it later," said Zeb.

"I'm here to listen when you want to talk," replied Jake.

Kate entered last. Helen advised her that Zeb looked a little like he'd been up all night. She also mentioned he was a bit touchy about it so it would be best not to mention it.

"Have a seat, Kate," said Zeb.

Kate sat in the big chair across from Zeb's desk. Jake pulled up a wooden chair and sat next to her.

"What've you got?" asked Zeb.

"Normally I'd say ladies first," said Jake. "But I got absolutely nothing. Seven dead ends. All with perfect alibis. Rambler went with me on the one Rez interview. The only thing I learned that was vaguely interesting was that the young Apache woman took a computer class at Eastern Arizona University with Curtis Lowe, but she didn't remember him. I called him, and he didn't remember her either."

"What's her name?" asked Zeb.

"Yulu Rozene," said Jake.

"Check her out further," said Zeb, writing down the name of Yulu Rozene.

Kate pulled out a notebook.

"Six of the seven women I talked to had iron clad alibis for the night of the murder," said Kate. "It seems they were all on the Rez at a four-day Holiness Ceremony to cure Bear, Snake and other sicknesses. There were over twenty-five women that were present, and everyone vouched for their presence."

"Did you find out who the sickness ceremony was for?" asked Zeb.

"Curing them and the others present from what Sun Rey and others had done to them," replied Kate.

"Who was the elder woman present?"

"Beulah Trees. She said you would vouch that she spoke only the truth, but that wasn't necessary. I could tell she spoke with one hundred percent truthfulness."

Zeb inhaled deeply. Beulah had blessed his love with Doreen. She would never allow a lie to slip through her lips.

"And the seventh woman on your list?" asked Zeb.

"Sonja Trees, Beulah's granddaughter."

"Could she state her whereabouts during the time of the murder of Sun Rey?"

"No, and she was very uncooperative. She more or less refused to say anything," said Kate.

"What's her background?"

"Military, then some college. Currently working on the Rez in a bookstore."

"What did she do in the military?" asked Zeb.

"Military police," replied Kate.

"So she has plenty of weapons training," said Zeb.

"Yes, near the top of her class," said Kate.

"So she may have had the skills to shoot Sun Rey from a long distance?"

"She was trained well enough to do that," replied Kate.

"Look more deeply into her. I'll go have a chat with her grandmother," said Zeb.

"There's one more thing about Sonja Trees," said Kate.

"Yes?"

"Echo Skysong is her half-sister and best friend."

"Shit," said Zeb under his breath.

"What?" said both Kate and Jake.

Zeb rubbed his tired eyes. "Echo found the body of Sun Rey."

"We both have read the report," said Kate. Jake nodded in agreement.

"But it was how she found the body. It was with almost supernatural abilities. She saw the body from where no one could have possibly seen it. She claimed to have been able to smell it even though it was in stagnant, foul water. Something doesn't square up with her explanation."

"I take it you are placing Echo Skysong on the suspect list?" asked Kate.

"Right at the very top of it," said Zeb.

21

CEREMONY PART 2

The drive to Crazy Medicine Canyon was filled with equal parts of angst, dread, disbelief and hope. Zeb's mind jumped between these emotions with lightning speed. Each bump on the road jarred loose one thought and thrust it into the next. Could Echo possibly be the killer? No, no way he told himself. She wasn't a killer. Yet absolutely she could be. She was a professional soldier with extensive training, combat zone experience and had interacted with Special Forces for three years. She had the desire to kill someone specific in Afghanistan and that was taken away from her. Her half-sister/best friend had been brutally raped by Sun Rey. Zeb knew all too well how heavily the powerful hatred that accompanies revenge could bear down on one's very being. To kill the rapist of her half-sister didn't make convoluted sense, it made nothing short of perfect sense. What would he have done if someone had raped Doreen? His mind held but a single answer to that question.

As Zeb approached the canyon, he eyed the distant flames from Song Bird's fire. They appeared to snap and lick skyward with malevolent intent. He stopped a half mile or so before getting to his destination in order to change into the clothing Song Bird had given him the night before. In his ceremonial clothing he drove the final distance with an increased awareness. In the periphery of his truck's headlights Zeb saw a dozen varying species of nocturnal creatures creeping about. As quickly as he caught their movement in the corner of his eye, each disappeared as if they had never been there. He wondered if his eyes were playing tricks on him. Oddly, his hearing also seemed altered as he heard nothing related to what he thought he saw. Little did he know it was only the beginning of a long night of hallucinations with phantasms that were part pure reality and part delusional dreams. But mostly he was going to experience what lives and lies between the two separate worlds. Lastly, his eyes sought the slinking, skulking of a wolf, but none was to be seen.

"Dagot'e," said Song Bird as Zeb departed his truck.

"Dant'e," replied Zeb.

"I see you remembered to dress for the occasion," said Song Bird.

Zeb glanced around. He saw only Song Bird's truck. No evidence of Echo being present was anywhere to be found.

"Is this a solo journey for me tonight?" asked Zeb.

"Have you eaten anything in the last four hours?" asked Song Bird.

The medicine man had given him highly specific instructions about not eating. Zeb had followed them precisely.

"No, nothing since noon."

"Good," said Song Bird. "You must be hungry, then?"

"I could eat," replied Zeb.

Song Bird reached into a colorful pouch hanging from his belt and pulled out what looked like a small, spineless cactus. It was button shaped, larger than a silver dollar in circumference and about four times as thick. In the reflection of the fire it looked pretty but not much like sustenance.

"Here, eat this," said Song Bird.

"What is it?" asked Zeb.

"A ticket to another world that lives inside you every minute of your life," replied Song Bird.

"Is it peyote?" asked Zeb.

Song Bird sensed trepidation.

"There is no need to have any worries. I will be with you, so will Echo. You will be safe. I promise you," said Song Bird.

"I know it's against the law to take this," said Zeb.

"Against the laws of man but not against the laws of nature and of God," replied Song Bird.

Zeb looked at the large, greenish-blue button which suddenly seemed to have doubled in size. Then he looked at Song Bird who now seemed to be a glowing aura of numerous colors and distorted shapes. As Zeb held the psychoactive cactus to his mouth, Echo appeared. She seemed to have magically risen from the flames of the fire. She approached Zeb. In her right hand she held a peyote button, perhaps two-thirds the size of the one Zeb was holding. Dressed as she had the previous night, her beautiful appearance was otherworldly. She held the button in front of her mouth.

"Shall we?" she asked Zeb.

Zeb looked past Song Bird, directly at Echo, put the peyote in his mouth and began chewing. The taste was horrifyingly earthy. It took all Zeb had in him to keep from spitting it out. Song Bird handed him some warm tea. He drank. It, too, tasted earthy. Zeb glanced at Echo. She chewed the dried peyote button with a beaming smile never leaving her face. Song Bird offered her some tea. She sipped it slowly.

"Your worlds are about to shift," said Song Bird. "For now enjoy the fire, but be careful the flames don't draw you in."

Once again barefoot, the medicine man placed Zeb on one side of the fire and Echo on the other. They had a clear view through the flames of each other, the darkness of the desert and the billions of stars in the sky.

"What do you mean our world is about to shift?" asked Zeb.

Song Bird responded with a dance. Each striking of his foot was accompanied by a vocal intonation that when put together became a story song in the form a question followed by a response. His words were Athabaskan. At first what he said was garbled nonsense, but forty-five minutes later Zeb began to understand every word even though it was spoken/sung and responded to in the native language of the Apache. Zeb watched as the entire world around him began to wobble like a gyroscope slightly tipped off its axis. Zeb tried to stand, but his legs would barely let him push himself up from the log. Through the flames Echo smiled beatifically at him. He tried to return the ecstatic smile, but his lips failed to move. He touched them. They felt like rubber, then wood, then bone. Zeb looked up through the flames. Echo seemed to be floating above her log bench seat. His vision of her body drifted through the flames toward Zeb slowly at first, then suddenly, like a rifle round. Then she was gone. Then she was standing behind him, her arms lifting him up. He couldn't see her but he recognized her smell.

"Dance," she whispered in his ear. "Dance to the rhythm of your heartbeat."

"I can't..."

But before he could finish his sentence Zeb found his bird spirit and was floating, flitting around the campfire with Echo who somehow managed to twirl constantly as she circled the fire. Song Bird beat a soft drum, hummed and sang words that had meaning in their sound. The trio danced for what Zeb determined to be hours. In reality very little time had passed when suddenly he fell to his knees and began to vomit. Purple, blue, green, orange, yellow and all variations of color spewed forth through his lips. He watched his physical reaction in astonishingly slow motion. Song Bird and Echo knelt beside him. Song Bird patted him on the back. As the spasms in his gut began to vacillate in rhythm to his breath, Echo began to vomit. Zeb lifted his head and watched. A rainbow projectile emitted itself from deep inside her. It was beautiful. He reached out to touch it.

Song Bird stopped Zeb's hand and whispered, "Just let it happen."

Zeb laid on the ground and watched the stars. In a short time Echo lay next to him. She began to giggle. The sound was infectious. He joined her. Soon they were rolling around laughing until their sides ached. Zeb noticed a shiny rock and showed it to Echo. They began to stack tiny rocks, one at a time, in a pile. Soon the small rocks reached a height of six inches. The fire reflected direct beams of color off the rocks. The radiance struck Zeb and Echo simultaneously, giving them unspoken pause. The beat of Song Bird's drum seemed ever present yet a thousand light years away.

Echo rolled away from Zeb. He was enthralled by the gracefulness of the way she moved. He tried to mimic it, but his arm landed on a small cactus. The spiny needles of the cactus pierced him in numerous places on his forearm. The pain was nearly intractable. Zeb's yelp brought Song Bird and Echo instantly to his side. The medicine man dampened the area with cactus juice, removed tweezers from his bag and proceeded to remove the spines almost painlessly. His actions caused tears to stream down Zeb's face. They were not tears of pain but rather tears of memory. Doreen's face was superimposed over Song Bird's countenance. Zeb reached out to touch the medicine man's face. His hand melted away and then elongated into space as it reached toward the stars. Pain was replaced by an overwhelming sense of joy.

Echo reached over and touched Zeb's arms. Her hand, her skin and his arm were all united as a single object, all of it foreign to anything he knew or understood. The softness of her smile was tactile. He followed her eyes to his and back to hers they returned, a thousand times in a flash of a second. He followed her gaze as it looked past him to the desert floor which began to vibrate and pulse to the rhythm of all the nature that engulfed them.

Echo moved next to Zeb and curled herself inside his arms.

"I didn't kill Sun Rey," she said.

A full bodied orgasm rushed through Zeb, not a sexual orgasm but a heightened sensitivity to her words. He knew she spoke the truth.

"I'm glad you didn't," he replied.

The pair just lay there, breathing shallowly until sometime later when they looked up to see Song Bird standing over them.

"Here."

Song Bird handed them a fruity nectar, thin and not too sweet. Zeb swallowed some. Echo swished it around in her mouth. Her actions made Zeb feel foolish and gross. She was the returning warrior and yet compared to him she was light in spirit. Song Bird witnessed it all.

"There is no reason to feel shame," he said to Zeb. "There is only reason to feel alive and free of your earthly sins."

Zeb began to weep. Tears streamed down Echo's face. No more words were spoken until the first rays of the rising sun peeked over the canyon walls. Perhaps they slept. Perhaps they drifted between this world and another.

"I'm tired," said Zeb eventually. "Exhausted."

"I could eat," said Echo.

Song Bird had prepared a feast of dried meat, berries, oranges, sweet bread and tea. They ate. Song Bird cleaned up the site. Within a few moments only the dying embers of the fire held any indication that someone had been there.

"Tonight we shall talk. Meet me back here at sunset."

With those words Song Bird ambled to his truck and slowly drove away.

Zeb turned to Echo with a million questions. She was even more beautiful in the morning light.

"Have you experienced peyote before?" asked Zeb.

"No," replied Echo. "I have heard about the journey from my ancestors, but their words failed to describe what I just felt."

"I didn't know..." began Zeb only to have Echo complete his sentence... "that all the universe is truly one thing."

Zeb and Echo lay side by side on a blanket as the sun moved overhead. Intermittent sleep came over them. By mid-afternoon both were alert and awake.

"Come to my house and I will cook us something to eat," said Echo.

"I should check into the office," said Zeb. "I have a murder case on..."

Realizing his words and that she had known of his suspicion of her as a suspect, he felt terrible.

"Now you know I didn't do it," said Echo. "So you've eliminated one suspect. I'd say that's a pretty good day's work."

"I'll follow you," said Zeb. "I don't know where you live."

"Some kind of sheriff you are," joked Echo. "You don't even know where one of your former suspects spends most of her time."

They both laughed heartily. Through the power of peyote, the weight of some of the world, of their lives, had been lifted from both of them.

22

BREAKFAST

Echo lived in a yurt on the southeastern edge of the Rez. In no time she whipped up a breakfast of machacha, fry bread and black beans. This time it was Echo watching Zeb eat.

"Didn't you say your mother told you it was impolite to watch someone eat?" he joked.

"You eat like no one has fed you in a while," laughed Echo.

Zeb realized he had been wolfing down his food and joined in the laughter. Breakfast led to tea and light conversation. Neither was ready to broach what had happened under the influence of peyote. It was just too new. When the conversation slowed, Zeb felt totally at ease. Nevertheless, it was time to go to work. Sun Rey's murder was becoming less fresh and more distant by the minute. He had work to do.

"Thanks for a wonderful breakfast and a night that I am certain we will discuss in depth at some point," said Zeb.

"I suspect we will," replied Echo. "And you're welcome for the breakfast. It was fun to cook for you. I don't quite remember when someone seemed to enjoy my cooking so much."

As Zeb stood to leave, she handed him his hat.

"How's that bump on your head?" she asked.

"Fine, almost healed. All that's left is a little embarrassment that someone got the jump on me," replied Zeb.

"I'm sorry," said Echo.

"Not your fault," replied Zeb. "Nothing to be sorry about."

Echo lowered her eyes. He could tell she wanted to tell him something.

"What is it?" he asked.

"That bump on your head should never have happened," said Echo.

"But it did," said Zeb. "And I'm still around to tell the tale."

"I..."

"What?" asked Zeb.

Echo looked away. "Nothing. Now that I know you I guess I just feel badly that you got hurt."

"Like I said, it's most certainly not your fault. It was my own for not having situational awareness. I can tell you it is unlikely it will happen to me like that again."

Echo thought back to Afghanistan. Lack of awareness and being less prepared than one should be were almost always the causes of injury or, worse, death.

Echo walked to the door and held it open for Zeb, then walked him to his truck.

"I will see you soon," she said.

"Tonight in Crazy Medicine Canyon," said Zeb. "God only knows what Song Bird has in store for us."

"I mean after that," said Echo.

"How about Friday night at my place? I'm not a bad cook. You eat a grilled T-bone steak and mixed veggies?"

"I lived on field rations for the better part of three years. A steak sounds great. I'll bring a fruit plate."

Zeb reached around and gave her an awkward hug goodbye. He felt as though he was looking at the world through fresh eyes as he made the drive home to change clothes and head to the office.

23

CURTIS IN THE WIND

"You look well rested and refreshed," said Helen.

"I feel good, very good, "replied Zeb.

"Jake and Kate have been hard at it. They wanted to talk to you as soon as you got in. They were expecting you a few hours ago. It has to do with Sun Rey.

"Ask them to come to my office as soon as they're ready," said Zeb.

A minute later both walked in. Kate placed an open laptop computer on Zeb's desk.

"This is Sun Rey's computer, the one left behind at the treatment center. We had Shelly, the woman who was doing the computer work for the BLM, drop by this morning and have a deep look at it."

"I thought you were going to have Curtis look it over," said Zeb.

"We both had a bad feeling about that," said Kate.

"We didn't feel we could trust him," added Jake.

"Okay. What did you find out?" asked Zeb.

"It took her all of ten minutes to find out some very valuable information," said Kate.

Zeb looked over at his office door. Helen had left it slightly ajar. He signaled Jake to close it quietly.

"What've you got?" asked Zeb.

"First of all, Sun Rey somehow managed to have access to the minutes of Senator Russell's committee meetings regarding the purchase and distribution of supplies and food to the San Carlos Reservation schools," said Kate. "He's managed to have that access for over six years."

"To what end did he use that sort of information?" asked Zeb.

"He, or someone who used his computer, we don't know the extent of Sun Rey's computer skills, managed to make it look like there were triple the amount of supplies and food sent to the San

Carlos schools. It is likely no one ever reviews anything. Checks for triple the real amounts of food and supplies actually ordered were sent to Levi Lowe."

"Yes, we all know he defrauded the federal government, and that's why he is sitting in federal prison right now," said Zeb. "So he must have been the brains behind it. He has the computer skills to pull it off."

"Except he never actually got the money," said Jake.

"What?" asked Zeb. "How can that be?"

"This was done very cleverly," said Kate. "The money was sent to an offshore account. There most of the overage was deposited and the rest, along with the actual amount due, was sent on to Levi Lowe. The amount sent to Levi Lowe was always ten to fifteen percent above what it should have been. I guess Levi had just about that much larceny in his heart. He kept it, and that's what got him nailed and sent to prison. The vast majority of the extra money stayed in an offshore account in the name of..."

"Sun Rey," interjected Zeb.

"Right," said Kate.

"That leaves a whole lot of unanswered questions," said Zeb. "First of all, at the trial the greater amount sent by the government would have been exposed, and Levi would have known he didn't steal that much. So why would he take the fall for a greater amount of money than he actually stole?"

"The federal prosecutors could prove he stole some amount of money. The rest, well, they couldn't ever find the rest of it. They assumed Levi had hidden it well enough to avoid them tracing it. After all, he is a computer expert," said Kate.

"Are you saying he didn't know who duped him?" asked Zeb. "I find that hard to believe."

"Oh, he knew," said Kate. "He took the fall because he was protecting someone."

"Who?"

"Not just one person," said Jake. "He was actually protecting two people, himself and Curtis."

"You've got my head spinning," said Zeb. "What are you talking about?"

"Sun Rey knew two inside secrets of the Lowe family. First of all, Levi was having an affair with one of Sun Rey's strippers from iCandy Gentlemen's Club."

"Jesus," said Zeb. "I've known him all my life. He's the last guy I'd expect of cheating on his wife. You're sure?"

Kate hit a button on the laptop she had placed in front of Zeb and up popped a video of Levi Lowe and a much younger woman having sexual intercourse.

"There are at least thirty tapes on the computer of him having sex," said Kate.

"Easy to see how Sun Rey blackmailed him. But, really, Levi chose time in prison over telling his wife?"

"His choice," said Kate. "Either way his life was going to crumble. Moreover, it looks as though he will be out in less than five years. My guess is that he will probably serve only three or four years. He made a choice."

"You said there were two reasons," said Zeb.

"Sun Rey was truly a deviant in the worst sense of the word. He also has proof on his computer that Curtis is gay," said Kate.

"That would kill his mother," said Zeb.

"A family with a closet full of secrets is ripe for blackmail," said Jake.

"It sounds like you two are thinking this is enough evidence to point the finger at Curtis when it comes to the murder of Sun Rey," said Zeb.

"We are," said Kate.

"Let's bring him in and have a little chat with him," said Zeb.

"I called his house earlier, over an hour ago. His mother answered. She is half out of her mind with worry," said Jake.

"Why?"

"Curtis went to the store thirty-six hours ago and hasn't returned," said Jake.

"Did he take his car?" asked Zeb.

"Yes," said Jake.

"Did you ever get over to the Lowe house and check the gun cabinet to see if any of the guns had been fired lately?"

"I did and none had, but that was before. Things have changed in the last thirty-six hours. The bad news is some of the guns and a lot of the ammunition is missing," replied Jake. "Here is the list of what should have been in the gun cabinet but wasn't, according to Angie." He laid a piece of paper on Zeb's desk. "But we have the murder weapon. It doesn't belong to the Lowes. It belonged to the U.S. government."

"If Curtis did the shooting, we've got to figure out who he got the gun from," said Kate.

"We'd better find Curtis," said Zeb. "Put a BOLO out on that old junker of his. Seek out any places he may have ever hung out. Check out possible sex partners and have a look into the people who played computer games with him."

"His life was one secret after another. It might be difficult to track down anyone he might be holing up with. He isn't one for leaving trails or sharing information with anyone."

"I don't care," said Zeb. "I want him found within 24 hours."

24

CEREMONY PART 3

Song Bird intently stirred the ashes of the fire with an ornately carved fire stick. The peyote, which had been out of Zeb's system for over twelve hours, was having latent effects on his mind. It seemed, for all intents and purposes, the old medicine man had become as ancient as the oak log Zeb was sitting on. Song Bird hadn't uttered a word to either Echo or Zeb for hours, but he continually fed them small portions of food and a variety of pungent drinks and clear liquids.

With each flicker of the flames Zeb's mind wandered far away only to return when the fire crackled, the wind blew or Song Bird made a sound by shuffling his feet. Zeb's thoughts spun with such rapidity that at times he was uncertain who he really was, where the peyote had taken his mind or even why he existed at all. He and Echo had once again been instructed to use each other's spines as resting supports. The warmth of Echo's back brought Zeb a comforting reality as he looked over the edge of the canyon wall toward the sky. He figured it was about an hour before sunrise. Then he giggled as he thought of how time meant nothing and figured what difference did it make anyway? He wondered where a thought like that even came from. All of a sudden he felt Echo's heartbeat synchronize with his own. At the same instant Song Bird broke a long silence.

"It is time for each of you to speak your truth," he said. "You can both lie on your backs and look toward the heavens."

Without speaking a word they did as Song Bird ordered. Zeb had said nothing for so long his mind tripped over the idea of speaking at all. He was thankful when Song Bird addressed Echo first.

"Echo," said Song Bird.

Zeb sensed anticipation of Song Bird's apparent question.

"To free your soul, what is it that must you tell us? What is that you must say to yourself out loud?"

Echo cleared her throat. She sat up. "May I have some water, please?"

Song Bird handed her a gourd with liquid in it. She smelled it before drinking. She handed it back to Song Bird and laid her body on the soft earth. Zeb turned to her. Tears were rolling down her cheeks. Seeing her cry provoked some hidden, empathetic reaction, and he too began to shed tears. Her voice vibrated as words pursed her lips.

"I lost someone I loved when I was in Afghanistan. His death was my fault."

"Sharing your truth will remove the deepest part of the pain," said Song Bird. "It will not only help you detach from the pain, but it will take away the thing that most injures your soul. It will help your suffering and make the pain less important. Most of all it will help you heal yourself."

Echo turned away from the men and stared into the oncoming dawn.

"You should not carry the death of someone on your shoulders. You should set them free. Would you not want to be free in death?" asked Song Bird.

"Yes, I would, but this is different. He was my lover in a time of war. He did something that I should have done myself and it got him killed. I failed as a soldier. I carry it with me every minute of every day. I feel like I have no choice but to carry him with me as well," said Echo. "I feel it is my duty."

"Say his name," said Song Bird.

From some private place deep inside Echo began to weep, slowly at first, then she stopped with a deep inhalation. When she quit shedding tears, she started to speak. Her voice seemed to be coming from far away.

"Hunter Foxwell. That was his name. He was a Specialist. We worked together. I gathered information from the Afghani women so he could lead his men and find the bad guys," said Echo. She chuckled and cried as the words 'bad guys' came out of her mouth.

"Tell us what happened," said Song Bird.

"No," said Echo. "I cannot, I will not speak of it."

"You must," replied Song Bird. "That is, if you want to unburden your spirit, transform yourself and clear all interference to your soul so that it can become one with God. Of course, you may also choose suffering, but you are a warrior, an American soldier, but first and foremost an Apache spirit warrior. You carry the essence of

Lozen. Lozen suffered as much as any Apache, and she told her story so others could learn from it. You must allow yourself to follow her lead."

Song Bird added some small dead branches to the fire. They crackled and shot sparks toward the sky. He reached inside his jacket and removed a bundle of sage, lit it from the edge of the fire and placed it on a stone. Then he returned to the ancient oak log. Silence prevailed for an amount of time that Zeb was unable to determine. Behind the canyon wall the first hint of dawn seemed to be appearing, but Zeb knew it could be his eyes playing tricks on him as they had all night long. Zeb wished Song Bird would not be so forceful with Echo, yet somehow it seemed necessary. Zeb wondered if he should even be part of the story she was sharing. Some of his thoughts told him he was invading very private turf.

"We are waiting to hear what happened," said Song Bird. "Take your time. Speak when you are ready. Find the words in your heart."

Echo found her strength, dug deeper and found words. At first her voice was so soft Zeb had to strain to hear it.

"I interviewed an Afghani woman. She told me her eleven-year old son was being repeatedly raped by the village chief. She said it was happening three times a week, always on Monday, Tuesday and Friday and always at the same time, eighteen hundred hours. I didn't know if she was telling the truth or not. Often Afghani people tried to use our team to work out vendettas they had against others. I sensed that, regardless of the situation with her son, she hated the village chief. On the other hand, she might have had good reason for us to know if he really was raping her son. I knew the chief by sight. He always carried a Shamshir sword at his waist. Rumor was he never took it off, not even to sleep. I told her I would look into it. Since I wasn't technically a field operative I couldn't look into it myself, so I passed the word along to Hunter."

The quiet stillness of the night became all-encompassing. In the near distance an owl hooted. Shivers shot up Zeb's neck. Lost in Echo's story, he had no thought of whether or not the owl was an omen.

"Hunter passed it along to his superiors. They denied his request because the tribal chief was supplying them with information on the Taliban. Apparently we were giving the tribal chief money, lots of it, as well as pornographic magazines in exchange for the location of the enemy fighters. When Hunter told me all this, I became irate. I made up my mind to sneak off base and see for myself. Inside I knew the mother wasn't lying. I could read it in her eyes. She was hurting for her son. However, she also hated the tribal chief for other reasons that I learned about later. I found out the chief had raped her years earlier and that the boy was actually his own son."

Echo paused and asked for another drink. Song Bird handed her a second gourd. This time it was full of warm water. She slowly sipped it. Hatred, not tears, filled her eyes.

"Thank you, Song Bird. I feel as though I am drying up inside," said Echo.

"Anger causes the insides of the body to create heat and dry up," replied Song Bird.

Zeb turned to Echo. At the same instant she looked over at him. For the first time since this transformation journey had begun he looked so deeply into her eyes that he quite literally looked past them. He felt like he was falling, maybe into her soul, as in a dream. She blinked and he was himself again. A single ray of sunshine sneaked through a crack in the rocks in the highest elevation of the canyon. Nature told Zeb it was almost seven a.m.

"Hunter agreed to have a look the next Tuesday. He took two of his buddies with him on recon. They saw nothing that would lead them to believe the mother was telling the truth. In fact, they saw nothing at all. I went back the next day and talked to the mother again. She said the tribal chief had been called away the previous night and had told her son to come over to him, as he always did, that night which was Wednesday. Back at the base camp I talked with Hunter who, needless to say, was frustrated with me because nothing had happened the previous night, and I had assured him it would. He said he didn't feel comfortable risking his friends' safety on something that might not be real. I volunteered to go with him. It was totally against protocol as I was not an official combatant. He said no. I will admit I seduced him to get him to allow me to go along," explained Echo.

"Was it right of you to use your sexuality to get what you wanted?" asked Song Bird.

Echo turned away and said something that sounded like a very meek, "No." She mumbled something else Zeb could not understand.

Song Bird responded as though he understood each word with perfection.

"Sexuality is for love and all the good that comes with love. If you abuse that, there is a cost," said Song Bird.

"There was a cost, a severe cost," said Echo. Her voice was full of regret, confusion and anger. "He allowed me to go along on the recon mission with him under the condition that I do nothing, no matter what I saw or heard. I agreed. I wanted to know if the mother was telling the truth. If she was, I would find out a way to deal with it later. We sneaked up to our vantage point where we could see inside the chief's house. Sure enough he was sexually abusing the young boy, his own son. I became irate. I was so full of hatred I wanted to kill the tribal chief with my bare hands right then and there. Hunter, who had been abused by a priest one time when he was a boy, said to leave it to him and that he would take care of it. I asked if I could go with him when he did. He knew I was an expert shot and would make a perfect back up. He said no. I begged and pleaded. I wanted to see the chief die with my own eyes. In fact, I would have killed him myself if Hunter hadn't throttled me back. He told me he would find a way to get it done, but it would have to look like someone other than US Special Forces killed him. Even though my blood was boiling I agreed. We were short timers then. We had only days left in our field deployment. Somehow I knew Hunter would get the job done and done correctly. I had every confidence in him."

"Did your blood continue to boil?" asked Song Bird.

"Like it was lit by the fires of hell," replied Echo.

"That is not good," said Song Bird.

"It felt good at the time," replied Echo. "It felt like the only thing I wanted to feel."

"Do you see how the devil set a snare and trapped you like a helpless rabbit?" asked Song Bird.

Zeb started to say something. He wanted to defend Echo whom he felt had every right to be filled with hatred at the situation. Song Bird silenced him with a mere glance.

Echo continued. "I do now, but then it was different. On the night before we were to leave Hunter asked me to go out on patrol with him. Once again this was totally breaking the rules of engagement, and both of us could get in huge trouble if something happened or if we got caught. He asked me to back him up as he was going to take the tribal chief out of the picture once and for all. It was a Sunday night so the chief, if he followed his routine, would be in his home by himself. His family would be away as was their routine. We sneaked up to the chief's house through the brush. We looked inside but saw nothing. Then we heard moaning from the bedroom. Hunter figured the chief was looking at the porno mags and taking care of business by himself. We sneaked into the house and checked it out. It was empty except for the bedroom. It was entirely dark in the house except for a single candle in the bedroom. We gently pushed open the door. Inside the chief, naked except for his Shamshir, was sodomizing the young boy. Lost in the throes of ecstasy, the chief didn't notice us. Hunter sneaked up, grabbed him and whispered in his ear in the local dialect that he was about to meet Allah. I was standing in the darkness about ten feet behind them as Hunter kept one hand over the chief's mouth and pressed a knife against his throat. The boy, who was on his hands and knees, turned around. He must have panicked because he grabbed the Shamshir from its casing and, in an instant, thrust the blade through both the chief and Hunter. The boy then ran out of the house. The boy never saw me. I pulled the blade out of Hunter who was still alive, but just barely. He asked me to get him out of there and back to the base. As I carried him he became weaker and weaker. I could feel the life ebbing out of him. It was horrible. He told me to lay him down behind the area we all used as the head and get help. He told me to tell everyone that I found him, carried him as long as I could and left him there. Before I got back he died. I explained the blood on me by saying I found him and carried him as far as I could and as close to the first aid unit on the base. Killing only led to more killing. I lost in almost every way possible."

The sun slipped over the canyon rim creating a new dawn as Echo finished her story.

"The investigation was over quickly, and Hunter became a KIA. The boy who had been continually raped was executed, beheaded by the first act of the new tribal chief."

Echo began to sob. The pain leaving her heart filled the canyon.

"This is the first time I have told anyone what really happened."

She rolled up her sleeve to expose the Fallen Soldier Battle Cross tattoo that honored Hunter and several others from her company. Further up her arm the initials HF, SB and DL were etched in dark blue ink. Zeb eyed the tattoo with a double take. No. This couldn't possibly be the arm that held the gun that whapped him on the back of the head, could it?

The sunrays breaching the entirety of the rim of Crazy Medicine Canyon told Zeb it was roughly fifteen minutes past seven a.m. He knew it was Wednesday, but any further specific details seemed ridiculous to even consider. His mind had travelled far and wide over the last several hours. Somehow the entire world had changed, changed in a way for which he had no words. It seemed as though everything he had known was not wrong, but somehow incomplete. Most of all, the suffering Echo had endured seemed beyond the pale. His heart felt the pain in Echo's heart as she wept. A morning breeze rippled the leaves in the trees. The clarity in Song Bird's eyes belied compassion.

Looking away, Zeb became transfixed on the moon in the early dawn sky. What was it Jake and Song Bird had taught him about that? Something about transition? Something about why God had night escape so quietly on the heels of the oncoming day? Right now that too seemed almost irrelevant. In the eastern sky he saw Venus. He knew from Song Bird and Jake that this month it was the morning star. He took that as a good sign. Venus was the Goddess of love. Her star symbolized true love. Like himself, he wondered if Echo could ever love again.

Zeb's meandering mind was interrupted by Song Bird's hand resting gently atop his head. The medicine man's palm generated a massive amount of heat that seemed to drive itself right down Zeb's spine. From the top of his head to the bottom of his feet he became alive with electric fire.

"Now it is time for you to release the interference from your soul, your heart and your mind," said Song Bird. "Are you prepared to be set free? Are you prepared to set yourself free?"

Zeb didn't know how to answer. He did, however, have a pretty good idea of what Song Bird meant. The interference in his soul, heart and mind was a weight the true gravity of which he had only now come to realize. Hearing Echo's story had somehow shaken some new truth loose inside of him.

Song Bird's hand had somehow dried Zeb up. Thirst that had evaded him now overcame him. He asked for a drink. Song Bird handed him a gourd full of something that tasted much sweeter than water.

"Yes, I think I am ready to say what needs to be said," offered Zeb, his eyes staring off into what was hidden behind the sky. "My heart has been hurt for as long as I can remember, perhaps since childhood. It seems as though my desires and goals, when I achieve them, get taken away."

"Perhaps you release them too soon," noted Song Bird.

A long held tightness in Zeb's chest loosened.

"When my wife, Doreen, was murdered by Carmelita Montouyez, I could only think of revenge. I became obsessed to the point of becoming a drunken bum who dwelled only on his own sorrow and pain. When I realized that alcohol wouldn't solve my problem, I allowed my booze demented brain to make a very bad decision. That decision was to kill Carmelita Montouyez. A sword, held by my hands, slowly pierced her heart. I can still see the look on her face and feel the pressing beat of her heart against the tip of the sword as I slowly tortured her to death. Some days it is all I see. Some nights the vision of it visits me in my sleep. I cannot move forward. I am stuck as if I were buried up to my chin in quicksand."

Zeb hesitated and looked around. Echo and Song Bird were hanging on every word. The fact that he was telling them the truth and that they were hearing it was almost as frightening as what he had done. He continued.

"I fear that my heart full of hatred almost got Helen killed and might get me killed as well. I might deserve it, but I am not ready to die and certainly my actions should have no bearing on someone killing Helen."

"We must always be cognizant of how our actions will affect everything else and everyone else in our lives," said Song Bird. "There is an invisible web that interconnects us with all that is woven by an unseen hand."

"I do not know how to move forward," said Zeb, a painful tear trickling down his cheek.

"You can begin by knowing that what is done is done and over. You own it. It is yours and no one else's. You need not carry it like some sort of badge of honor or foolish cloak of disgrace. No matter how you see it, your actions have led you to this point. The consequences of what you have done may be over or they may not. Either way, you must live your life as a man who has learned complex lessons from his actions."

Zeb lowered his head as the rays of the sun glinted in his eyes. He had never considered his true feelings. He had only acted with hate and revenge in his heart and ended up drawn into perpetual stress from doing so. He stared at his hands. A realization struck him like a bolt of lightning.

"I am my own worst enemy," said Zeb.

"Indeed you are," said Song Bird. "How heavy the burdens of carrying one's own hatred as though it were gold?"

Zeb glanced at Echo. She returned an understanding, hopeful smile and beaming eyes.

"We are birds with broken wings," said Echo. "We need to learn to fly again."

Song Bird grabbed them both by the hands, and the trio began to move slowly in a circle around the dying embers of the fire.

"The life path of all humans is but a circle," said Song Bird.

After five exhausting minutes they all began to laugh joyously. Zeb felt the bliss right down to his bones. Echo felt paradise in her heart. Song Bird could see what they felt. Their hearts had opened just far enough to begin the process of easing themselves of long held burdens and sins.

25

TROUBLE FOR CURTIS LOWE

Helen took the frantic call from Angela Lowe, Curtis' mother.

"Curtis has been shot. He's bleeding. Do something. Send the sheriff." Mrs. Lowe shouted. Her voice was panic stricken.

Helen tried to remain calm as she glanced at the clock. It was two minutes past ten a.m. Less than thirty minutes earlier Sheriff Hanks had called and said he was running late and would be there in forty-five minutes. Jake and Kate would have to handle this one.

"Have you called 9-1-1?"

"Yes, of course, they are on the way. But please send Sheriff Hanks over. He's the only one who can figure this out. Hurry! Please!"

"Angela, Sheriff Hanks is out of the office right now. He is out of contact until later this morning. I can send Deputies Jake Dablo and Kate Steele over right now. They should be there in three minutes or less."

"Please hurry."

"Is Curtis alert?"

"Yes, he's talking to me," replied Angela Lowe. "But just barely."

"Is he making sense?" asked Helen.

"Yes and no. Honestly, I can't tell. I can see that he is in terrible pain. There is blood everywhere."

"Where is the wound?"

"He was shot in his chest, shoulder and arm," replied Angela.

"Did you think the bullets hit the heart or major arteries?"

"No, I don't think so."

Mrs. Lowe was a registered nurse at the local hospital. Helen knew she was quite prepared to handle such things as gunshot wounds and had probably treated as many such injuries as most doctors. But this was her son and that made this an entirely different story. There was no way to make her rational.

"Hold on one second while I tell the sheriff's deputies to get over there."

Helen held the phone against her chest and called out to Jake and Kate. She quickly explained the situation, and they were out the door and on their way to the Lowe household.

"The deputies are on their way right now. Stay on the phone with me until they get there or until the ambulance arrives."

"I'm so scared," said Angela. "Who would do this?"

"That's what I wanted to ask you. Does Curtis have any enemies?"

"No, not that I know of. He practically never leaves the house. He lives in the basement playing those stupid, online, interactive war video games. He even played with some actual soldiers while they were stationed in Afghanistan. One of them was from around here. But really he's just a quiet boy without many friends. I worry about him. I can't believe he would be hanging around with anyone who would shoot him," said Angela. "You saw him when he worked at the sheriff's office. You've seen him around my house since he was little. You know he's a good boy."

Helen kept her lip zipped. Looks could be deceiving and often were. This was neither the time nor the place for a mother to hear the ugly truth about her son.

"Has he said who he thinks shot him?" asked Helen.

"No. He told me that he got out of his car and was walking toward the house when a red truck, a gray motorcycle and a couple of light colored cars drove by. He has an eye for details like that. I was in the house. I thought I heard firecrackers going off. Then I looked out the window and saw Curtis lying on the ground, curled up in a ball, clutching his chest and shoulder. I grabbed my cellphone and a gun and raced outside."

"Why did you grab a gun?" asked Helen.

"I don't know, instinct I guess. There was that drive-by shooting last year, you remember?"

"Yes, of course, some gang-bangers from Tucson," said Helen. "I remember it well."

"No, wait. I grabbed the gun because I could see the blood. I put two and two together and figured someone had shot him. I took it in case I needed to defend myself."

Helen knew the conversation was being recorded and held back from asking any further questions that might implicate Angela. Helen couldn't help but wonder who kept a loaded gun by the door unless they suspected something bad might happen? If you were a criminal or a cop, then maybe, but a civilian? It didn't make sense other than there was no real man in the house. Off the top of her head, Helen didn't remember any break-ins at the Lowe residence. In the background Helen heard the police siren and the whoop-whoop of the ambulance racing to the scene.

"They're here now. Thanks, Helen," said Angela as she dropped the call.

Helen dialed Zeb's cellphone. He answered on the third ring.

"Someone just shot Curtis Lowe?"

"Is he dead?" asked Zeb.

"No. Kate and Jake are there now and so is the ambulance."

"I'll head directly to the hospital," said Zeb.

Minutes later Zeb walked through the doors of the Safford Hospital ER. The admitting nurse took one look at him and pointed to Room 1.

"Doctor Yackley is with him. Your deputies are too. Try not to stick around too long. He's hurt pretty badly, and Doctor Yackley needs room for staff in there. Don't get in his way."

Zeb tipped his hat. "Yes, ma'am. Thank you."

An IV drip had already been inserted, Curtis' clothes had been cut away and preliminary preparations for removing the bullet fragments were taking place. Doc Yackley was working steadily on the wounds. Curtis was drifting off into unconsciousness. Zeb stood by his deputies.

"Did he say who did this?" asked Zeb.

"He claims he didn't see anything," said Jake.

"He was shot in the chest in broad daylight and he didn't see anything? That's bullshit," said Zeb. "He had to be facing whoever shot him."

"Zeb, Jake, Kate, take it outside. He's out cold. I prefer to work without the background chatter, unless you can sing my favorite Patsy Cline songs. You can't find out anything now anyway. I'll let you know how he is once I get the lead out of him," said Doc.

Kate and Zeb abruptly left the room. Zeb loitered momentarily to ask Doc a question.

"Thanks, Doc. Is he going to be all right?" asked Zeb.

"Maybe," said Doc. "Maybe not. Depends on how much internal bleeding I find and how quickly I can stop it. Between you and me, his odds are fifty-fifty."

Zeb nodded and left the room. Another murder, even an attempted murder, was going to be tough on the city. People were going to be beating a path to the sheriff's office demanding answers. Zeb had little else on his mind as he met Jake and Kate in the hallway.

"Did Curtis say anything to you two?" asked Zeb.

"One thing," said Jake.

"Which was?" asked Zeb.

"He took one look at us and said, 'I hate all cops'. Then he passed out," said Jake.

"I hope he pulls through," said Kate.

"He will," said Jake. "He's young and a youthful body has a lot of resilience. He'll make it."

"Doc says its fifty-fifty as it sits right now."

"Does his mom know that?" asked Kate.

The three of them spotted Angela Lowe pacing back and forth in the waiting room. She motioned to Zeb. Kate and Jake stepped toward an exit door to give Angie and Zeb some privacy.

"What did Doc tell you? Don't lie to me," said Angela. "I saw the wounds."

"He's got better than a fighting chance. It isn't going to be easy, but given the fact he's young and healthy there's a really good chance he'll pull through just fine."

Zeb had colored the truth and felt badly about it. He felt even worse as Angela collapsed in his arms. He held her momentarily before helping her into a chair. He got her a bottle of water.

"I'm scared to death," she said. "I saw him. I've treated a lot of wounds like this one. I know you gave me the sugar coated version, but I also know from the look on your face that there is hope my son will pull through."

"It's a good time to get something to eat and spend a few moments in the chapel," said Zeb. "A little prayer can go a long way. Curtis is going to be in surgery for a while."

"Thank you, Zeb. I really appreciate all your help," said Angela.

Once again Angela threw her arms around him. This time her body shook as she wept uncontrollably. Zeb held her until the body spasms stopped.

"I'll be checking in. One of my deputies will be around if you need anything," said Zeb. "We'll do whatever we can."

Zeb asked the admitting nurse to get one of Angela's friends to stay with her for a while. The nurse stepped into the nurse administrator's room and stepped back out with a woman who was a close friend of Angela's. Slowly she and Angela made their way down the long hallway toward the cafeteria. Zeb doubted she would eat much, but she needed the distractions of food and prayer. After watching her walk away, he went to meet Jake and Kate.

"I want one of us here when Curtis wakes up," said Zeb. "We need to find out what he knows and what he meant when he said he hated all cops."

"Probably something to do with his old man being in prison," said Jake.

"Maybe," said Kate. "But maybe it has to do with the shooting."

"None of us shot him," said Jake.

"We aren't the only cops in the area," replied Kate.

"Do you have someone in mind?" asked Zeb.

"Do you?" replied Kate.

"I think we all have some ideas," replied Jake.

26

RODRIGUEZ

Zeb headed to the office. Zeb's mind was as clear as the blue sky over Mount Graham as he pondered the peyote ceremony he had just undergone. A powerful second thought, his upcoming steak dinner with Echo, felt good in an anxious sort of way.

The shooting of Curtis gave Zeb definite pause. It could have been an initiation rite from a Tucson gang, like the one that occurred last year. Also, it wasn't unreasonable to believe that Curtis had pissed someone off trying to figure out who was responsible for putting his father in prison. It could even be another oddball, like Curtis, who spent their life in their mother's basement and was pissed off because Curtis had kicked his ass in computer gaming and rubbed it in once too often. Zeb assumed, based on what he knew of Curtis, that he was just dumb enough to expose his real name in the gaming world. In any case Zeb was fairly certain whoever shot Curtis wasn't bright enough to keep it a secret for too long. Odds were good the shooter would expose himself sooner rather than later.

One thing, above all else, stuck in Zeb's brain. Why had Curtis made such a curious hospital bed statement to Jake and Kate that he hated all cops? It may simply have been Curtis' state of mind from being shot and lying there bleeding. It might have been that the cops were the first on the scene and the words just spontaneously came out of his mouth. Zeb knew from experience that gravely injured people who were in shock often made incoherent statements. He'd know more when he interrogated the injured young man, which he hoped would be very soon.

Arriving at the sheriff's office, Zeb found FBI Agent Rodriguez's truck parked in the sheriff's personal parking space. Zeb nudged the nose of his truck against the tailgate of Rodriguez's vehicle, blocking it from any possibility of going anywhere, and jammed the gearshift into park.

"Goddamn Rodriguez," he muttered. "He just keeps asking for it. He's gonna get what he asks for sooner or later."

Inside the sheriff's office Rodriguez was chatting it up with Helen who was doing the very best her polite nature would allow to ignore him.

Only a few days earlier Zeb would have grabbed Rodriguez by the collar and gotten into a face-to-face confrontation with him. The peyote ceremony had somehow changed what he felt an appropriate reaction would be. Just blocking his truck was enough.

"Agent Rodriguez," said Zeb.

"Sheriff Hanks," replied Rodriguez.

"I saw your vehicle."

"Yeah, I thought you wouldn't mind if I used your parking space, since it was empty anyway."

Helen surreptitiously peeked out the window and saw what Zeb had done. Quietly she said, 'Yes!"

"I assume you are here to see me about something?" asked Zeb.

Rodriguez handed Zeb a manila folder. When Zeb began to open it, Rodriguez suggested it was a matter that might be better served by privacy.

"Please, come into my office and have a seat," said Zeb, holding the door open for the agent much to the surprise of the agent and consternation of Helen.

Agent Rodriguez casually took the chair across from Zeb, never once taking his eyes off the sheriff. Zeb placed the folder on his desk and ran a finger slowly across it a few times before rolling his fingers, quietly wondering exactly what kind of surprise might be waiting inside the agent's little gift.

"Open it," said Rodriguez.

"Now?" asked Zeb.

"Of course. It's for your eyes only," said Rodriguez.

Zeb removed the Randall knife from his belt and used it as a letter opener. He placed the knife on his desk. Rodriguez placed himself in a slightly defensive posture. All too often in his career he'd seen the damage a knife could do and how quickly it could inflict serious harm.

Zeb removed three 8 x 10 glossy pictures from the envelope which he immediately recognized. They had all been taken in San Iglesias, Mexico on the Feast Day of Santo Diego. The first picture was a picture of Josh hidden behind some trees aiming a rifle in the general direction of the church. He had been providing cover for Zeb who was waiting for the cartel head to show up at the Mission San Iglesias to make his yearly generous donation. Zeb was ticked off at himself for putting Josh in such imminent danger. The second image was Carmelita and Zeb sitting on a bench outside the mission. The final picture was Zeb and Carmelita, naked, in her bedroom. Zeb looked up at Rodriguez but said nothing. Every thought he'd had regarding Rodriguez being in the pocket of the cartel was feeling more like the truth. Zeb asked Rodriguez a question he already knew the answer to.

"What exactly is your point?"

"Seriously?" asked Rodriguez.

It appeared Rodriguez may not have been kidding when he had said he was Carmelita's lover. It was proof positive the agent had been a tool of the cartel. There was only one way this was going to end--badly.

"Why didn't you kill me when you broke into my computer?" asked Zeb.

"What the hell would I want with your computer?" asked Rodriguez.

Zeb did a double take. The emphatic FBI agent appeared to be telling the truth. If it wasn't Rodriguez who had broken into the office and banged him on the head, who had? Zeb unconsciously rubbed the injured area. Then again, if Rodriguez had been working for the cartel while simultaneously being an FBI agent, he would have the art of lying perfected.

"I heard about that little incident," said Rodriguez. "I was surprised someone could get the upper hand on you so easily."

"I'm going to open my desk drawer," said Zeb. "I have something I want you to look at."

Rodriguez fingered his gun. Zeb removed a piece of paper, placed in on the desk and slid it over to the agent. Rodriguez eyed the paper and read it aloud.

"The best revenge is revenge. This isn't over. We will meet again."

"From you?" asked Zeb. "Just curious."

Rodriguez eyed it from every angle before speaking.

"Looks a lot like my handwriting."

Zeb leaned forward and slipped the .45 caliber Kimber Ultra-Carry II from its holster.

"Is this the day we meet again?"

"Not when you've got a gun pointed right at my heart and an itchy trigger finger," said Rodriguez.

"Then what's this all about?"

"Just wanted to see the look on your face when you looked at my dead lover, Carmelita. I just wanted proof you were the one who stuck a sword through her heart and tortured her to death," said Rodriguez.

Rodriguez rested his arm on the desk. He had cleverly slipped his second weapon from his sleeve and now had it aimed directly at Zeb's chest.

"For what it's worth, I never loved her," said Zeb.

"But you did love Doreen."

"Indeed I did. I loved her enough to avenge her murder," said Zeb.

"Perfect answer. That is exactly how much I loved Carmelita."

The buzzer on Zeb's phone hummed from the outside office.

"Helen keeps a pretty close eye on things, doesn't she? I bet you'd hate to lose her," said Rodriguez.

"Keep her out of this. This is between you and me," said Zeb. "If anything happens to her, there are a number of people who won't hesitate to see that you have breathed your last breath."

Rodriguez stood, pivoted and walked toward the door. Zeb followed closely on his heels. There were no circumstances under which he would allow Rodriguez to put a bullet in Helen.

Rodriguez stopped at the door. Without turning around, he spoke.

"I hear your boot heels," he said. "Don't worry, Helen is safe. I agree wholeheartedly, this little tango is a dance that is only between you and me."

He opened the door to Zeb's office only to walk directly into Jake and Kate.

"Yes, it is," said Zeb. "It's just between you and me."

Rodriguez stormed out of the office.

"What was that all about?" asked Jake.

"It's private," replied Zeb.

"I'll add that to my list of things you don't want to talk about," quipped Jake.

"We just got a call from the hospital," said Kate. "Curtis is out of surgery and has been moved to a private room."

"Great. I'll head over to the hospital right now," said Zeb.

27

WHAT HAPPENED

Zeb stopped at admitting to see what room Curtis was in. He ran into Doc Yackley in the hallway as Doc was leaving Curtis' room.

"How's the patient? Can I talk to him?" asked Zeb.

"His mother is in there with him now," said Doc. "She's pretty shook up even though she knows it could have been much worse."

"I don't imagine anyone likes to see their kid lying in a hospital bed recovering from gunshot wounds," replied Zeb.

"Just go lightly on him when his mother is in there," suggested Doc.

"I know Angie. We go way back. She and Helen are friends. She called the office and specifically asked for me when Curtis was shot. I think she trusts me. Nevertheless, I will watch my ps and qs. How's he doing?"

"An angel must have been dancing on his shoulder when he took the bullets. I've seen people with worse injuries from peeling potatoes. There were two bullets, both .45's. One went in and out of the back of his upper arm. The other went right through his chest wall and out his back, didn't even nick a bone. Damn miracle if you ask me. An inch either way and you've got a major artery, a rapid bleed out and likely a quick death," said Doc.

"Do you anticipate a full recovery?"

"More or less. There is nothing from the injuries that should make a whole lot of difference, physically that is. But he seems to be the kind of young man that might have some psychological terror from the whole thing. It isn't like his life has been a piece of cake recently," said Doc.

"You don't know the half of it, Doc."

"Want to tell me? It may make a difference in his recovery."

"I'd like to, but I can't right now. It involves an ongoing investigation."

"Is Curtis somehow related to Sun Rey's murder?" asked Doc.

Zeb smiled. "We've got a lot of open cases, Doc. All I can say is that Curtis is involved in one of them."

"Do you think it has to do with him taking a couple of slugs from a .45?"

"I hope not, Doc. Enough of the amateur sleuthing on your part."

"Fine. Let's take a walk. I need a cigarette," said Doc.

"Thought you gave that evil business up," said Zeb.

"I did," said Doc. "A long time ago."

The men stepped outside a side door, well-hidden from the view of any potential passers-by. Doc pulled a solitary cigarette from the inside of his white coat and lit it with a zippo lighter he pulled from his back pocket.

"Is Curtis doped up?" asked Zeb.

"Yup."

"Can I talk with him?"

"Yup."

"Think he'll give me straight answers?" asked Zeb.

"He'll more likely give you dopey answers. His mind is still in a post-surgical fog, but my best guess is that he will likely chat it up. Like I said, please be careful what you say around his mother. I gave her some Valium because she was so jittery. It's got to be tough on her with her husband in prison and her son having been on the receiving end of a pair of gun shots," said Doc.

"Can I consider his answers to be legit, or is he too doped up from the drugs?" asked Zeb.

"No two people are alike. Some people are actually more honest in this state of mind. The drugs act almost like a truth serum. Others start spinning lies faster than a politician on the day before an election," replied Doc. "He's a young kid, so you never know. I would guess, based on experience, no matter what face he puts on, he's scared to death. That might work to your advantage. He might give you something unexpectedly true. But that's just an educated guess."

Doc inhaled the cigarette with two deep drags, dropped the butt of his cigarette to the ground and crushed it with the heel of his cowboy boot.

"I've got to get back to the old salt mine," said Doc with a wink. "Go easy on the boy. He's had a bad day and a bad couple of years. I suspect all kinds of nasty shit is brewing up inside of him."

Inside the door Doc went one way and Zeb headed the other, directly to Curtis' room. He peeked through the glass and saw a mother talking to her son. From the drifting of his eyeballs and rolling of his eyelids Curtis appeared to be about half conscious. Angela Lowe had obviously been crying. Zeb tapped lightly on the door. Angela motioned him in. She blew her nose and stuffed the handkerchief away as Zeb approached the bed.

Inside the room Zeb took off his hat and stood solemnly at the edge of the bed. Curtis had fallen asleep and was purring softly. Angela stood, walked toward Zeb and threw her arms around him and began to sob. Zeb rubbed her back and gave her what assurance he could, that everything would be all right.

"Angie, he's got youth and luck on his side. I just talked with Doc. He said it was practically a miracle that the bullets did such little damage," said Zeb. "That's something to be grateful for."

Angela Lowe steadfastly held onto Zeb, as if she might crumble if she loosened her grip. Zeb could feel her weakness and her strength. His mind went to Levi Lowe's prison cell. He should be here, holding his wife, comforting her. Eventually she let go. As she returned to her chair next to Curtis, she passed by a mirror, ran a few fingers through her hair and grabbed a tissue to wipe away runny mascara.

"Oh, my God. I look a fright," she said.

"You look fine," said Zeb as she quickly straightened herself up a bit while looking in the mirror.

"I am so pissed off at Levi for being in prison, I can't tell you..."

"I know he'd give his right arm to be here. I'll talk to the warden and see if I can arrange a visit, if you'd like," said Zeb. "The warden owes me a few favors. Levi is hardly a hardened criminal. I can probably even get him over here fairly soon."

"Oh, Zeb, you're an angel. You always were the good guy."

Zeb blushed, not out of embarrassment but rather because he helped put Levi in jail for something he probably had a lot less to do with than the criminal court had decided. He also thought of how little of the truth Angie actually knew. Zeb thought of how she had described him. He was many things, but certainly not always a good guy. He was grateful she chose to see his good side as opposed to his darker side.

"I'll take care of it when I'm done here," said Zeb. "A father should get to see his son under these circumstances, and he should be here for you."

Tears began to stream down Angela's cheeks. "Thank you so much, Zeb. I really don't know how to thank you."

"Come next election throw your vote my way," joked Zeb.

The brief moment of levity made the heaviness in the room lessen considerably.

"How's Curtis seem to you?" asked Zeb.

"Doped up. He says he's not even in pain. He keeps nodding in and out, so I figure the drugs are still doing their work."

"When he comes to, does he say much?"

"He keeps apologizing, like it was his fault or something. I don't quite get what he's talking about. Do you have any idea why he's apologizing?" asked Angela.

"Maybe. Nothing for certain. If he comes to, do you mind if I ask him a few questions?" asked Zeb.

"Certainly not. If he has any idea who shot him, we need to know who it is and find them right away."

"We will," said Zeb.

Angela reached over, placed her son's hand in her own and began stroking the back of his arm. She seemed lost in thought so Zeb remained quiet, observing the motherly love she was giving her son. Her actions reminded him of his own mother. Eventually Angela spoke. She asked Zeb a question that seemed to come out of the blue.

"You don't think this has anything to do with Levi being in jail?" she asked.

It was the kind of question that comes out of the mouth of someone who knows more than they want to say.

"Why do you ask?"

"Oh, I don't know," said Angela, "Just a thought that came over me. I've always felt like somebody on the Rez viewed this whole thing as a White-Apache conspiracy and, even though Levi ended up in jail, the Apaches thought he got away with something."

Curtis began to stir and his eyes opened to the sight of his mother.

"Hey," he said.

"Hey," she replied. Did you get a good nap?"

"I didn't even know I was asleep," said Curtis. "I thought I heard you and dad talking about me."

"You probably heard Sheriff Hank's voice in your sleep," said Angela. "He stopped by."

Curtis turned his head in Zeb's direction.

"I don't know who shot me, if that's what you're here for. If I did, believe me, I'd tell you," said Curtis.

"How are you feeling?" asked Zeb.

"Weird," said Curtis. "It's like a dream. Like a waking dream, but not a daydream."

"I've been shot and I came out of surgery feeling the same way," said Zeb.

"Really?" said Curtis. "Cool."

"Mind if I ask you a few questions?" asked Zeb.

"Shoot away," said Curtis, not realizing his pun.

"What's the last thing you remember?" asked Zeb. "That is, before you were shot."

Curtis rubbed the top of his head and put his palms against his eyeballs, as if to exaggerate how hard he was thinking.

"Take your time," said Zeb. "There's no rush. I want you to think as clearly as you possibly can."

"I am. I think I am anyway. I had just gotten out of my car. I remember dropping the keys on the floor of the car and digging around for them. Then I heard a motorcycle go by. It roared like it had cutoffs on the mufflers. I looked up to see who it was. The motorcycle was silver colored and sleek looking. I remember thinking that if I was ever rich I'd get one just like it."

"Not if I have anything to say about it," said Angela.

"Mom."

"Mom, nothing. No dangerous vehicles and that means motorcycles."

Curtis rolled his eyes.

"Then you got out of your car?" asked Zeb.

"Yeah."

"Did you lock it?" asked Zeb.

"You're kidding, right? That old junk heap is only worth a couple of hundred bucks," said Curtis.

"Okay, so you didn't lock it, but you got out and moved away from the car?"

"That's right. I got out and started walking up the sidewalk. I remember thinking how brown the grass in the yard looked, even for this time of year. I was carrying something, an apple or a banana, some piece of fruit."

"I found an orange on the sidewalk the next day," added Angela.

"It was an orange. That's right, an orange. I was a little bit hungry, and I picked one up at the Safeway store, actually two of them. I must've eaten one."

"Then what happened?"

"I just fell to the ground. It was like some invisible person tripped me. I thought I'd hit my nose and gotten a nosebleed or cut my head because I saw blood, lots of it. I figured I'd cut myself pretty badly so I shouted out so my mom could hear me. But I guess I fell because I was shot. At least that's what Doctor Yackley said. He said I was shot twice by a .45. He said I must have had a guardian angel. I guess he's right about that."

"You were shot on the front part of your body. We have it possibly pegged as a drive-by shooting..."

"Like the one last year when Jimmy Ellinghysen was shot. I remember that. Jimmy wasn't quite so lucky, was he?"

"He's out of rehab and walking with a cane these days," said Zeb. "He's coming around."

"Good. He was always nice to me in school, good guy."

"Do you think you might have turned around and been shot by someone in a passing car or truck?" asked Zeb. "If this was a drive-by shooting, you would have been facing the street based on the location of your entry wounds."

"I don't have any memory of turning around," said Curtis. "I'm getting really tired."

"Can we stop for a while, Zeb?" asked Angela

"Sure. Curtis needs his rest. I can ask him more questions when he's feeling better," said Zeb.

"Thanks for your help," said Angela. "If he mentions anything, I'll be sure and relay that information to you."

"Thanks, Angie, I appreciate that."

Angela Lowe stood and gave Zeb a long hug. Zeb glanced at Curtis. Through Curtis' half-opened eyes, Zeb thought he saw both anger and confusion.

28

THE POWER OF LOZEN

Zeb called the warden at the federal prison in Safford from his truck. The warden agreed to allow Levi Lowe to visit to his son at the hospital. Then Zeb called Kate.

"Meet me at the Lowe residence."

"You got something, Zeb?" asked Kate.

"I don't know, maybe. I need your help determining the location of the shooter. I just talked with Curtis. What he tells me doesn't make sense."

"Is he lying to you?"

"I don't know. He's pretty doped up."

"One other thing. What's your favorite wine?" asked Kate.

"What?"

"Your dinner date stopped by and asked me. I thought it was Merlot, but since you're on the phone, I thought I'd ask," said Kate.

"Merlot is fine. Is she still there?"

"Yes?"

"Being that she was so incredibly accurate in figuring out the trajectory of the shot that killed Sun Rey, maybe she can lend us a helping hand," said Zeb.

"I'll have her follow me."

Five minutes later Kate, Echo and Zeb stood on the sidewalk where Curtis' spilled blood was already beginning to fade. Zeb thanked Echo for coming.

"What do we know?" asked Echo.

"Curtis Lowe was shot with entry wounds in the right chest and right upper arm/shoulder area," said Zeb. "Doc said it was practically a miracle that there was no major damage. Curtis even denied having any pain when he got shot. He says it felt like he tripped on something, cut himself and then saw blood."

"Check," said Kate.

"In combat I don't know of anyone who felt much of anything until after the injury took hold," said Echo. "He certainly could be telling the truth."

"He claims he was walking up the sidewalk toward the house, just after having parked his car, when he was shot," said Zeb.

"Did you have a long talk with him or just ask him a few questions?"

"It was a brief chat. His mother, Angela, was present too."

"Could she verify what he said?" asked Kate.

"I didn't ask, but I think she would have said something. I'll ask her later. We're going back over there when we're done here."

"So you don't really suspect this was a drive-by shooting?" asked Kate.

"If he's telling the truth, it couldn't have been. He had his back to the street, and both bullets entered him on the front of his body, according to Doc," said Zeb. "The shots would have come from over there."

Zeb pointed to a small grove of trees behind the neighbor's house, about seventy-five feet away from the sidewalk.

"We'd better talk to the neighbor," said Kate.

The neighbor was a balding bachelor with a protruding potbelly and long, greasy hair that looked like it hadn't been washed in weeks. He brought up his neighbors, the Lowes with whom he said he wasn't close.

"I haven't seen Levi around lately, but, then again, I work nights, so I don't see much of anyone. Guess that's why I'm still a bachelor."

"Have you walked by those trees on the south side of your house lately?" asked Zeb.

"No, sir. No reason to go over there."

"We'd like to have a look at that area," said Zeb. "With your permission, of course."

"Sure, there's no one else to ask. I live alone. I work 60 hours a week at the copper mine in Morenci. You can verify that by calling my supervisor, Al Cashton."

Kate made a note.

"I'll give Mr. Cashton a call," said Kate.

"My name is Del Tripton, Jr. Named after my daddy. He worked the Morenci mines too. Am I a suspect?" asked Del.

"No," replied Kate. "We just need to verify what you told us."

"If I was under suspicion, it would be the most exciting thing to happen to me since the cave-in back in oh-nine, the spring cave-in, not the winter one."

Zeb, Kate and Echo nodded. The man didn't wear his loneliness well at all.

"Mind if we look around at that edge of your property line, by those shrubs and those two thorn trees over there?" asked Zeb.

"Sure 'nuff. Need some help?"

"Thank you, we're fine, Del. We really appreciate your cooperation."

"Imagine that, my yard being a possible crime scene."

"Yes, sir," replied Kate. "Imagine that."

Del Tripton, Jr. suddenly perked up.

"Ladies, there's a dance at the VFW tonight. Either of you looking to do some drinking and dancing on my dollar. I ain't much to look at, but I can dance like Fred Astaire and John Travolta combined."

Kate held up her engagement ring. The man frowned. "How about you, young lady?"

"Thanks, I've got a date," replied Echo. "But it is awfully nice of you to ask. I do appreciate the gesture."

"I'd say this town has some real lucky men that get to date the likes of you two. Kind of figured it would be a long shot for either of you to want to go dancing with me. If I were only younger, richer and better looking," he said, closing the door and patting his belly affectionately.

Fifteen minutes later Kate and Zeb had scoured the area and had no more information. If someone had fired from here, they had picked up their casings. The mostly dead grass was sparse, and no obvious footprints were anywhere to be seen.

"Nothing," said Zeb.

"A whole lot of nothing," agreed Kate.

Echo stood silently off to one side. She held her right hand over her head with the palm facing the sidewalk where Curtis had fallen. Then she lifted her palms upward, outstretched. "Usen," she said. Kate and Zeb became quiet. She turned to them and spoke again. Her words were confusing. Then Zeb remembered what he had heard about Echo having the power of Lozen.

"There was a whirlwind in this thorn tree not long ago."

"What does that mean?" asked Zeb.

"It's complicated," replied Echo. "I have never talked about it with anyone. Sometimes I'm not so sure I understand it myself."

"What do you mean a whirlwind in the thorn tree?" asked Kate.

"Leaving a trail is like whispering a secret."

"I'm sorry, I'm not following you, Echo," replied Kate.

"It means the shooter shot from here. Right here, or at least he stood right here. If we look around, we will find evidence of his being here," explained Echo.

"His? It was a man?" asked Kate.

"Yes. Of that I am one hundred percent certain."

They soon discovered some recently fallen needles from a nearby pine tree had covered his tracks. Echo walked to the base of a nearby tree where she found an imprint of a knee. Zeb and Kate joined her.

"Looks like the shooter knelt here and steadied his arm against the tree," said Zeb. "I'm surprised he didn't get him right through the heart."

Kate paced off the distance between the bloodstains where Curtis had fallen and the tree. It was seventy feet. Definitely not a sure shot with a .45 caliber handgun.

"The shooter took a chance," said Zeb. "He must have been desperate."

"Maybe it was his only chance at a shot," said Kate. "Maybe one of the vehicles traveling the street blew his cover?"

"Wait a second. Curtis said he stumbled when he was walking down the sidewalk. Maybe he really did have a guardian angel looking over his shoulder. Maybe the stumble was perfectly timed in such a manner to have the shooter miss his mark."

"That makes sense," said Echo. "Only a true marksman would try for a kill shot with a hand gun from seventy feet. The shooter got cocky."

"And Curtis got damn lucky," said Zeb.

"Lifesaving lucky," added Kate.

Both Zeb and Kate were dying to understand how Echo knew what she knew.

"How did you know?" asked Zeb.

Echo answered with a single word, "Lozen."

The way she said it made it sound sacred and mysterious. It felt like one of those things that shouldn't be probed, rather it was something Echo would explain if and when she chose. Kate was polite enough not to ask. Zeb knew better than to ask.

Zeb moved closer to Echo. Seeing that the two wanted a private moment Kate moved away.

"See you at eighteen hundred hours," said Zeb

"I'll be on time," replied Echo.

29

HOSPITAL

"Let's go back to the hospital. I want to see the interaction between father and son," said Zeb.

"What do expect to see?" asked Kate.

"No idea," replied Zeb. "I have no idea what their relationship is, other than Curtis was trying to raise money to pay a lawyer to get his dad out of prison."

Zeb and Kate arrived at the hospital just as the prison guards were leading Levi Lowe into the hospital.

Zeb motioned the prison guards to wait.

"What are we doing?" asked Kate.

"I want to see the expression on both Curtis' and Levi's faces when they first see each other," replied Zeb.

"What do you hope to see?"

"Some truth," replied Zeb. "Maybe the real story of what is going on."

Zeb approached his old friend Levi. They shook hands but exchanged no words. Levi entered the room with the guards, Zeb and Kate on their heels. Levi Lowe stopped dead in his tracks when he saw his son hooked up to all the medical equipment. Curtis looked at his dad and began to cry.

"I was just trying to raise money to hire you a better lawyer and get you out of prison," said Curtis.

"May I give my son a hug?" Levi asked the guards. They looked toward Zeb. Zeb nodded. Levi bent over his son and whispered in his ear. "Don't say anything incriminating." He hugged his son and spoke loudly enough for all to hear, "I love you. You are going to be all right. Everything is going to be all right."

"Thanks, Dad."

Doc Yackley walked into the room.

"Levi, glad you're able to see your son. Don't worry, he's in good hands. He did really well for someone who caught a couple of .45s the hard way. He's a tougher kid than I thought. Takes after his old man."

"Is his arm going to be okay?" asked Levi.

"Should be able to use it one hundred percent," replied Doc. "It's gonna hurt for a while, but we got pain medication and PT for that."

"Thanks, Doc."

"The nurse is going to give him a dose of morphine in the drip line in about two minutes, so do your talking now. The drug will make him sleepy," said Doc.

"I'll be around later to check on you, son," said Doc.

"Thank you, Doctor Yackley," said Curtis.

"May I speak with my son in private?" Levi asked the guards.

"No. We have to be with you at all times," replied one of the guards.

"Zeb, you know me. I won't do anything. Can you assure the guards it will be okay for me to have a few private minutes with my son?"

"Sorry, Levi. Not in my jurisdiction," replied Zeb.

Father and son talked innocuously about how each other was doing. The nurse came in, pumped some morphine into the line and within a minute Curtis could barely keep his eyes open.

"Let's go," said the guard. "He's out of it."

Levi kissed his son on the forehead, turned, said goodbye to Zeb and Kate and headed out the door.

"It's all so sad," said Kate.

Zeb stuck his head out of the hospital room door to make sure the guards were walking Levi out of the building. When he was certain, he approached the doped up Curtis.

"Curtis, can you hear me?" asked Zeb.

Curtis' eyelids fluttered, and he opened his eyes.

"Sheriff Hanks? When did you get here?"

"Just now. I have a couple of questions. Feel like talking?"

In his doped up condition, Curtis agreed.

"Who hit me on the head? Did you?"

"No," replied Curtis.

"Who did then?"

Curtis looked confused.

"Didn't you already ask me this?"

"I did," replied Zeb. "But you said you'd tell me later."

"I did?"

"Yes, you said you wanted to get it off your chest," said Zeb.

The injury combined with the morphine made Zeb's statement sound exactly like the truth.

"Promise you won't tell anyone?" asked Curtis.

"It'll be our little secret," replied Zeb.

"I probably shouldn't tell you this, but since you're okay, why not?"

The drugs were doing exactly as Zeb had hoped.

"Who hit me, Curtis?"

"Agent Rodriguez."

Zeb stepped back. His anger carried the strength of a summer thunderhead, but peyote had taught him the lesson of collecting his power and using it when the time was right. To be ruled by anger was a burden and served no purpose. It was a lesson Zeb was practicing.

"Agent Rodriguez?" asked Zeb. "Curious choice of friends for someone like you."

"He was helping me get the information off the computer," said Curtis.

"Why? How was he your friend?" asked Zeb.

"I barely knew him. He approached me because he knew that I had seen him with my dad several times," said Curtis. "We got to be friends, or should I say we got to a point where we could help each other."

"You told me you didn't know who it was the first time I asked you," said Zeb.

"I know. I lied. Sorry."

"Everyone lies," replied Zeb.

"It was kind of like playing war," continued Curtis. "We were getting information from your office computer. It was supposed to be like a clandestine op. Agent Rodriguez is a war veteran you know. He was a sniper."

"I know," said Zeb. "I know."

"I'm so tired, and I can't even keep my eyes open."

Zeb patted Curtis on the head, and he fell asleep.

"You were right about suspecting Agent Rodriguez," said Kate. "You want me to go pick him up?"

"No, that won't be necessary. We have to gather some more information from Curtis when he can talk to us with a clear head. What he told us, considering the morphine and since no attorney was present, wouldn't be admissible as evidence against Rodriguez anyway. We can only hope it isn't the last time he talks to us," said Zeb.

Zeb and Kate's boot heels clicked loudly as they walked down the empty hallway of the hospital.

"Let's call it a day," said Zeb.

"Good idea," replied Kate. "I've promised Josh to cook his favorite meal tonight."

"Geez, thanks for reminding me. In all the hubbub it skipped my mind," said Zeb.

"You forgot that you're cooking Echo supper tonight?"

"Well, I didn't forget. I would've remembered when I got home because I left the steaks out to thaw."

"You're going to have to work on your dating skills," said Kate. "A woman likes to think you've been thinking about her all day."

"Really? You're kidding? I never knew that."

Kate rapped her knuckles against Zeb's forehead.

"Exactly as I thought."

"What?" asked Zeb.

"Rocks. You've got rocks in your head."

30

DINNER

Echo arrived exactly at six carrying a bottle of wine. She handed it to Zeb as she passed over the threshold.

"Merlot," she said. "I thought it would go good with grilled steak."

"Thanks, it will."

"Don't sound so enthusiastic. I would have done almost anything for a good bottle of wine in Afghanistan."

"I suppose the Army feeds its soldiers steak on a regular basis," joked Zeb.

"No, but we stole a cow from an Afghani group that had been harassing us. We butchered it and ate like kings for a week."

Zeb didn't know whether she was pulling his leg or not. He simply shook his head as he helped her remove her light coat. Force of habit had him double checking to see if she was carrying a weapon of any kind. She wasn't, as far as he could tell. He was half hoping she was carrying in case Rodriguez made some sort of surprise appearance. She would be perfect back up.

"How are you doing since our Crazy Medicine Canyon adventure?" asked Zeb.

"It was good for my soul," replied Echo. "It made me realize the importance of honesty."

"I can relate to that," said Zeb.

"I also realized that mortal wounds don't always come from a bullet or an IED. I think I was well on the way to being permanently injured instead of healing."

Zeb nodded. There was nothing he could add to that.

"How about you?" asked Echo.

"I guess it made me realize I may not always be the best judge of character."

"You sound like you're talking about someone specifically," said Echo.

Her pointed remark caught Zeb off guard. He hung his head, lifted it up and looked Echo straight in the eye.

"I am."

"Is this about Curtis Lowe getting shot?" asked Echo.

Zeb did a double take. That wasn't at all what he was talking about, but now it was on his mind. There was a constant nagging in the back of his mind that Echo could have been the shooter? After all, at the time of the shooting a motorcycle with a description quite like hers had driven by. His mind was spinning. Ordering it to slow down was no easy task.

"In a roundabout way, I guess," replied Zeb. "What makes you ask?"

"I am friends with Curtis. He and I have talked a lot. I hope you find out who pulled the trigger on him," said Echo.

Zeb rubbed the base of his skull where he had been whacked during the break-in at the sheriff's office.

"How is that healing up? Did you figure out who hit you?" asked Echo.

"I had a little help from some morphine," replied Zeb.

"I should have guessed. Special Ops uses morphine sometimes. We called it truth serum. When you went back to the hospital, you got Curtis to talk, didn't you?"

"He wanted to confess," said Zeb. "He's caught up in a world of guilt."

"Maybe more than anyone knows," replied Echo.

"Do you know something I don't?" asked Zeb.

"I know a lot you don't, and you know a lot that I don't," she replied.

"Why so coy?"

"Like I said, Curtis and I are friends. I don't want to betray his trust. He's suffering much the same way you and I suffer. His dad is in jail. He just got shot, twice. He's in physical pain. His emotional world is upside down."

"Is he looking for revenge?" asked Zeb.

"Maybe. Maybe he's already taken his revenge," said Echo. "I know him, but I don't know him well enough to answer that."

"Do you think his revenge was breaking into my office and stealing what was on my computer?"

"Pretty good chance that's what he was thinking. If he made the sheriff's office, meaning you, look foolish by being broken into, it might just be the revenge he wanted against you for helping put his dad in prison."

"I didn't put his dad in prison. I merely helped with the background connections and local stuff. His dad admitted to everything. No one made him confess. He gave himself up."

"Curtis didn't tell you someone threatened to kill him if he didn't get the information from your computer?" asked Echo.

"No, he didn't. Who wanted to kill him?" asked Zeb.

"Someone connected to Sun Rey," said Echo.

"Go on, this is getting interesting," said Zeb. "You seem to know an awful lot about this."

"I spent three solid years in Afghanistan extrapolating information from women who feared for their lives if they talked. It's my area of expertise. Getting information from Curtis was like shooting fish in a barrel."

A strange thought ran through Zeb's mind. What if she were interrogating him right at this very moment?

"Do I need to watch what I say around you?" asked Zeb.

"Of course you do. Now let's have a drink. Why don't you open the bottle of Merlot?"

For some unknown reason pangs of paranoia ripped through him. Dark thoughts of Special Forces, black ops and poison inserted into a wine bottle through the cork with a syringe flew through Zeb's brain. The whack to his skull didn't kill him, but any one of a number of poisons could. His mind shifted into high gear. He would make her drink from the bottle first. But what if she had taken an anti-dote in advance? Maybe she knew he was a lightweight when it came to red wines and would give up just enough control for her to get the upper hand. She hadn't carried any weapons on her when she arrived, but she had been trained by and worked with Special Forces for years. There could be a thousand ways to kill him that he might never think of. He glanced over at his wedding picture. Doreen seemed to be wearing a knowing smile, one he had never noticed before. Did that mean Doreen knew he was on his way to meet her? Did it mean he should trust Echo? He opened the bottle and set the corkscrew so it was not between himself and Echo.

"A little bit of paranoia is a good thing. It keeps you alert and on your toes," said Echo. "Too much of it leads to mistakes."

"You're right."

"Of course I'm right."

"Are you reading my mind?" asked Zeb.

"No, just reading you. Old training habits die hard."

Zeb poured two medium-sized glasses of the Merlot. He watched as Echo held the glass up to the light. Zeb mimicked her.

"Nice color," she said.

Zeb thought it was close to the color of blood.

"I learned that Merlot comes from the French word that means blackbird. I guess it refers to the color of the grape, not the wine," said Echo.

Zeb looked again. He saw only the color of blood.

Echo checked the aroma. Zeb followed course.

"What do you smell?"

"Vanilla. Oak."

"Very good," replied Echo. "There is also a hint of coconut if you let it waft up all the way."

Zeb couldn't detect the coconut smell.

Echo clinked his glass with hers. "To your health."

"To yours and to the truth," replied Zeb.

He watched as she took a sip. Once again he followed suit. They each took a second sip and a third.

"You were going to tell me something about the truth," said Zeb.

"Yes, of course."

"Why would someone connected to Sun Rey want to kill Curtis?"

"You'd make a lousy interrogator," said Echo, sipping again from the glass. "You need to gain someone's confidence before you ask the hard questions. Why don't you start with something simple like why didn't Curtis tell you someone threatened his life?"

"I don't think he trusts authority figures. He said he hates all cops."

"Maybe he's got a good reason for not liking law enforcement officials. For instance, the law put his dad behind bars at a time when he probably needed him the most in his life?"

"That makes sense," said Zeb. "He's young and things get overly exaggerated in your mind when you're full of spit, vinegar and hormones."

Echo took a long drink of the wine and asked for more. Zeb obliged, re-filling his own glass as well.

"Yulu Rozene," said Echo, "might just be another reason Curtis has a chip on his shoulder."

"One of Sun Rey's rape victims," added Zeb.

"Yulu and I were hired by Levi Lowe to handle the records on the distribution of food and supplies to the school on the Rez. This was back when we were in high school and before I enlisted. She continued to do it long after I left and went into the Army. When she was raped, she told Levi and somehow Curtis found out. Curtis knew that Yulu and I were friends. Being the young fool that he is or was, he threatened Sun Rey. Stupidly he did it not only by e-mail, but face to face. He was foolish."

"He might have been born a fool, but I hope by now he has learned a lesson or two," said Zeb.

"Let's hope so. In any case, he was then threatened anonymously by someone," said Echo.

"Sun Rey?"

"No, someone with a much bigger set of balls, someone with a military background from the sounds of it," said Echo. "Someone who could easily do some deadly damage."

"And you know that exactly how?" asked Zeb.

"By the language he used. It was strictly military lingo."

"You're sure?"

"As sure as I can be," replied Echo.

"Why should I trust you to be correct?" asked Zeb.

Echo sipped the Merlot again and placed her glass on the table. She sat back seductively, or so it appeared to Zeb. She nestled next to Zeb on the sofa. She leaned over and kissed him on the ear. His eyes widened as she whispered softly.

"Did not Sister Peyote teach you anything?"

Zeb, in a move totally out of character, leaned over and put his arms around Echo, holding her close. She felt warm and safe. There were no feelings that he was betraying Doreen. He liked the way it made his heart and mind feel.

They sat there quietly, Zeb thinking clearly. Echo was doing her absolute best to help him, but his unnecessary paranoia had caused him to doubt her.

"Did Yulu kill Sun Rey?" asked Zeb, already knowing the answer.

"If she did and I knew she did, I would consider it justice served. But she didn't. She doesn't have the skill, not by any stretch of the imagination."

"Do you know who did?"

"No, I'm sorry to say I don't. If I did, I might just pin a medal on that person," said Echo.

31

DARK DISCOVERIES

Zeb ran a finger across the keys of Sun Rey's co-opted computer. Mike Patterson, the PI who took it from Sun Rey's room at the treatment facility, had earned the extra two grand it had cost Zeb. The original eight grand Zeb paid for all of the information Patterson had obtained on Sun Rey was also a steal. Today he was hoping for more. The computer hadn't yet been thoroughly vetted. There was only one person he could ultimately trust to extrapolate the information.

"Helen, get me the BLM on the phone."

"Anyone in particular?"

"A federal contractor working on their computers, Shelly somebody. I didn't catch her last name."

"Shelly Hamlin," replied Helen. "She's a smart gal. I like her."

"Yes, that's her. I want to talk to her, here, as soon as possible about getting any and all information from Sun Rey's computer. I'll personally foot the bill, so let the BLM know it's on my dime. If they balk, tell them I'll pay two days of her regular pay out of my budget."

Helen put in the call. Shelly could be there in fifteen minutes. Zeb called Jake and Kate into his office.

"Sun Rey's computer needs to be examined with a fine toothed comb. We need to break it down, hard and fast," said Zeb.

"I don't think Curtis is in any shape to have a look at it," said Kate.

"At this point in time, I don't think we could trust him, even if we looked over his shoulder every minute," said Zeb.

"What's the plan?" asked Jake.

Zeb briefly explained what he hoped to find on the computer Sun Rey left behind at the treatment facility in DC.

"It's a long shot, but there could be something on the computer that could lead to finding Sun Rey's murderer. If we're lucky enough, we might link Sun Rey to some other nefarious deeds, including the possible wrongful imprisonment of Levi Lowe."

"God only knows what else we might find," said Kate.

"Did Sun Rey have a relationship with Agent Rodriguez that you know of?" asked Jake.

"Curious question," said Zeb.

"Criminals of all ilk make for strange and certain bedfellows," replied Jake.

"Maybe we'll find out if and to what extent, they knew each other if we can dig deep enough into the Sun Rey's computer," said Zeb. "Sun Rey was a stickler for details."

Helen tapped on the door. At her side was Shelly Hamlin, the smart, punky looking IT expert.

"Looks like a party," said Shelly. "Hope I'm not too late for all the fun."

"You just might be the life of the party," said Zeb.

"Cool. I could dig that. What do you need?"

"I need to know all the secrets that are on this computer," said Zeb.

"More than I've already given you?"

"Yes," said Zeb. "Much more."

"I get four hundred bucks an hour for this kind of work," said Shelly unabashedly.

"No wonder you can afford such fancy clothes," said Zeb.

"I make no apologies for what I charge. I'm the best at what I do. Pay my fee or find someone who can do what I do for less."

Zeb put his hand on her shoulder. Shelly was not unaware of the sheriff's hard ass reputation.

"You'd better be worth it."

Shelly rolled her eyes. "I'll be worth ten times that, Sheriff Hanks, and likely much more."

"I certainly hope so," said Zeb.

"What am I looking for?"

"I don't know for certain," said Zeb.

"If you did, it would save you money. A shot at a known target is better than a shot in the dark," said Shelly.

Zeb gave her a cold, hard glare.

"I'm just sayin'."

"Okay. Start with anything linking Sun Rey to an FBI Agent by the name of Frank Rodriguez, anything on your old friend Curtis Lowe, his dad Levi Lowe and any of these women." He handed Shelly a list of Sun Rey's rape victims.

"Is that all? I was hoping to get rich today. I guess I could always keyboard slowly."

"There could be more, but let's start there. We'll see how rich we can make you and if you're worth what you think you are."

"Oh, I am. Make you a deal. If I don't get what you want, you don't pay me. If I do, you pay double what I charge. How's that sound?" asked Shelly.

"Sounds like you're a gambler," said Zeb.

"Just trying to pay my bills," replied Shelly.

"Let's stick with our original deal," said Zeb. "You can only shake this money tree so hard before it drops a branch on your head."

"A girl's gotta ask. Say, could I get a triple espresso and two sugared donuts. It makes me work faster," said Shelly with a calm, knowing smile.

"You got it," said Zeb.

Zeb turned to Jake and nodded in the direction of the 322. He was back in a flash.

"That's a weird place," said Jake, setting the donuts and espresso on the desk.

Shelly sipped the espresso, took a bite of a donut and leaned back.

"This is going to be fun."

"Do you have something already?" asked Zeb.

"Sun Rey kept good records, creepy, but detailed and complete."

"Good," said Zeb.

"Sun Rey kept records on everyone, and I mean everyone, including all of your employees, Sheriff Hanks, and their personal lives. You want the birthdates of Helen's grandchildren and what they got for Christmas last year or is that irrelevant?"

"Irrelevant," said Zeb.

"Kidding," replied Shelly.

"It seems he had access to his father's, Senator Russell I mean, personal data bank. Do you want me to start with what he knows about all of you?" asked Shelly.

The room quieted to a dark silence. Fireball glances shot back and forth amongst Zeb, Kate and Jake. Shelly observed it all. The looks were more than telling. It was obvious there were secrets that weren't going to leave the room.

"Senator Russell's personal date would be a good starting point," said Zeb. "Let's begin with Levi Lowe."

"This is strange," said Shelly. "Beyond what I already told you. Levi was paid for something described vaguely as San Carlos Reservation subcontracting. The money went through an offshore account in the Cayman Islands. The account was paid by order of a BIA subcommittee subcontractor in DC. However, Sun Rey acted as the middleman. From the time he got the billing until the time the original bill was actually paid, the amount was more than tripled, sometimes quadrupled. Aha, this is interesting."

"What?"

Everyone in the room asked the question in such harmony that Shelly could barely contain her chuckling.

"Sun Rey had three accounts set up, one in his name and two in Levi Lowe's name. You already know the results of that. Sun Rey skimmed roughly two-thirds, turned around and paid Levi Lowe his actual price and put an extra ten to fifteen percent in the other account. That was enough, as we all know, to put Levi Lowe in prison. The weird thing is both of Levi's accounts are openly linked to his account here in Safford. No wonder they caught him. There's a direct trail. Sun Rey was not only obsessive compulsive about keeping his records, but he was smart enough to set up Levi Lowe from the onset. He's no fool."

"No, just a pathologic crook," said Kate.

"Don't care for him, do you Kate?" said Shelly. "Based on what I see here, I can understand why."

"Since I'm paying you by the minute, keep looking and keep the small talk to absolute minimum. There has to be more to it. I know Levi, and he wouldn't go to jail for that small amount of money. He'd turn state's evidence first. He's no fool. There just has to be more to this picture," said Zeb.

"He ended up in jail, didn't he?" asked Shelly. "How smart can he be?"

Zeb placed his hands on Shelly's shoulders and ground down hard, much harder than he normally would on a woman. She tersely brushed his hands away.

"None of that, Sheriff Hanks, or I am through."

"I apologize. I shouldn't have done that," said Zeb. "I was wrong, frustrated I guess."

Zeb instantly felt a kinship with her. She was tough. She took no prisoners. If there was something to be found, she would find it. He could trust her even though she was going to do things her way, not his.

The rest of the gathered crew drank office coffee and ate day old donuts. Fifteen minutes later Shelly's chair squeaked, and she oozed out a quizzical and rather odd sounding, "hmmm."

"Hmmm?" asked Zeb. "What kind of hmmm was that?"

"I found a personal, at least I think it's personal, account of Senator Russell. It may be an account related to his campaign. I can't really tell. Nothing marks it as anything related to something specific. However, it appears Sun Rey had some special interest regarding it as he made some very cryptic notes on it. The dude makes comments on everything. Wait a second, there's an addendum."

"What does it say? What does it mean?"

"Senator Russell, actually Sun Rey acting on his behalf, paid Bank Menatep 250,000 US dollars to the personal account of Vladinski Arsendev," said Shelly.

"What the hell does that mean?" asked Zeb.

"There's a reference to a gambling note owed to the Russian mob by Curtis Lowe. It looks like Curtis was doing more than just playing war games online. He was gambling with some big, bad fish. Here's one more thing. This is ugly."

"What is it?"

"The Russian mob was going to cut off Curtis' hands if he didn't pay up in full and immediately."

"When was this?" asked Zeb.

"A little over four years ago."

"Right about the time Levi Lowe confessed for a much larger crime than he actually committed," said Zeb.

"Levi agreed to keep his mouth shut about what Sun Rey was doing in order to save his son's hands and probably his life. Sun Rey didn't seem to have much concern about getting caught," said Jake.

"He lacks a conscience," said Kate. "Act now, screw worrying about what you've done."

"It makes sense that Sun Rey would pay Curtis' debt to the Russian mob with the government's money in exchange for keeping himself out of jail and ruining his father's reputation. That kind of business, your son defrauding the government, might make re-election quite difficult," said Jake. "Taxpayers can get mighty finicky about things like that around election time."

"So Levi agreed to some fairly easy federal prison time for getting Curtis' gambling debt paid off, albeit fraudulently, not to mention saving his son's hands from being chopped off at the wrists by the Russian mob? In return Curtis kills Sun Rey? There has to be more to it than that," said Zeb.

"The amount of time Levi will ultimately do won't amount to more than four or five years. From the looks of it Senator Russell would likely keep Levi on the payroll or give him a payoff of some kind. That seems to be the way he operates," added Kate.

"Like I said, there has to be more," said Zeb. "Something else that would push Curtis over the edge."

"Shelly, keep checking to see if you can find a criminal connection between Sun Rey and Curtis."

An hour and four hundred bucks later she had something. She found what she was looking for in a batch of hidden video files.

"I think Curtis was being blackmailed by Sun Rey," said Shelly.

"For what?"

"For this," said Shelly, pointing at the screen.

Curtis was the main actor in a highly graphic homosexual pornographic film written and directed by Sun Rey under the nom de plume of Raysun.

"And these. More film clips. Dozens of them."

"Didn't see that one coming," said Jake.

"But here is what you might be looking for specifically...a motive...in writing."

It was a note from Curtis to Sun Rey.

"If my family ever finds out about my secret life, I will put you down like a sick dog, Sun Rey. Don't think that just because I seem weak and am bisexual that I won't. And don't think for one minute that just because you and I were once lovers that I wouldn't hesitate to kill you."

"It's a clean motive," said Jake. "But from what you tell me about Curtis, in spite of his angry note, he just doesn't seem like the killing type."

"In a moment of anger a person can do just about anything," said Zeb.

"Or he might have hired someone," said Jake.

"Unless the killer was from far away we'd have heard something," said Zeb. "At least I hope we would have."

The door to Zeb's office opened slowly. All eyes turned. It was Helen. She had a report in her hand.

"Am I interrupting something?"

Shelly politely closed the laptop, shielding it from Helen's eyes.

"No. What have you got there?" asked Zeb.

"It's two reports, one from the FBI and one from the DIA about the fingerprints on the missing gun from the Tucson National Guard Armory, or should I say the gun that shot Sun Rey."

Zeb took the reports from Helen.

"Looks like we're going to have a busy day tomorrow. Everyone be here by eight-thirty."

Zeb hung around a few minutes before locking up. His mind was working overtime, and his brain was tired. A good night's sleep would serve him well.

At home Zeb made himself a peanut butter and jelly sandwich, downed it with a beer and was watching Jimmy Kimmel's monologue when the phone rang. Even though he knew the time he looked at the wall clock when he saw it was Helen.

"Don't forget you've got a final interview with Sawyer Black Bear tomorrow."

Zeb scratched his head. He hadn't had any interviews with Black Bear. Jake and Kate had handled everything. Helen managed to put her two cents into the mix as well and seemed to be pushing hard for Sawyer Black Bear. The unusual later in the evening phone call from Helen was likely for emphasis.

"I know what you're thinking, Zeb. You're thinking you haven't even met Sawyer Black Bear. Am I right or am I right?" said Helen.

"You are right. So what's up?"

"Do I have to be your total memory? You told Jake and Kate to handle everything and if they thought he would be good for the job to set up a short interview with you for final approval."

"It's all coming back to me now," said Zeb. "What time is that appointment?"

"First thing in the morning. With your approval he will start tomorrow right after he signs the papers."

"What do you think of him, Helen?"

"He's as smart as a whip, sharp as a tack and reminds me of a sassy, young Jake. I suspect you are going to be very happy with him."

"Is he faster than a speeding bullet, more powerful than a locomotive and able to leap tall buildings in a single bound?"

"Zeb Hanks, button your lip. He's a good man, and he's going to be a great deputy for Graham County if you give him half a chance."

"You make him sound invincible. I like that. But a sassy young Jake, that might be tough to contend with," said Zeb.

"I would say it is exactly what you need to keep on top of your game," said Helen.

"Okay, okay. I'll see him first thing in the morning."

"Goodnight, Zeb. Be sure and say your prayers."

Zeb hung up the phone and turned off the TV. He knew Helen's late night call was a courtesy reminder of the final interview with Sawyer Black Bear as well as a way of checking in on him. Zeb picked up Black Bear's file. It was indeed impressive. Among the oddities was the fact that he'd shattered his right hip falling from a horse while chasing a car thief. While in pursuit he had lassoed the bandit through the open window of the driver's side. As he yanked the three-hundred-pound car thief through the window, he fell from the horse and landed on his hip. He got his man. Zeb figured Black Bear must be one tough hombre. Maybe it was time to bring a little bit of the old west back to Graham County.

32

TROUBLE

Helen unlocked the   door to the sheriff's office at exactly eight o'clock. Today was no different from any other day in that respect. She would expect Kate and Jake to walk through the door in the next five minutes. They would have coffee, tea and donuts. She had previously told Sawyer Black Bear to arrive at eight fifteen. Helen had warned him to make a good impression by being on time. Actually it was a little test of hers to check his promptness. If he lacked punctuality, he likely was a time waster, something Helen detested. Zeb had already told her he would be in at eight-thirty.

"Good morning, Kate."

Deputy Steele placed a bag with two fresh blueberry muffins on Helen's desk.

"A great start to a great day," said Helen.

A minute later Jake placed a fresh, steaming cup of chamomile tea on Helen's desk.

"Straight from the Town Talk to you," said Jake.

She tapped the back of his hand. "Jake, you're the best."

Jake tossed her a wink. She returned a smile.

"What time is Black Bear coming in?" asked Jake.

Helen glanced at the clock on the wall. "If he's smart, he'll be here in the next five minutes."

Four minutes later he walked through the door.

"Morning, Black Bear," said Jake, offering his hand.

"Do you prefer Sawyer or Black Bear?" asked Kate, also extending a hand.

"It's been Black Bear since I was knee high to a grasshopper, so it might as well stay that way. But really, either is okay," replied Black Bear.

"I am going to call you Sawyer. It just feels more comfortable to me. I've always been afraid of black bears," Helen said.

Her response brought a universal chuckle that came to a sudden halt when an unexpected guest entered the front door. It was FBI Agent Rodriguez. He nodded wordlessly at everyone present and made his way to Helen's desk where, with lightning speed, he did a double draw of his Springfield 911 .45s. He held one to Helen's head and pointed the other at Black Bear. Black Bear noticed both bore silencers.

"Starting with you, young man, put your right hand in the air, unbuckle your holster with your left hand and let it drop to the floor. If you have a second gun, drop it too."

He had a second gun. He did as Rodriguez ordered.

"Now flat on the floor. Over there, by the half wall."

Black Bear did as he was ordered. Rodriguez handed Helen a pair of zip tie plastic handcuffs and pointed toward Black Bear.

"Be quick about it. You've got two more to go."

Jake was next to drop his weapons and head to the floor. Kate was last. When they were all tucked away and out of sight, Rodriguez had Helen Duct Tape their mouths shut.

"What do you want?" demanded Helen. "Haven't you done enough already?"

"Shut up, if you want to live though this," said Rodriguez. "What time are you expecting Sheriff Hanks?"

Helen glanced at the clock. He was due in exactly two minutes. Helen didn't know exactly what lie to tell or what good it would do.

"Sometime later his morning," said Helen.

Rodriguez put the gun against her face as he had done the first time he had broken into the sheriff's office and terrorized her. Helen began to tremble.

"He's due any minute, isn't he?"

Helen shook her head no. Rodriguez tapped the silencer at her daily reminder calendar. She had penned in the 8:30 meeting with Zeb, Kate, Jake and Sawyer Black Bear.

"You are such a bad liar," said Rodriguez.

Tears fell from Helen's eyes. Rodriguez pushed a box of tissues in her direction and ordered her to wipe them off.

"I don't want the sheriff seeing them when he comes in. Now sit at your desk and act as naturally as you can. Greet Sheriff Hanks as if everything is normal. Got that?"

Helen nodded. What was she going to do to signal the sheriff? What would he notice that would seem out of place? Before she could make any decisions she heard Zeb's truck pull into its parking spot. So did Rodriguez. Guns drawn he peeked out the window. Behind the half wall someone was moving.

"I'll shoot the first person who makes another sound," said Rodriguez.

It was then Helen noticed the extensions on his guns. They had to be silencers. She began to panic. Was Rodriguez going to shoot Zeb in cold blood right there in front of her? If so, he would have to kill everyone. Rodriguez placed himself so Zeb wouldn't see him when he entered the office. Time slowed to a crawl as Helen watched the door handle to the office turn. Slowly, ever so slowly the door opened. Walking through the door Zeb noticed the bag of muffins sitting on Helen's desk.

"Morning, Helen. I see I'm not the first to arrive. Beautiful fall day must have gotten everyone up early. I noticed everyone's vehicles, including one with a South Dakota plate. I take it Black Bear is here?"

Helen froze. She nodded ever so slightly.

"You okay? Shoulder bothering you? You're awful quiet. Did I forget something?"

At that moment Zeb felt the cold, harsh metal of a gun barrel in the middle of his neck. He didn't even have to look.

"Rodriguez, you're a dead man."

"The circumstances would speak to quite a different outcome, Zeb, my friend."

"I'm no friend of yours."

"That's right. You killed someone near and dear to me. I think it's time I returned the favor."

"You're not only dead, you're an asshole, Rodriguez. There's a special place in hell for people like you."

"You mean for people like us, don't you, Sheriff Hanks?"

If looks could have killed, Rodriguez would have been a dead man.

Rodriguez forced Zeb to kneel by Helen's desk, placing Helen between the kneeling Zeb and the gun toting Rodriguez. He ordered her to handcuff Zeb with zip ties.

"I'm sorry, Helen. I never meant for this to happen. If I can do anything to stop him, I will," promised Zeb.

Helen's prayers became audible. She prayed for Zeb, for Jake, Kate and Sawyer Black Bear. It was at that exact moment Zeb heard a faint, muffled sound outside the sheriff's office.

"I thought I told you to be quiet back there," said Rodriguez.

"Sheriff Hanks, get up off your knees. I want you to look into the eyes of the others you have condemned to death by your foolish actions, by your lust for blood."

Zeb stood. Rodriguez grabbed him by his zipped tied wrists and dragged him to the half wall where his deputies and Sawyer Black Bear were bound.

"The only trouble I'm having is how to make you suffer the most," said Rodriguez. "I suspect you are the least close to this Black Bear fellow so he should go first. You probably won't even feel any pain as you watch him die. The problem comes with who is second to die. Deputy Kate is as loyal as anyone could ever be. She stood beside you and even helped you with Mexico. Then, there is your old pal and former sheriff, Jake Dablo. How many times have you saved each other's lives? How many lives of others have you taken? How many bodies have you buried in the desert? Then there's Helen, not only loyal and true, but a blood relative. She goes next to last, right before I blow your brains out. I might as well make her suffer with you."

From the corner of his eye. Zeb saw Echo Skysong parking her motorcycle. She started walking toward the office then stopped. Holding her hands in the air for a moment she returned to her motorcycle. Zeb breathed a sigh of relief until he saw her reach into her saddlebag and withdraw a gun and a knife. She chambered a round in the gun and slipped the knife into a sheath she wore strapped across her heart.

"Helen, why don't you join your friends? That way I can confine the mess to a smaller area."

Helen began to weep.

"Stay strong." Zeb whispered to her. "Everything is going to be all right."

"Oh, how odd it is to hear you speak with such faith, Zeb. I am happy for you," said Helen.

"Nonetheless, you are a fool to think that anyone can save you now," said Rodriguez.

Behind him Zeb could hear the tiny, creaking sound the doorknob made when it turned. Helen had oiled it a dozen times, still it squeaked. If he lived, he made a vow to never get a new doorknob. Sawyer Black Bear, who had been placed at the edge of the half wall, witnessed the door slowly opening. He coughed surreptitiously to cover any noise. He noticed the woman coming through the door was barefoot. From the look in her eyes and on her face she was a true warrior. Stealthily she closed the door. Moving along the wall she watched and listened.

"Sawyer Black Bear, you are going to be the first to buy a bullet. Want to take it sitting or standing?"

"You're making the first day on the job, that is if I get the job, a tough one," said Black Bear.

"You're hired," said Zeb.

"Bad timing on your part," replied Rodriguez. "A buddy of mine got killed in a military cargo plane that crashed on its way to the supply buildup in Kuwait back in '91. Shit happens."

Black Bear's eye caught Echo's. She gave him a sign that indicated he stall for one minute.

"Does the condemned man get any final words?" asked Black Bear.

Rodriguez lifted the gun and pointed the barrel directly at Black Bear's heart.

"Make it quick."

"To answer your first question, I'll take my bullet sitting. Just a weird preference I guess. Actually, I have thought about dying on my feet or going down sitting, and dying on one's feet is such a cliché. But, on the other hand, I am going to die with my boots on."

"Quit stalling," growled Rodriguez.

Black Bear sat on a chair facing the FBI agent. Rodriguez kept the gun trained directly on him. Rodriguez's second gun was aimed in the direction of the area where he had gathered everyone else. Echo had moved to within three feet of Rodriguez. Everyone worked to keep their eyes off her. In her hand she held her boot lace.

"I'm the kind of guy who always believed the hero would come in at the last moment and save the day," said Black Bear.

"Well, you're shit out of luck today," said Rodriguez.

"You never know where or when a meteorite is going to land."

"Enough of this bullshit. You've said your piece."

"I guess I have," said Black Bear, slowly lowering his head.

At that exact instant the barefoot Echo stepped close enough to flip the boot lace over Rodriguez' head and tug back forcefully on his windpipe. Simultaneously, in a singular motion she kicked her right foot in the air, knocking the gun from his right hand and, with a move only a ninja could perform, gracefully lifted her left leg over the top of his left arm, dislocating Rodriguez' elbow and shoulder by twisting down and back. Reflexively the gun fell from his left hand. Somewhere in the midst of the sudden, chaotic action, a bullet was fired from Rodriguez's gun into the hardwood floor. Echo kept continual pressure on the boot lace. When Rodriguez fell to the ground, she let go of the lace, grabbed him by the head and twisted his neck, breaking it with an awful, sickening sound. He crumpled to the floor, gasping his final breaths. He'd never seen it coming.

"Who the hell are you?" asked Black Bear.

"A warrior woman," replied Echo. "A direct descendant of Lozen."

"Thanks for saving my life," said Black Bear. "I humbly thank you."

"You'd have done the same."

Zeb's eyes locked with Echo's. They were calm and crystal clear. Zeb had never witnessed such an unbelievable display of the true power of a warrior. He nodded once in her direction.

"Well done," he said.

"It had to be that way," Echo replied. "Everything was on the line."

Once again, Zeb nodded.

Walking over to the body of Agent Rodriguez, Zeb pulled a piece of paper from his back pocket and dropped it on the dead man's chest. Black Bear walked over to read it.

THE BEST REVENGE IS REVENGE. THIS ISN'T OVER. WE WILL MEET AGAIN

"Hello and goodbye," said Zeb. "The best revenge has the final word."

33

BLACK BEAR JOINS THE TEAM

"Jake, take Black Bear and arrest Curtis Lowe. Bring him here. Be careful, he could be armed," said Zeb.

"That candy ass isn't going to shoot anyone," said Jake.

"That candy ass has already killed someone," replied Zeb. "And he's armed to the teeth. You saw the gun cabinet and the ammo. Don't forget he was the state shotgun shooting champ when he was fifteen years old."

"I shouldn't be so glib, but, man, in my day the girls would have beaten him up," said Jake.

"I guess this isn't your day anymore, old timer," said Black Bear.

Jake smacked the new deputy on the back of the head with an open hand. As they walked out the door on their way to arrest Curtis, Jake said, "Did I ever tell you about the Graham County lie detector test?"

"No, sir, you haven't," said Black Bear mockingly. "But my dad did. He says he taught it to you. Only we called it the Pine Ridge polygraph."

Jake jabbed the younger man in the ribs with his elbow. "You know, kid, I think we are going to get along just fine." He flipped the new deputy the keys. "Here, you drive."

"What's the address?" asked Black Bear.

Jake pointed a finger in the general direction they were headed. "I'll tell you as we go."

"There, that's the house."

Jake pointed to a stucco house with a woman sitting on the front steps. The woman was holding her head in her hands. It was Angela Lowe. She didn't even move as Black Bear and Jake walked up the sidewalk.

"Angie?" asked Jake. "Is everything okay?"

When she didn't respond, Jake and Black Bear looked inside the open front door. The house looked like it had been tossed by the DEA.

Stepping next to her, Jake saw a .45 tucked under her dress.

"Angie, could you please hand me the gun?" asked Jake.

As she reached for the weapon and laid it on the ground, Black Bear kicked it away. Angie began crying.

"I almost killed my own son," she said.

"Is he here now?" asked Jake.

"He's gone, long gone, gone to hell most likely," replied Angie.

Black Bear drew his weapon and entered the house. He signaled to Jake he had things under control. Jake sat next to Angie.

"Want to talk?"

"I said I almost killed my son. He almost killed me. I think he missed me on purpose when my gun jammed."

"What happened?"

"What do you mean what happened? I just told you. We had a gunfight, right here in this house. My son and I had a gunfight in our own home. I missed him twice. He missed me once. Then he left in my car. He stole my car. He's a thief and a murderer."

The two-way radio on Jake's shoulder hummed. He tapped to answer.

"Jake?"

"Yes, Zeb?"

"I've got reports of shots fired in the vicinity of the Lowe household. Does it involve you or Black Bear?"

"No. There were shots fired. Three shots it appears. It was Curtis and Angie Lowe who fired the shots."

"Who were they shooting at?"

"Each other."

"Everyone okay?" asked Zeb.

"Depends on what you mean by okay. No one was injured as far as we know, at least not physically. I am talking with Angie right now."

"Is that Zeb?" asked Angie.

"Yes, ma'am."

"Can you ask him to come here? I think he can straighten this whole thing out," said Angie

"Zeb, you copy that? Angie would like you to be present when she makes her statement."

"I'm on my way."

Black Bear stepped out from inside the house.

"What did he take with him?" asked Jake.

"Just what you'd expect. Guns and ammunition. He also took a few personal items that I noticed were gone from their usual place," Angie answered.

"Personal items?" asked Jake.

"He is an avid collector of 70's and 80's horror films paraphernalia."

"Like knives or hatchets? That kind of thing?" asked Jake.

"No, they were more like masks. He loved the masks that the main characters in those movies wore," said Angie.

"Which movies?"

"All of them. For sure *Friday the 13th*, Leather Face from the *Texas Chainsaw Massacre* movies, Freddy Kruger from those *Nightmare on Elm Street* movies. *Child's Play*, *Hellraiser*, Mike Myers from the *Halloween* series. One of his goals was to be a makeup artist in the movies."

"You didn't find any of that strange?" asked Jake.

"I thought it was just a lonely young boy acting out his fantasy. Actually, to show me they weren't evil movies, he had me watch some of them with him."

"Okay. How about the ammo? How much ammunition did your son take with him?"

"There were two thousand rounds in the cabinet. He broke into it and filled a rucksack with as much as he could carry." Angie's tears turned to anger as she spoke.

"Do you know what weapons he took?" asked Black Bear.

Zeb stepped out of his truck just in time to hear her answer.

"An AR 15, two modified shotguns, a .45 and a .38. The AR 15 and the shotgun have scopes on them."

"Is he going after someone?" asked Jake.

"An FBI agent, Frank Rodriguez," replied Angie.

"Do you know why?" asked Jake.

"Revenge. His blood is hotter than the flames that lick the gates of Hades," replied Angie. "One of them, and I would bet it will be my son, is going to be dead by sundown."

"He won't be dead by Rodriguez's hand, I can tell you that with one hundred percent certainty," said Zeb.

Black Bear responded immediately to the puzzled look on Angie's face.

"Rodriguez has already met his maker. His spirit no longer walks among the living."

Angie fainted dead on the spot.

"Get a glass of water and a wet towel," ordered Jake. "And don't speak until I tell you to."

"Just trying to give a grieving mother some relief," said Black Bear.

Slowly, the wet towel and a cold glass of water brought Angie around. When she came to, she had one question.

"Did Curtis kill him?"

"No," replied Zeb. "Your son did not kill Agent Rodriguez."

Angie took another sip of water. She seemed very calm for someone who just took a potshot at her own son. Zeb waited for her to speak.

"I suppose you're wondering two things—why I shot at Curtis and why he was after Rodriguez with such a vengeance?"

"Those would be good starting places," replied Zeb.

"I shot at him to wound him. I was trying for the leg. I didn't want him killing anyone. I think when he returned fire, he missed me on purpose. He is a much better shot than that. He could have killed me had he wanted to."

"Okay," said Zeb. "I understand you were trying to stop him. Did you try talking to him first?"

"Of course. I sure didn't want to shoot him. He was so hot under the collar that nothing was going to stop him from getting revenge on Rodriguez."

"Do you know why he was so determined to kill Rodriguez?" asked Zeb.

"Seriously, you have to ask?"

"Yes, Angie, I need to hear what you know. You may know more than I already do," replied Zeb.

"Rodriguez was the lead agent on Levi's case. My son blamed him the most for his father being in prison."

"Right, makes sense."

"My son believed beyond a shadow of a doubt that Rodriguez was in cahoots with Sun Rey."

"Are you talking about Sun Rey blackmailing Curtis?"

"Yes."

"And Curtis believed Rodriguez was behind that?"

"Yes, of course."

"What made him believe that?"

"He was certain Sun Rey had told Rodriguez that he was gay and that he had made those horrible films. It sickens me to even talk about it. He hated Sun Rey for that and, in turn, hated Rodriguez. He said he knew that Rodriguez was working directly for Senator Russell."

"What? Say that again," said Zeb.

"Curtis was certain Rodriguez was working for Senator Russell, and the linkage to the offshore accounts my husband received funds from were a plot between Rodriguez, Sun Rey and Senator Russell."

"Did he have proof of that?" asked Zeb.

"Likely not enough to make a legal case, but more than enough to make him blame Rodriguez for being a middle man."

Zeb looked at Black Bear and Kate. "What do you figure he's going to do with all that ammo once he finds out Rodriguez is dead?"

"Suicide by cop," said Kate.

"What other option does he have?" asked Black Bear.

"He could always surrender," said Zeb.

"And the Pope might turn Muslim," said Black Bear.

"Angie, any idea where Curtis might be right now?"

"He's been tailing Rodriguez."

"And?"

"Rodriguez has been staying at Senator Russell's hunting lodge. Since there's no way Curtis knows Rodriguez is dead, I imagine he's at the senator's hunting lodge setting a trap for him."

34

SENATOR RUSSELL'S LODGE

The opulent lodge of Senator Russell sat on a knoll half way up a canyon. Insiders facetiously knew the property as The Little Grand Canyon Hunting Lodge and Chalet. Locals called it Home of the Fat Cat. Essentially it was a hunting lodge, but in reality it was a private fortress for an ultra-wealthy man who made no bones about flaunting what he owned.

Zeb and Jake knew the area around the lodge best. Zeb had Black Bear ride with him and gave him enough information so that he had at least a cursory idea of the layout. Jake and Kate followed in Jake's truck. There was a pullout a half mile from the first decent vantage point of the house. Zeb decided they would rendezvous there. He put in a call to Helen with Black Bear's phone so she would know what was going on. Zeb used Black Bear's phone just in case Curtis had placed a tracking device of some kind on his phone or the two-way radio. At this point he was not about to put anything past Curtis Lowe. The trucks parked behind some oleander trees that had sprung up around some large boulders. The nearby scrub brush stood as tall as the top of the truck cabs, hiding them well enough that someone could walk within twenty feet of them and miss them entirely.

Zeb knelt and began drawing a map in the sand. The others joined him on bended knees.

"This is the house. It has front and back entrance doors. The front door is a half screen door. The top half is screened. There are two wide, floor-to-ceiling windows in the front of the house. There is a wrap-around deck with plenty of juts and turns on the deck with flower pots, statues and other obstacles that someone could hide behind. In other words, there are more than a few places someone could take a pot shot at us as we approach if they were so inclined," said Zeb.

"Do you think Curtis is waiting on the inside of the lodge?" asked Black Bear.

"That's where I'd be waiting," said Jake.

"Agreed," added Kate.

"His point of entry, if he's in the house, would probably be the back door as it is least likely to be seen by someone approaching the house."

"How should we make our approach?" asked Kate.

"The front of the house faces east. The back is angulated toward the southwest. Let's team up and head in from the north and south. As I remember the terrain, there is considerably more cover on those sides. There's a continually flowing small creek that runs under the house. Other than that, just the usual vegetation."

"Any questions?"

"I'll partner with Kate," said Jake.

"That works," said Zeb. "Black Bear and I will take the north side."

"Curtis is loaded for bear, but he isn't looking for us," said Zeb. "So don't spook him."

"Shoot to kill?" asked Black Bear.

"Only if he shoots first or your life is in danger, otherwise shoot to injure. There is still a lot of information I'd like to get out of him."

The four officers un-holstered their sidearms and each carried a 30.06 as they split up and headed toward the house. Each team carried a set of binoculars. They hadn't moved a hundred yards before they saw the truck Curtis had taken from his mother's house. It was parked in a small ravine and covered with branches. Zeb pointed it out with hand signals to Kate and Jake.

As they neared the house, Zeb took out his binoculars.

"Damn it," he whispered.

"What?" said Black Bear.

He handed Black Bear the binoculars.

"Shit. Bad scene."

Zeb took a chance and tapped lightly on the two-way.

"What?" asked Jake in low whisper.

"Look at the front porch."

Jake took out his binoculars.

"What the fuck?"

"I know," replied Zeb.

Looking toward the porch, Zeb recognized Senator Russell's fancy cowboy boots and two other young men in suits. They were all hog-tied and trussed up in three rocking chairs like lambs for the slaughter. Each of the men had horror masks covering their faces. One of the men had black hands. Zeb assumed it was his former deputy, State Senator Devon Dawbyns. The third man was likely one of Senator Russell's top aides.

Senator Russell's chair had been pulled up tightly against the double entry front door. The other two men were tied in their chairs snuggly against the floor-to-ceiling windows. Though it was hard to tell since their heads were covered with masks, it appeared their heads were all tipped up and stretched toward the door and windows.

"Something look funny to you, Jake?"

"Yes, I see what you're talking about."

"What's going on?" asked Black Bear.

Zeb handed him the binoculars for a closer look. Closer examination of the situation revealed that Curtis had pulled Senator Russell tightly against the double doors. He had tightly taped the AR15 to the back of the senator's neck. He had placed Dawbyns and the other man up against the windows, drawn the shades, punched out a pane of glass and attached taped shotguns to the back of their necks as well.

"Do you see Curtis?" asked Jake.

"No. I don't see any movement."

"He's probably in the lodge," suggested Jake.

"Let's regroup and come up with a plan B," said Zeb. "Let's all meet back at the trucks. Stick a knife in all four tires of Curtis' getaway vehicle. He's not leaving here without us."

35

ACTION

"We've got ourselves one fucked up hostage situation," said Zeb.

"Do you think he has demands?" asked Black Bear.

"Probably the immediate release of his father from prison," said Jake.

"He's not getting that," said Zeb.

"Death by cop," said Kate.

"He might just get his wish, if that's what it is," said Zeb.

"What's our next move?" asked Black Bear.

"Move back toward the house from the north and south, like we did before. I want to see if Curtis will talk with me. Everyone keep out of sight and stay low so he can't get a pot shot at you. I don't want anyone getting hurt," said Zeb. "Safety first."

Everyone stealthily crept into place. Each had their 30.06 aimed at one of the windows in case a weapon appeared. When they were all in position, Zeb shouted toward the lodge.

"Curtis, this is Sheriff Hanks. I'd like to talk to you."

A minute passed with no response.

"Curtis, I talked with your mother. She forgives you. She wants to make a fresh start. She understands you want to set your father free from prison. Can you hear me, Curtis?"

Another long minute of silence.

"Maybe he's not inside the lodge," said Black Bear.

Just then an explosion went off in the lodge. Thankfully, all three of the hogtied victims still had heads on their shoulders.

"Or maybe he is," added Black Bear.

"Did you notice something odd when that explosion went off?" asked Zeb.

"Yes," replied Black Bear. "None of the men hardly even flinched, and none of the glass blew out of the windows."

"I think it was a decoy explosion," said Zeb. "I think he's trying to draw us inside."

"Do you think his plan is to end up dead and take all of us with him?" asked Black Bear.

"Or kill all of us and escape," replied Zeb.

Zeb's two-way radio buzzed. It was Kate.

"We spotted something taped over the top of the archway of the door and at the top of the windows. Jake is certain they are plastic explosives."

Zeb took out his binoculars. He couldn't make out exactly what it was. He handed the binoculars to Black Bear.

"I'm going to move in closer for a look. Cover me."

"Stay low. Be careful," warned Jake.

"A Lakota knows how to make himself invisible when he has to," whispered Black Bear.

Black Bear snaked through the underbrush with amazing speed and dexterity. He returned with a treasure trove of information.

"It is definitely C4 explosives above the front door and both windows. Since I can't see much past the crack in the front doors or the broken panes in the windows, I am assuming the blasting caps are strung together and attached to a single detonating cord. I could smell gas coming from the back of the house. I think that was the original explosion. I am fairly certain it was remotely set and almost one hundred percent certain it was a decoy," said Black Bear.

"It looks like a hell of a lot of C4," said Zeb.

"More than enough to blow the front half of the lodge to kingdom come," said Black Bear. "Certainly if it blows, it will kill the three men."

"Shit. We got ourselves a bad situation," said Zeb.

Zeb hit the two-way and copied Jake and Kate in on what was happening. They had more or less already come to the same conclusions. Zeb decided one more time to try and reason with Curtis.

"Curtis," shouted Zeb. "If those men die, you could get the death penalty. Is all of this worth dying for? We know Senator Russell was in on the scam to put your father in jail. We know your dad took the hit and did the time to save you from embarrassment and keep his marriage with your mother intact. He has made a lot of sacrifices for you and for your family. Do you want that all to be for nothing?"

No response was forthcoming.

Jake called on the two-way. "Maybe he's already dead. Maybe the C4 is on a timer? Maybe he's alive and waiting for us to move in close so he can take us all out?"

Sitting on a hill one hundred fifty yards behind Zeb, Jake, Kate and Black Bear was Curtis Lowe. In his arms rested a 30.06. At his side was a detonator attached to a cord that could blow the entire lodge to smithereens at any given moment. He was simply biding his time. He had embarrassed his family with the pornographic films. He had failed to get his father out of prison. His mother would never forgive all his transgressions. There was only one way to go out--in a blaze of glory. From the computer records he knew State Senator Devon Dawbyns was Senator Russell's toady. The third man with Senator Russell and Devon Dawbyns, one of Senator Russell's campaign money bundlers, just happened to be in the wrong place at the wrong time. Senator Russell had his dirty hands mixed up in every part of the entire mess. He had covered for and enabled Sun Rey, stolen from the San Carlos and taken money from any group that would give it to him in exchange for whatever they wanted. His death would make the world a better place. Killing Zeb, Kate, Jake and their new deputy felt right to Curtis. He hated all cops and would feel nothing taking their lives. At this moment it was simply a matter of choosing the perfect moment. He would know it when it arrived.

"Curtis, I am giving you one last warning," shouted Zeb. "Then we are coming in."

Hidden behind them Curtis smugly laughed as he double-checked the detonator. Once he blew the lodge apart Zeb and his deputies would move toward the building. With his 30.06 he could easily pick them off one at a time. The fools were standing in pairs. He fantasized killing two of them with a single shot. In his mind it was all a video game.

Zeb caught something out of the corner of his eye. It was the detonating cord. He turned to Black Bear and pointed it out.

"He's behind us," said Zeb.

Zeb tapped the two-way and whispered to Kate. "Take cover behind a tree or a rock between the hill behind us and the lodge."

"What?" asked Kate. "We'll be sitting ducks."

"We are sitting ducks. He's on that hill behind us."

Kate and Jake did as they were ordered. They scanned the hillside but saw nothing.

"There," said Jake, eyeing a glint of sunlight off the barrel of Curtis' gun.

"Do you have a shot at him?" asked Kate.

"I don't think so. I can't see him clearly. Plus, I would want to see the detonator to see if it's armed. I'd hate to lose three men because I was in a hurry."

Across the way, Zeb and Black Bear were hatching a plan of their own. They would follow the detonating cord and get as close as they could. At that point they would have enough information to reassess the situation. If the detonator was armed, they would have to carefully kill Curtis, making sure he didn't have time to press the detonator or accidentally fall onto it when they shot him.

Zeb tapped the two-way. "We're moving in on him. Sit tight for now. Radio silence."

"Good luck."

Zeb followed Black Bear who followed the cord through the underbrush. With adrenaline rushing through his veins, Zeb had no trouble keeping up with his younger deputy. Fifteen minutes later they eyed Curtis Lowe. He had placed himself strategically between two large, round boulders. He was leaning against a third boulder with the detonator between his legs and set to blow. A 30.06 with a scope and two boxes of ammunition were at his side. If they shot him and he fell forward, his fall would ignite the detonator and the lodge would blow, taking Senator Russell, State Senator Devon Dawbyns and the third man with it.

"Any ideas, Sheriff?"

Zeb slipped his Randall knife from its sheath and cut the detonating cord.

"That's why you're the sheriff," said Black Bear with a smile. "What next?"

Curtis made the decision for them. Unaware the cord had been cut and unable to see any of the four sheriff's officers who were after him, he chose one last hurrah.

"Sheriff Hanks. Do you like explosions?"

Zeb and Black Bear took cover and aimed their weapons at Curtis.

"Yes, as a matter of fact, the fourth of July is my favorite holiday," shouted Zeb in response.

Hearing the sheriff's voice so close caused Curtis to grab his weapon and tighten into a ball. He also placed one hand on the detonator.

"I'm going to blow them all straight to hell," said Curtis.

"No, you're not," replied Zeb. "There's no need to kill anyone. It's all over now. Put down your weapon, take your hand off the detonator and walk out slowly with your hands over your head."

"Are you serious?" asked Curtis. "It's either death or jail for me. I've got nothing to live for, and I sure as hell ain't going to prison like my dad."

"There's no need for anyone else to get hurt," said Zeb. "Come out now. Please."

"Screw you and your flunkies, Sheriff Hanks."

Curtis pressed down hard on the detonator. When nothing happened, he tried it a second and a third time.

"I cut the detonating cord," said Zeb. "There isn't going to be an explosion today. It's all over. Put down your gun and put your hands in the air. This time it's an order, not a request."

Curtis aimed the 30.06 in the general direction he had heard Sheriff Hanks' voice coming from and fired off a couple of rounds. They missed Zeb by a good thirty feet.

"He's aiming blindly," whispered Black Bear. "What do you want to do?"

"I don't want to kill him, but he wants to die," said Zeb. "At the very best, he's going to go to prison for a long time. Probably the rest of his life. Would you want that?"

"No way," replied Black Bear. "I'd rather be dead."

"Well, then..." began Zeb.

His comments were interrupted by Curtis rising from his hiding place and walking in a straight line toward Senator Russell's lodge. He stopped, planted himself and took aim at Senator Russell. Before he could squeeze the trigger all three deputies and Sheriff Hanks fired off rounds. Four 30.06 rounds struck Curtis in the chest. Curtis Lowe crumpled instantly into a dead heap.

36

OUR PATHS WILL MEET AGAIN

Sheriff Hanks and his deputies stood over the dead body.

"Jake, call the ambulance."

"Who's going to tell his mother?" asked Black Bear.

"Me," replied Zeb. "It's my job."

"Maybe we'd better go untie Senator Russell and the others," said Kate.

"I can only imagine what they are thinking after hearing four shots," said Zeb. "I don't know exactly how dirty they are, but none of them are clean in this deal. Let's let them sweat a little first."

Gradually Sheriff Hanks and his deputies walked down to the lodge and untied the men.

"I guess this makes us even, Sheriff Hanks," said Senator Russell.

Zeb said nothing. In another place and time Sheriff Hanks would have drawn his weapon and placed a bullet between the eyes of Senator Russell. But this was the new west. The ways of the old west were dead and gone, at least for the time being.

"I suspect you want to see Levi Lowe out of prison," said Senator Russell.

"I think that would be fair," said Zeb.

"Since he and I have both tragically lost sons, I have compassion for him. I will contact the parole board tomorrow and do what I can."

"You can get it done, Senator Russell. I am certain of that. Good day, Senator Russell."

"I'm certain our paths shall cross again," said Senator Russell. "Probably sooner rather than later.

"Time will tell," said Zeb. "Time and circumstance."

Zeb and Black Bear did a quick pivot and a slow walk to Zeb's truck.

"Sounds like you have a love-hate relationship with Senator Russell," said Black Bear.

"Let's just say it's complex and multi-layered," replied Zeb.

"How about us?" asked Black Bear.

"What about us?" asked Zeb.

"I was wondering if I really got the job or if you were just stalling back there with Rodriguez?" asked Black Bear.

"Well, let me think," said Zeb. "I'll consider what just happened to be the practical part of your interview."

"Do you make all your deputies undergo trial by fire?"

"Nope, just you so far," replied Zeb. "But I think it's a good way to test a man's mettle."

"I'll take that as I passed the Zeb Hanks interview process," said Black Bear.

"With flying colors," replied Zeb. "But, remember, this was just another day on the job."

Black Bear grinned. He was going to like working with a man like Zeb Hanks because it seemed as though there was nothing normal about him. They were going to be a good fit.

"Good, because I haven't had this much fun since I was arrested the first time," said Black Bear.

"That's a tale I'm going to want to hear," replied Zeb.

"I'll tell you when you know me a little better," said Black Bear. "That way you won't judge me."

"I'm learning to let go of judgment," said Zeb. "I'm working on changing a few things around here. I'd like to make Graham County and the surrounding area the safest and best place to live in Arizona."

"Mighty noble of you. I watched my mother and father try and do that up on Pine Ridge. They failed. I wish you luck."

The ride back to town was peaceful as the men swapped stories and began to know and understand one another. At times Zeb felt like he was talking to Jake Dablo, Jimmy Song Bird and a little bit of Eskadi Black Robes all wrapped into one person. It felt good. It felt like home.

37

PEACE AND HARMONY IN THE GILA VALLEY

Helen placed the contract on the table in front of Sawyer Black Bear. She had placed three tabs, each one next to his printed name.

"Sign here, here and here, please," she said, pointing to the lines for emphasis.

"I take it once I put my John Hancock on the dotted line, not once, not twice, but three times, I officially will be an employee of the Graham County Sheriff's Department?"

"You're a quick study," replied Helen spritely. Anyone listening to her or watching her would easily see that she had a special liking for Deputy Sawyer Black Bear.

Sawyer smiled and signed his name three times. His mother might have been a radical back in the day with the American Indian Movement, but she also taught her son proper manners.

"Thank you," said Helen.

"That's all there is to it?" asked Deputy Black Bear.

Helen smiled knowingly. The look on her face did not escape the new deputy.

"No, there is the swearing in ceremony. Come with me."

Sawyer Black Bear followed closely on Helen's heels to the conference room. The entire western facing wall was filled with the photographs of every man or woman who had ever been employed by the Graham County Sheriff's Department. Black Bear took the time to look closely at each picture.

"Not too many Indians and not a lot of women," he said.

"Times are changing," replied Helen. "You are proof of that, aren't you?"

"Yes, ma'am, I guess I am."

"Stand over there next to the Arizona state flag," said Helen.

Helen eyed the newest employee through her cellphone and snapped the picture. She glanced quickly at it.

"Now, let's try one that makes you look like you're happy to be here," she said.

"You mean I should smile?"

"That's the general idea. I've been here over thirty years and I'm still smiling."

"I don't want the camera to steal my spirit," said Black Bear.

"If anything can steal your spirit, it isn't going to be the camera on my cellphone," said Helen.

Sawyer Black Bear's beaming smile lit up the room. Seconds later Sheriff Zeb Hanks, Deputy Kate Steele and Deputy Jake Dablo walked into the room. Following them were Josh Diamond and Echo Skysong. Each approached Black Bear singularly, gift in hand. Zeb handed him his official Graham County Sheriff Officer's badge. Jake handed him his gun and holster, Kate his official sheriff's shirt and Josh a specially made boot gun and holster. Finally, Echo handed him a Native American amulet that she and Song Bird had created.

"It has been blessed by both a Lakota medicine men and Jimmy Song Bird," said Echo, placing it around his neck.

Helen sneaked out of the room and returned with a plateful of blueberry muffins surrounding a bear claw.

"My favorites," said Black Bear. "How could you have known?"

"I had a little pow-wow with your mother on the phone," replied Helen.

Helen's surprising remark brought out a solid round of laughter. The new team, barely into its infancy but having already survived a trial by fire, was coming together.

'I'm going to have to learn a few things pretty quickly," said Black Bear.

"Such as?" asked Zeb.

"Like what makes Graham County click?"

"Cotton," replied Jake.

"The people," added Kate. "Both the good ones and the bad ones."

"Good place to settle and raise a family," said Josh.

"Copper is king," added Zeb.

Echo drew a step closer to Zeb and slipped one hand into his. With her other hand she pointed toward Mount Graham and spoke with great reverence.

"This is a sacred area. It always has been and always will be. We will always call this place home."

Zeb squeezed her hand. Josh gave Kate a kiss. Jake and Helen hugged like only old friends can. Today there was peace and harmony in the Gila Valley.